THE
Arrangement

MELISSA TEREZE

First Edition June 2019
Published by GPC Publishing
Copyright © 2019 Melissa Tereze
ISBN: 9781073694198

Cover Design: Melissa Tereze

Find out more at: www.melissaterezeauthor.com
Follow me on Twitter: @MelissaTereze
Follow me on Instagram: @melissatereze_author

All rights reserved. This book is for your personal enjoyment only. This book or any portion thereof may not be reproduced or used in any manner without the express permission of the author.

This is a work of fiction. All characters & happenings in this publication are fictitious and any resemblance to real persons (living or dead), locales or events is purely coincidental.

ALSO BY MELISSA TEREZE

ANOTHER LOVE SERIES
THE CALL (BOOK TWO)

THE ASHFORTH SERIES
PLAYING FOR HER HEART (BOOK ONE)
HOLDING HER HEART (BOOK TWO)

OTHER NOVELS
ALWAYS ALLIE

MRS MIDDLETON

IN HER ARMS

BEFORE YOU GO

FOREVER YOURS

THE HEAT OF SUMMER

FORGET ME NOT

MORE THAN A FEELING

WHERE WE BELONG: LOVE RETURNS

NAKED

CO-WRITES
TEACH ME

TITLES UNDER L.M CROFT (EROTICA)
PIECES OF ME

For you, Brittany Neal.
1992-2019
Because the world should know your name

CHAPTER ONE

The sun bounced off the still dock water, the sandstone buildings shining in all their glory as another summer's day blazed outside. The office building sat positioned in the perfect spot when the British weather behaved accordingly. Sam knew that the moment she stepped inside, enquiring about purchasing it. The estate agent hadn't been interested in her enthusiasm, clearly only there to make his commission and leave, but she knew. She felt it. To this day, three years on, she could still smell the fresh paint. She could recall the pride and sense of ultimate accomplishment as she pushed the doors open on a dreary Monday morning, a spring in her step. Of all the moments she'd enjoyed in her life, setting up her new business was up there with the greatest. The thought of being on cloud nine, daily, did wonders for her mental health.

But then everything turned into a blur. A single moment in time that seemed to have rushed by, her knowledge strained as she focused on the water below her office window. How could something feel so good, yet so terrible at the same time? How could life give you everything, only to take it all away? That was some cruel twist, Sam was well aware of that, but it didn't make life any easier. It didn't make her days here any less painful. No, it still hurt.

"Mrs Phillips?" A light knock on her door tugged Sam from the depression she was slowly but surely heading towards. The more she thought, the worse her night at home would be.

"Come in." She fixed her tailored black suit and stepped away from the window.

"Hi, I'm sorry to bother you..." Cheryl, her assistant, said, "but I brought that website address you wanted."

"Web address?" Sam took a seat on the edge of her desk, crossing her legs at the ankles. "I don't believe I asked you for any address."

"When we were at Cork on Friday, we got talking..." Cheryl scratched the back of her neck and frowned. "I told you about the website I'd been using...you said you'd like to have a look at it."

"I've no idea what you're talking about." Sam fidgeted as she gave a half-hearted laugh, her eyes unable to meet Cheryl's. Over the last eighteen months or so, her drinking habits had become somewhat unpredictable, but surely she wasn't at a stage where she didn't remember her nights out. *This could become an issue.*

"Anyway, it's just a business card." Her assistant stepped further into the office and slipped it onto the desk beside Sam. "If you don't want it, it can go in the bin. I don't need it."

Sam nodded, watching Cheryl disappear into the corridor, the door closing over behind her. She slid her hand across the desk and her fingertips connected with the glossy card. *What the hell is she talking about?* Sam lifted the business card and held it up in a better light.

Hush.

Hush? She continued to study the card, at a loss as to what her assistant was offering her. Or rather, what she, herself, had requested. The black, glossed card didn't provide a great deal of information, but it did have a website printed across the bottom of it. If Sam was to take a guess at what that website would hold, she would guess that it was something she wouldn't like. Something she knew nothing about. Something she *didn't* require.

She dropped the card back down to her desk and turned her body, pressing number one on the black handset next to her. "Cheryl, can I see you in my office for a moment?"

"I'll be right there, Mrs Phillips."

Sam stood and gathered herself. While she could log onto her computer and take a look at *Hush* herself, she didn't have any plans to do so. The longer she waited for her assistant, the more unease grew in the pit of her stomach.

"Yes?" Cheryl poked her head around the door.

"What is this?" Sam tapped her pristine manicured fingernail against the card. "What am I going to find if I look it up?"

"Exactly what you asked for, Mrs Phillips." Cheryl smiled. "Don't worry, they're all women for women only. Strict policy."

"Excuse me?" Sam raised a perfectly defined dark eyebrow. "Women for women, what?"

"T-The agency." Cheryl's brows drew together. "Is everything okay with you? You seem a little bit..."

"A little bit what?" Sam stood tall, squaring her shoulders.

Cheryl adjusted her blouse. "Forgetful."

"No, Cheryl." Sam's hands balled into fists. "I think *you* are mistaken."

"Right, yes. I'm sorry. I must have got it wrong."

"I don't know what you *think* you're doing bringing me this, but it's unacceptable *and* unprofessional."

"Yes, I'm sorry." Cheryl bowed her head and sighed, her mousy-brown hair framing her face. "Let me go out and get us some lunch."

"I have lunch." Sam glowered. "Take a break, do anything. Just...don't try something like this again."

"I'm so sorry. If you need anything..."

"I don't." Sam lifted her handbag from the floor beside her desk. "I have a meeting at one. I won't be back here."

"Mrs Phillips."

"Yes?" Sam turned around, eyeing her assistant.

"It could be good for you..."

"Pardon?"

"Looking that website up. It could be good for you."

"Get out!" Sam slammed her palm on the desk. "Right now. Get out!"

Cheryl shuffled out of her boss' office as fast as she could, her heels clicking against the marble corridor flooring. Sam dropped down into her office chair, cradling her head in her hands. She didn't need this. She didn't want her staff, her assistant, meddling in her life. She'd somehow managed to keep it that way for two years, so why now? Why was Cheryl suddenly concerned about her personal life? Why couldn't people just leave well enough alone?

I can't do this. I'll never be able to do it.

Sam caught a tear before it settled on her cheek, placing her index finger under her eyelid. Waterproof mascara became her best friend over the last couple of years, but she shouldn't be crying at work. This office, at one time, was her safe haven. Her sanctuary. Her peace.

Get yourself together and get back to work, she admonished herself, standing and clenching her jaw. She fixed her suit, the lapels sitting impeccably in place, and straightened her back. She was the owner of this business, and Cheryl would do well to remember that if she wished to have a job by the time summer came to an end. Sam left her office, turning out her light as she went, and headed straight for the small cluster of desks in the open space at the end of a glass-walled corridor.

"Mrs Phillips." Cheryl gingerly rose from her seat.

Sam's nostrils flared. "Miss Webb?"

"Stains has just called. He's had to cancel."

Sam turned her wrist towards herself. "Forty minutes before the meeting is due to take place? Seems he's not the *only* unprofessional one today."

"He's had a personal emergency."

"Whatever." Sam lowered her voice. "I'm taking the rest of the day off. Finish up the paperwork and go home."

"Yes, Mrs Phillips."

"See you tomorrow."

Sam pushed her apartment door open, the room brightening with its automatic lighting. Dropping her bag to the floor, she kicked her heels off and pushed them to one side with her bare, pedicured foot. She cradled a bottle of rioja, her usual wine glass clean and ready on the granite worktop in front of her. Lifting a controller from the side table, she pressed a button and soft, sensual music played around her apartment. Being a property developer for the rich meant that she could afford such luxuries, but it didn't feel as good as it once had. She still had a home away from the city, but it stood unused, two years on from when she closed the door without looking back. Sam didn't know the condition it was in, but someone went there once a month to clean it and keep it in working order. While she didn't plan to return there in the near future, she would hate to see it turn to ruin.

She stepped out of her pants, her underwear pooling at her feet with them, and lifted the silk blouse from her body. Her suit jacket had already been shed before she'd left her car, still thrown over the back seat of her Range Rover. Turning the taps, she allowed her waterfall shower to reach the perfect temperature and turned, facing herself in the mirror.

Shit, I look old.

She took in the outline of her eyes, sunken and dark from her lack of sleep. Sam wasn't a good sleeper, she never had been, but everything became worse once she moved into the apartment. Looking back, she thought moving was the right thing for her, but now, as she looked at her thirty-seven-year-old body, she wasn't so sure. Sam sighed as she stepped into the shower, the tension leaving her shoulders as the water cascaded over her skin, soothing her aching muscles.

During her drive home, she'd thought about the website Cheryl left with her. She felt guilty, disgusted with herself for even considering such a ridiculous idea. She also felt an intrigue, one that hadn't lessened since she climbed out of her car some fifteen minutes ago. Would it be the worst idea in the world to take a look at an escort website? She knew that's what it would be. The moment *'women for women'* fell from Cheryl's lips, she could have bet her entire wealth on it. As the guilt ate away at her deep down, the intrigue pushed it further, drowning it in her belly.

Looking isn't doing anything wrong...

Sam finished up in the shower, pulling a huge bath sheet from the hook outside the cubicle. As she stepped out, wrapping it around herself, her hand settled on the sapphire necklace sitting on her chest. Her eyes closed and her breathing remained calm. This could be the worst idea she ever had, but as with most things in life...she wouldn't know if she didn't try.

Her damp feet padded down the hallway, where she landed back in the kitchen. Pouring a glass of wine and moving towards the dining table that sat in front of the floor-to-ceiling windows, Sam pulled out a chair and lifted the lid of her laptop. Her browser already open, she searched the term 'hush escorts' and her face flushed as a webpage sat at the top of the search results. *Do I really want to do this?* The cursor hovered over the link. *Is this really the right way to go about things?* Sam wasn't sure about anything this day had thrown at her, but she'd already answered her questions as her finger clicked the mouse and sent her to a high-end webpage.

"Okay, I'm here. I may as well continue." She sighed, taking her wine glass and sipping slowly. "Hmm..." She narrowed her eyes, perusing the women on offer. It didn't matter what she thought of any of them because nothing would come of this. She wouldn't pay another woman to spend time with her, not in a million years. If she couldn't be content with herself, she had serious issues.

"I want you to find love again. I don't ever want you to be alone."

Sam squeezed her eyes shut, refusing to allow herself to cry. She'd done enough of that this afternoon, and now it was time to push everything from her past to the back of her mind once again. After all, it was what she was good at. Taking a deep breath, Sam's eyes returned to the screen. In front of her she found an array of women, all beautiful, but not what she was looking for. Of course, had she been single and looking for something fun, she would find what she required here, but she wasn't. She was married, regardless of whether her wife was around or not. She was married, and she always would be. A woman like Lucia, her wife, was someone who could never leave your life.

She'd hate this.

Sam lowered her eyes to the keyboard. That sense of guilt rushing through her again. She lifted her wine glass and drained it of its contents. Moving back into the kitchen, Sam took the bottle of rioja from the worktop and carried it back to the table. Refilling her glass, she sat back in her seat and focused on the screen.

"Okay, just look..." Sam's deep brown eyes bored into the screen. "Alicia, twenty-nine, looks like she would eat me alive." Sam laughed, moving onto the next woman. "Brianna, nineteen, nope!" She swiftly moved on. "Alexis, twenty-five, enjoys dinner dates." Sam clicked Alexis' profile, apparently interested without realising it. "Okay, she's beautiful." Sam wasn't particularly bothered by a woman's appearance, but Alexis *was* incredibly attractive. Not in a seductive kind of way, but a natural beauty. Nothing about this woman looked false, and if dinner dates were what she enjoyed, Sam could certainly indulge in that, too.

Her phone sounded out beside her, shocking her from the screen. "Hello?"

"Did you eat?"

"No, not yet." Sam smiled, closing the lid of her laptop. "I'll grab something now."

"I left you a beef ragu in the fridge. Eat it; I'll know if you haven't."

"I really wish you wouldn't just let yourself into my apartment." Sam ran her fingers through her dark, caramel-highlighted hair and relaxed back against the chair. "I know you're my sister, and I know you're only looking out for me...but I'm fine."

"I called the office," Lindsay said. "Cheryl told me you didn't leave in a good mood."

"Cheryl really should mind her own business."

"And you really should be thankful that you have people who care about you," Lindsay countered. "I know you're fine, Cheryl does too, but we can still worry when we need to."

"Are you coming over?" Sam asked, changing the direction of their conversation. "I could use some company."

"I'll be there in half an hour."

"Thanks, sister."

"Love you," Lindsay replied.

"Love you more."

CHAPTER TWO

Sam sat cross-legged on her corner couch, her arm draped over the back. Lindsay arrived at her place twenty minutes ago, and she was waiting for the questions to begin. They always came in one form or another, but Sam would prefer her sister to come out with it and say whatever she had to say. As she glanced at the sixty-five-inch TV on the wall, she felt Lindsay's eyes on her. Burning through her. Trying to figure her out. Searching for something...anything. Sam cleared her throat and made herself a little more comfortable. Her eyes scanned the open-plan apartment, a sense of loneliness swallowing her up into a world that she didn't recognise. This wasn't her. The bright white walls. The chrome on black. The granite. This apartment had nothing in it that resembled the woman Sam was—not the old Sam, anyway—but this is what her life had become. Something unrecognisable. Something she, herself, didn't know.

"Mum sends her love."

"I'll call her tomorrow," Sam said, her eyes landing on her sister. "Dad?"

"He's just Dad." Lindsay smiled. "He's working with a new firm. I don't see him much."

"Well, you're welcome to come and stay here with me."

"Do you need someone to stay with you?" Lindsay's voice wavered. "You know you only have to ask, Sam."

"I don't *need* anything. I'm simply offering you somewhere to stay if Mum is getting to be too overbearing."

"You know what she's like. If she's not fussing around one of us, she doesn't know what to do with herself."

"Yeah, that's Mum."

"So, how's the office?" Lindsay reached for her wine glass. "Busy?"

"I'm always busy." Sam stretched her legs out, sighing. "I took the afternoon off when a meeting was cancelled and went for a drive."

"Go anywhere nice?"

"Usual place." Sam shrugged as she sipped her wine. "Had some cleaning up to do. She looked a mess."

"I'll bet she looks gorgeous now..." Lindsay settled her hand on her sister's leg. "You always did make sure of that."

"Oh, she was always gorgeous without my help." A smile crept onto Sam's mouth. "Incredibly beautiful."

"You know... she'd hate this." Lindsay glanced around. "You, in here alone."

"I've been here alone for two years, Linds."

"Exactly. That's what she'd hate more than anything. This time you've spent here. Time that could have been spent picking up the pieces. Finding someone you could share your time with."

"Have you been speaking to my assistant?" Sam narrowed her eyes. She could usually read her sister like a book, but tonight she was failing miserably. In all honesty, she had no idea what Lindsay was thinking.

"Cheryl? Yeah. I told you I'd called the office earlier."

"I'm talking about me. Have you been talking to her about *me*?"

"No, why?" Lindsay twirled her hair with her index finger. "Should I?"

"She just...she's convinced I need to go out and find someone." Sam's deep brown eyes closed, her teeth tugging on her bottom lip. "She left me something today. Something she said I'd asked for."

"What?"

"I'm not sure I should say." Sam shook her head ever so slightly. "I've already made the mistake of thinking about it..."

"Thinking about what, Sam?"

"A uh..." Sam hesitated for a moment, running her slender fingers around the rim of her wine glass. "Just a..."

"Huh?"

"An escort." She placed a hand over her face. "A fucking escort."

"You...with an escort?" Lindsay raised an eyebrow, proud that her sister was willing to move forward. "Sam Phillips...paying a woman to spend time with her?"

"Exactly. You see how stupid that sounds?"

"Actually, I think it's a genius idea." Lindsay beamed as she sat forward. "Absolutely genius."

"How the hell do you come to that conclusion?" Sam stared at her sister incredulously. "I mean, really?"

"You don't want to commit to another woman. I don't believe that is how you should live your life, not at all, but that's your decision. If you *do* choose to remain loveless, an escort is one way to curb any cravings you have."

"I don't *have* any cravings."

"That may be true, but coming home every night and locking yourself away is not good for you, Sam. Find a woman who just wants to spend time with you. To converse with you."

"Those women don't *want* to spend time with me. They're doing it for the money. Big money, I might add. Do you have any idea how much an escort charges?"

"Nope."

"One-thirty," Sam roared. "An hour!"

"Like you'd notice if that disappeared from your account."

"That's not the point." Sam groaned, swinging her legs off the couch and standing. "Do you want another?" She pointed at her sister's wine glass, gaining a nod from Lindsay. "The point is...that I don't think I should be spending my time with escorts."

"Why? What's wrong with it?"

"There's nothing *wrong* with it. If that's how people choose to make a living, that's up to them."

"Really, because you sounded a little judgy." Lindsay loved her sister, but at times, she could be infuriating. Sam needed this. She believed Sam knew that, too.

"I'm not." Sam returned to her sister, handing her glass over. "You know I'm the least judgmental person around."

Sam flopped down on the couch, resting her head against the low back. "Can you imagine what Lucia would say?"

"I know what she'd say."

"Oh, and what's that?" Sam's jaw clenched. "Since you seem to know exactly how I should live my life."

"She'd tell you to be happy, Sam." Lindsay shifted, resting her head on her sister's shoulder. "She'd tell you to stop wasting time sitting around. She'd tell you to go home and live your life."

"I am home."

"No, you're not." Lindsay sighed. "This will never be your home. I've never seen anyone looking so uncomfortable..."

"I-I don't know."

"And that's okay." Lindsay leaned up, pressing a kiss to her sister's cheek. "You'll know when the time is right, but if you're waiting for some kind of blessing from Lucia, you know you already have it."

"Y-Yeah." Sam closed her eyes briefly, willing her tears to disappear. "Maybe. I don't know."

"Tomorrow is another day." Lindsay smiled. "I'll stay the night. Keep you company."

"You know what? I'd like that."

"Good, because I'm not leaving."

Sam woke to the sound of cups clanging around her kitchen, startling her before she wished to rise. *This is why I live alone.* She groaned, throwing back the thin sheet that had covered her during the night and climbed to her feet. *God knows what I'm about to be faced with.* She brushed her dark hair from her face and made her way out into the open-plan space. She found Lindsay in the kitchen, trying to work her new coffee machine, muttering expletives as she did.

"Need some help?"

"Only you could have a fucking coffee machine with an app attached to it."

"It gives you options, Linds. It's fascinating."

"No, it's a ball ache," her sister retorted, moving away from the machine and groaning. "I just want a cup of black coffee. How hard can that be?"

"Okay, but what strength do you want?"

"Strength?" Lindsay's eyes widened. "Just one strong enough to prevent me from throwing you from the window."

"Well, that was rude." Sam pushed her sister out of the way and prepared a coffee she knew she'd enjoy. While her sister was only seven years younger than her, her immaturity often shone through. Polar opposites in every aspect of their lives, Sam settled down early on in life, marrying her wife at the age of twenty-seven, yet Lindsay was still partying hard at the age of thirty. Work was nothing to Lindsay, compared to Sam and her dedicated professionalism. Lindsay worked at a local bar, occasionally taking on photography gigs when someone contacted her, but Sam was at the office by eight am each morning, working until the evening rush hour traffic had died down.

"Why are you awake so early?" Sam turned to face her sister. "Even I'm not awake at six each morning."

"Couldn't sleep. Unfamiliar place."

"Mm, I know that feeling." Sam pursed her lips, turning her attention back to the coffee machine. "Here. Try that."

"So..." Lindsay sipped, moaning her approval. "Alexis?"

"What?" Sam almost spewed her coffee down the front of her pyjamas.

"Alexis." Lindsay winked. "She looks nice..."

"You've been going through my laptop!"

"Hardly. It was open on her page."

"That doesn't make it okay," Sam admonished her sister. "Why can't everyone leave me alone?"

"I'm your sister... I don't have to leave you alone." Lindsay looked pointedly at Sam. "I should be the one you come to when you have a dilemma like this."

"I don't have a dilemma. You just like to match-make."

"Wrong. I like to see my sister happy."

"And I was perfectly happy in my own little bubble before you and Cheryl came in and ruined it."

"That's not very nice." Lindsay pushed out her bottom lip. "I love you and want the best for you."

"You know what's best for me?" Sam slammed her coffee cup down. "Letting me get on with my business and staying out of a love life that will *never* exist."

"She wouldn't like this..." Lindsay called out as Sam walked away towards her bathroom.

"You know what?" Sam turned around. "She may not like it, but you know what I didn't like?"

"What?"

"Her dying. Her leaving. We were supposed to be together

forever so don't stand there and tell me she wouldn't like that I'm single and lonely. If she was here, that wouldn't be the fucking case!"

"Sam, I'm sorry."

"Yeah, and I'm sure Lucia is too." Sam slammed the bathroom door shut and rested back against it, sinking down to the floor.

Sam steadied herself, tucking her white silk shirt into her black fitted pants. Slipping her feet into her heels, she squared her shoulders and gave herself the once over in the mirror. Lindsay was still outside but knowing that she'd looked up Alexis annoyed Sam. She didn't want to reprimand her sister, but she couldn't allow this kind of behaviour. It wasn't acceptable and Sam wouldn't tolerate it, regardless of who it came from. Whether it be Lindsay or Cheryl, she didn't like the recent turn of events. It left her feeling uncomfortable. Unsure. Apprehensive.

Lifting her phone from the bed, Sam checked for any messages, finding none from Cheryl. While she fully believed that her assistant was treading on thin ice, Sam wanted to apologise. She wanted to put the escort situation to bed and get on with her job. A job that had provided everything Sam and Lucia could ever need. *Yet it didn't save her.* Sam picked up the framed photo sitting on her bedside table, her fingertips brushing gently against the glass. *God, I miss you so much.* Sam swallowed down the lump in her throat as she returned the photograph to its place with shaky hands.

"I'll see you tonight." Sam's voice wavered, her back connecting with the bedroom door. "Just you and me. Always."

"Sam?"

"I'll be out in a moment," she called back to her sister. "If you have to leave, that's fine."

"I-I do have to leave, but I wanted to see you before I did," Lindsay stuttered. "Please, come out..."

Sam slowly turned the handle, praying her eyes didn't give her away. "I'm okay. See?"

"You've been crying." Lindsay leaned against the frame of the door. "If that's because of me, I'm sorry."

"It's not. I'm sorry about this morning." Sam waved off her sister's apology. "No more of this, okay?"

"Which?"

"Trying to find someone to spend my evenings with. I'm perfectly fine coming home and preparing for the next day. I don't need a woman in my life. I have everything I need." Sam squeezed her sister's shoulder and smiled. "Now, you should go home before Mum has a fit about where you've been all night. Tell her I'll call her tonight after dinner."

"Why don't you come to Mum's for dinner? You know she'd love us all to be together." While Lindsay wanted to push their conversation regarding Sam's loneliness, she wouldn't. Her sister had been through enough emotion already this morning.

"I don't know what my schedule looks like yet," Sam said. "Let me have a look at my day once I get to the office and I'll call you." Sam was fully aware of her schedule for the day. She merely didn't want to get into something with Lindsay right now.

"That works for me." Lindsay kissed Sam's cheek. "I am sorry about this morning."

"It's forgotten about."

Sam watched her sister leave, throwing her a wave as she slipped out of her apartment door. Releasing a deep breath, she gave herself a moment before leaving too, not wanting to share the lift with Lindsay this morning. She felt suffocated. She needed to come up for air, and that couldn't happen while her concerned sister was standing beside her, sharing the same space.

Sam closed her eyes and calmed herself. Of course, she appreciated everything her loved ones had done for her in the two years since Lucia passed away, but they couldn't look after her forever. They had their own lives, their own problems. Before Sam foolishly opened her laptop last night, she didn't believe she had any issues to contend with. But now, after spending an hour showering and allowing her thoughts to get the better of her, she felt differently.

CHAPTER THREE

"I understand that, Stains, I really do..." Sam pinched the bridge of her nose. "But I'm not prepared to scrimp on contractors because you want the job done for less. I'm sorry, but we know what happens when we make shortcuts."

"What?"

"Problems arise. In some cases, people lose their lives." Sam had dealt with this man before, and the second time around, she continued to have issues with him. "Those people who will move into that apartment block, paying a lot of money to do so, wouldn't appreciate a shoddy job. I'm not about to provide one. You sign off on the estimate, or you find someone else. I won't have my name, my *wife's* name, tarnished when the shit hits the fan."

"Sam, love..."

"Don't, Roger!" Sam gritted her teeth. "Make your decision. You have until the end of the week or I'm pulling out."

Sam returned the handset to the receiver, squeezing her eyes shut as she felt a headache approaching. Pressing the speakerphone, she called outside to Cheryl. "Come to my office."

"Be right there."

Cheryl sounded perky this morning; Sam had recognised that the moment she walked through the double doors at eight am. She wanted to believe that Cheryl was being her usual self, but after yesterday's exchange of words, she couldn't.

"Mrs Phillips?" Cheryl appeared in her doorway. "How did the call with Stains go?"

"How do you think?" Sam glanced at the door, motioning for Cheryl to come inside. "Have a seat..."

"He wants you to change the estimate, doesn't he?" Cheryl relaxed into the high-back leather chair facing her boss.

"Of course he does." Sam nodded, gathering paperwork in her hand. "He's always been a tight arse, but he won't have me on board if he continues."

"No, I know." Cheryl smiled. "I don't know how he expects you to do it for less, I really don't."

"I can't." Sam shrugged, turning her full attention to her assistant. "He believes I'm adding on for my own gain. Has he seen my accounts? My portfolio?"

"I'm going to assume he hasn't."

"About yesterday." Sam held up her hand. "I'm sorry."

"No, I am," Cheryl countered. "I shouldn't have stuck my nose in your business. I was just doing what you asked me to do."

"I don't recall the conversation we had at Cork, I really don't, but that doesn't mean that I had any right to speak to you how I did."

"Don't worry about it." Cheryl crossed her legs. "I won't mention it again."

"You said you use the website..." Sam drummed her fingers on her desk. "Often, or...?"

"Depends what mood I'm in." Cheryl smirked. "There was a time when I used it more than I should..."

"Because?"

"Because I was lonely," Cheryl admitted.

"And you're not anymore?"

"Actually, I'm dating someone."

"Oh, that's great." Sam smiled, clasping her hands together. "About time you let your hair down."

"Trust me, I let my hair down. That website was epic at times."

"I'm sure it was." Sam wanted to remain neutral, but the more Cheryl talked, the more she needed to know. "Did you always book the same woman?"

"Pretty much."

"Well, I'm glad you've found someone now." Sam nodded. She may be intrigued, but her assistant didn't need to know that. "It looks good on you." She noted that glimmer Cheryl had in her eyes. "Perhaps you could bring her by the office some time?"

"Maybe I will." Cheryl stood, fixing her skirt on her thighs. "Drinks on Friday?"

"Always." Sam winked. "Friday is our reserved 'thank fuck the week is over' night..."

"And I will certainly drink to that when Friday comes." Cheryl backed up, opening the office door. "I'm going to lunch in twenty. I'll see you later."

Settling back in her seat, Sam reopened the webpage she'd closed thirty minutes ago when Roger Stains called. It was a bad move on her part to even consider browsing the internet, but she'd already fallen into the possibility of hiring an escort, and she wasn't sure she could back out now. Not after Cheryl had all but sang the agencies praises. She clicked on Alexis' ad details and picked up her personal phone. The website gave the option of calling or sending a text message; Sam opted for the latter. The thought of making a phone call and hearing another woman's voice, a woman she was interested in paying, would surely make her crumble into a thousand pieces.

Oh God! What have I done?

Sam's hand trembled as she set her phone down on her desk for the fifth time in around forty minutes. Alexis had responded, opting to meet Sam at a restaurant this evening. Her heart was in her mouth but she couldn't back out now. It was just dinner, after all.

What if she expects sex?

Sam's stomach churned, the possibility of spending the evening with another woman causing bile to rise in her throat. Sam wasn't stupid; she knew what most escorts evenings entailed. Would hers be the same? Alexis didn't look like some of the women in their profiles. She looked less inclined to expect sex at the end of their evening.

I'm not paying her for sex. I'm paying her for dinner.

A million and one thoughts whirled around Sam's head, her eyes blurring as she stared at the blank computer screen in front of her. Should she just go home and pretend she'd never sent the message? Should she cancel? No, she couldn't. Deep down, she didn't want to. Perhaps it *would* be nice to not sit at home alone. This could be the start of something new, but what that something was, Sam had no idea. In all honesty, she didn't know what she wanted from this evening. The only certainty she was aware of…was that tonight, she would be alone with a woman for the first time in two years.

A sudden panic set in, sending Sam's pulse racing. She collected her phone from her desk and dialed her sister's number. "H-Hello?"

"Sam, is everything okay?" Lindsay's voice quivered. "Sam?"

"I made a mistake."

"I don't think you've ever made a mistake in your life…"

"No, I have. This time… I definitely have."

"Okay, calm down and talk to me."

Sam's breathing quickened. "I booked her." Her voice trembled. "I booked a fucking escort."

"Okay, stop," Lindsay said. "Just breathe, Sam. This isn't the end of the world."

"Oh, I think it is." She dropped her head to the palm of her hand. "What the hell am I doing? Have I lost my mind?"

"No, you're just ready to explore."

"How can I explore an escort, Linds? I'm paying a woman to have dinner with me. What the hell is there to explore?"

"I-I don't know." Lindsay sighed. "But at least you've made some kind of step."

"To what? Whoring myself out, effectively?"

"You know that's complete rubbish." Lindsay laughed. "If you want to book an escort, that's your business."

"It still doesn't feel right."

"Okay, but what happens if you meet her and sparks fly?" Lindsay asked, the line suddenly becoming silent. "Sam, hello?"

"Sparks?" Sam snorted. "What planet are you on, Linds?"

"Hey!" Lindsay admonished her sister. "You don't know *what* the outcome of tonight will be. That woman could fall head over heels in love with you!"

"And you need professional help if that's what you really think," Sam quipped. "I have to go. My work won't do itself."

"Avoiding!"

"I'm not. I'm just not prepared to listen to you talk rubbish anymore."

"Fine."

"I'll call you tonight when I realise I've made a mistake again and run out on a beautiful woman."

"Step one, accomplished."

"Excuse me?"

"You just referred to her as a beautiful woman…"

"So?"

"You've just gone from 'whoring yourself out' to meeting a beautiful woman in a matter of minutes."

"No, I was simply stating the obvious." Sam cut the call and threw her phone down onto her desk. She should have known that her conversation with Lindsay would be pointless, but she could still pretend it had been worth her while.

Sam relaxed back in her seat, kicking her heels off beneath her desk. She swivelled around in her chair, facing the water through the gigantic windows Lucia had installed when Sam bought the building. The light they let into the office was incredible, but Sam had every trust in the woman she loved. Lucia always had an eye for the finer things in life, and that extended to her wife's office. This room had been a personal project of Lucia's, with Sam banished from it until her wife had given her the key the morning they officially opened. The desk sat central in front of the panoramic windows, providing Sam with a view that was simply breathtaking. When the dark nights approached, it was as though she was staring out into the abyss, only the occasional light from a ship sailing down the river reminding her what sat outside the comfort of her office.

When she worked late during the summer months, the pink and purple hues in the sky were enough to bring tears to her eyes. Hues that Lucia was conjuring up only for her wife. That's when it hit the hardest, when Sam was alone in the office, contemplating ending it all. For months after her wife's death, she wondered how she could continue coming into the office every day. She wondered how any of this was normal behaviour. Then it hit her, as it always did. Lucia didn't want Sam to retreat inside herself. She didn't want her to live a life of loneliness, only conversing with those closest to her. She wanted Sam to live her life. A life they were supposed to live together.

"Babe?" Sam dropped her bag, closing the heavy wooden front door as she slid her blazer from her shoulders. "Luce?"

"In here, honey," Lucia called out to her wife, the scent coming from the kitchen confirming her whereabouts. "I made you your favourite."

"You're too good to me." Sam approached her wife from behind,

her arms settling around Lucia's waist as she leaned in, kissing the skin of her neck. "I thought you were coming by the office this afternoon?"

"I got held up with an old client."

"Anyone I know?" Sam asked, taking a glass of red wine from the kitchen island worktop.

"No, he's a client from way back." Lucia stirred the tomato sauce on the stove before lowering it to a simmer and meeting her wife's eyes. "It was awful."

"Why?"

"He lost his wife," Lucia said. "Jude...she was wonderful. I worked with her when I first started out." Lucia was an architect, meeting Sam when she was just twenty-five. "She had a stroke. He turned off her machine."

"Sorry to hear that." Sam took Lucia's hand, pulling her against her. "Can I do anything to make it better?"

"Just having you home for dinner is good enough." Lucia leaned in, her lips softly pressing against Sam's. "But it got me thinking..."

"Uh-oh." Sam smirked. "That's never a good sign."

"Hey!" Lucia swatted her wife's shoulder. "It got me thinking about us. If that time ever came..."

"Babe, don't." Sam lowered her eyes. "I don't want to talk about death with you. Nothing is going to happen. We're both healthy and thriving."

"I just want you to know that I'd want you to move on. If anything happens to me, mourn me, but find someone to share your life with."

"Luce..."

"That's all I'll say about it, but I mean it, Samantha. I want you to find love again. I don't ever want you to be alone."

"Nobody could ever compare to you..."

"And I wouldn't expect them to." Lucia smiled as she cupped Sam's face. "That doesn't mean you wouldn't deserve to be happy again. Or me..."

"Uh, I've got no plans to die and leave the most beautiful woman in the world alone."

"Good. Me neither."

Sam closed her eyes, remembering her wife's voice. At one time, it was too painful to hear Lucia, but as the months wore on… things became easier. Now, she often replayed their videos. Their wedding day. Anything that kept Lucia alive inside her. As much as she wanted her wife to walk through her office door, Sam had made peace with the fact that it would never happen. As she slept alone night after night, she knew she would never breathe the same air as her wife again.

Lucia had that something about her. Whenever she walked into a room, she stole people's breath. Sam's included. That had never lessened over the course of their relationship and their marriage had only secured them more. Her dark Italian eyes gave off an intrigue that Sam had never witnessed before, and the moment Lucia spoke, her soft, sensual voice lulling Sam into another world, she knew she would love her forever. She knew that wherever they were in the world, together or apart, she would never love another woman like she loved Lucia Phillips. When she told her wife that nobody could ever compare to her, she meant it. As the years passed since Lucia's death…that fact still remained. Nobody on the planet held Sam's attention for even a fraction of a second. Not that she had been looking, but still, not a single woman had come close to turning Sam's head. None.

"I'm leaving for the day," Cheryl said, startling Sam as she stepped into her office.

"Christ!"

"Sorry, I didn't mean to scare you."

"No, you didn't." Sam placed her hand over her chest and spun around in her chair. "I was just thinking. Must have gotten carried away."

"Did you need anything before I go?"

"No, thank you." Sam smiled. "Enjoy your evening."

"Any plans?" Cheryl asked, her light jacket draped over her arm.

"Nothing," Sam lied. "Home. Dinner for one. The usual."

"You're more than welcome to come over to mine if you wanted some company."

"Thank you, but I have stuff to do at home." Sam slid her thick, black-rimmed glasses down her face, sitting them perfectly on her nose. "I'll see you in the morning, okay?" She focused her attention on the blueprints in front of her. "I'm leaving in the next hour or so."

"Okay, goodnight, Mrs Phillips."

CHAPTER FOUR

Sam stopped at the dock entrance, gathering herself for a moment before she turned the corner and made the biggest mistake of her life. Since she'd left the office, she'd continuously wondered what her wife would make of the evening she had planned. Sitting in a high-end restaurant with another woman. An escort. Talking freely about life and one another. Sam didn't know the first thing about how to approach this evening, but it was too late to back out now. There wasn't enough time to turn around and head home, leaving Alexis sitting alone in a bar. Even if she did have time for that, Sam would never do that to another woman. Regardless of who she was.

She steeled herself and blew out a deep breath, pushing her thick, dark hair away from her left shoulder. The temperature was hovering above average this evening, so she'd opted for a little black dress, falling just above her knee. Her dark, smoky eye makeup would hopefully hide the puffiness of them since she'd spent thirty minutes crying before she took a shower.

Okay, the sooner I get inside...the sooner I can leave.

She walked towards the corner of the dock front and turned, heading for the restaurant she'd arranged to meet Alexis at. Long summer nights brought a stress-free vibe to the city. Patrons relaxing on the outdoor seating of the local bars, live music enticing customers to come inside and try a craft beer or two. Where Sam was headed was her usual choice of dining, but nothing about this meeting felt as relaxing as it usually would. Of course, she could go in there in business mode, but what impression would that give to the woman she was paying this evening? On the other hand, how could she attempt to be calm and collected when her heart was beating harder than it had in a long time?

Sam quickly removed her phone from her bag and pulled up her assistant's details.

S: You know when you book one of the women...do you pay for everything?

Her phone buzzed, giving her less time than she thought she had to think up a response.

C: Why are you asking such a random question?
S: Intrigued, I suppose.
C: Well, yes. You pay for her and everything else.
S: Okay. Thanks.
C: Who did you book?
S: What? I didn't...
C: Sure. Enjoy your evening.
S: I will. Home in my PJs.
C: Sure you are.

Sam chose not to respond and instead, shoved her phone back into her bag. Cheryl wasn't stupid, she knew that, but she didn't have the time for a million and one questions from her assistant. Once she answered one question, it would snowball and she would never make it inside.

She pushed the heavy glass door open to be greeted by a familiar waiter. This tapas bar had become a regular for her and Lucia over the years, and every time she came back, Sam was welcomed just the same.

"Sam, it's been a long time..." Xavi, the waiter, held out an arm. "Your usual table?"

"Oh, no." She cleared her throat. "I'll wait at the bar for another."

"Of course." He smiled, his chiseled look fitting in perfectly with the dim Spanish surroundings. "Please, follow me."

Sam moved through the foyer and towards the bar, glancing around for any sign of Alexis. Discovering that she wasn't yet there, Sam calmed her nerves and took a seat on the high bar stool in front of the distressed wooden counter top. *Perhaps she's going to stand me up.* Sam pondered that thought for a moment, relieved that it could be a possibility, but then the doors opened and the first thought on Sam's mind was to run out the back door. Alexis was incredible. Her long, naturally blonde hair fell over her shoulders and sat above her midsection, the colour of an organic honey. The bluest eyes lit up the entire restaurant, causing Sam to swallow hard. But it was the effortless beauty radiating from Alexis that suddenly felt intimidating to Sam, which caught her attention above all else.

Her eyes found Alexis' and Sam could do nothing other than smile. She climbed down from her stool, and Alexis leaned in, kissing her on the cheek.

"You must be Samantha."

"Sam."

"Whatever you prefer." Alexis gave her a full, beaming smile. "Have you ordered?" she asked, elegantly pulling herself up onto the stool next to Sam's.

"No, not yet."

"May I order?" Alexis crossed her impossibly long legs. "This bar has some of the best cocktails around."

"You come here?"

"All the time," Alexis said. "Usually with friends. Not clients."

"Oh." Sam's hands trembled. "Okay, whatever you think is good."

Alexis nodded, turning her attention to the barman. Upon arrival, she'd noticed the older woman's beauty. She'd also noticed it the moment she was contacted earlier today. Alexis didn't make a habit of just meeting with any client who contacted her. If she didn't get a good vibe, a positivity, she would simply decline. When Sam's name and profile popped up for her to read through, Alexis was blown away. Now, sitting beside her, she knew she'd chosen the right one out of a long list of potentials.

Sam hadn't realised it in the moments that Alexis approached her, but this woman made her feel comfortable. Nothing seemed forced. Okay, they'd merely spoken a few words to one another, but she imagined it to be different. Nerve-racking, perhaps.

"Am I late or did you arrive early?" Alexis turned her attention to Sam, placing her head in her palm.

"Oh, I think I was early. Habit, sorry."

"Don't apologise." Alexis laughed, sending Sam's heart rate soaring. "You look like someone who has never been late in their life."

"I think you could be right." Sam couldn't recall a time she had ever arrived late to anything. She'd like to believe it was the businesswoman in her but growing up had been the same. Her parents had drilled it into both Sam and Lindsay that punctuality was important in life. Unfortunately, Lindsay never lived by that, and Sam knew that was why she struggled to hold down a permanent job during the day.

"Sam, your table..." Xavi approached Sam and helped her down from her stool. "You have company this evening."

"Business," Sam said, bristling.

"Yes, this way."

Once seated, Sam rested back in the booth, her eyes fixed on her hands sitting in her lap. It wasn't very often that she was a woman of few words, but something had genuinely caught her tongue tonight. Her guess, that something being Alexis.

"You've never done this before, have you?" Alexis asked, her voice low as the waiter brought them their cocktail order.

"N-No." Sam shook her head, glancing up at the waiter. "Thank you, Steve."

"Good to see you, Sam." He smiled as he acknowledged Alexis and left the table.

"But I did check online and it stated I'm to pay you before the evening gets going..."

Sam didn't like this. Not the money side of it. While she was perfectly happy to pay Alexis for their evening together, she didn't like doing business over the table of her most frequented restaurant.

"Don't worry. We can fix that later."

"No, I play by the rules." Sam reached for her purse.

"Samantha, it's okay."

"Sam." Her eyes shot up, her brow furrowed as her hands stilled. "It's just Sam."

Alexis noted the tone of Sam's voice. "Right, yeah." She nodded. "I'm sorry."

"Only my wife calls me Samantha." The words left Sam's mouth faster than the speed of light. Closing her eyes, she internally winced, her admission catching her off guard.

"You know, I have a lot of married clients. It's nothing to be ashamed of." Alexis tried to lighten the mood, effectively putting Sam at ease, but her client's eyes told a different story. This woman...she didn't want to be here. Perhaps she did to some extent, but this really would be a night of dinner and nothing more. That, to Alexis, was her ideal night.

"Excuse me?" Sam's eyes fluttered open.

"My clients...a lot of them are in relationships or married. What we're doing, it's actually quite normal."

"I'm not like your other clients." Sam shook her head. "I'm not a cheat. At least, I don't think I am." Her words hung in the air as she contemplated them. Was she a cheat? This, what she was doing, could be considered that to some.

"This is just dinner, Sam."

"Alexis, you're wonderful..." Sam paused. "...but I don't know what I'm doing here. I don't know what to say to you or how to approach this."

"What do you want this evening?" Alexis asked, her sincere tone appearing to calm Sam as her shoulders relaxed.

"This. Dinner," she said. "Conversation with someone rather than the four walls at home."

"Then that is what you can have."

"If this becomes a thing." Sam motioned between them. "Us, meeting or whatever... I *only* want dinner and conversation."

"You mean, you're not booking me for sex?" Alexis placed her hand over her chest, feigning shock. "I'm horrified."

"Okay." Sam laughed, nodding. "I like you." She lifted her glass and sipped, surprised by how good her cocktail tasted. She was more of a wine woman, but when Alexis suggested something different, she found herself unable to overrule. "What is this?"

"It's called a Godfather Part Three." Alexis lifted her own drink and winked. "Cheers."

"Yeah, cheers." Sam narrowed her eyes. Were all escorts this polite and laid back or had she just chosen right?

"And that was why I became an escort."

"So, you're telling me..." Sam studied Alexis' face. "...that you enjoy good food, good company, and women...so that's why you're an escort?"

"Pretty much." Alexis shrugged. "And you should know, Sam, I don't agree to meeting with everyone who contacts me." As the evening wore on, Alexis found herself willingly flirting with the woman sitting across the table from her. It wasn't foreign, not by any means, but Alexis didn't usually react this way. If someone wanted nothing more than dinner or friendship, she would usually oblige, but tonight... she found herself being lured in by Sam's deep eyes. Her smile. Everything.

"No?"

"Oh, no." Alexis laughed from deep within her belly. "I've had some great clients, and I've had some terrible ones. I don't need to do this permanently. I do it because I enjoy this kind of evening."

"You don't have friends you can do this with?"

"I do, of course. But meeting someone new...someone who is kind and appreciative of my company gives me a real confidence boost."

"Well, I certainly have enjoyed your company."

Alexis simply smiled, enamoured by the woman holding her attention in every way possible.

"Is this the only thing you offer?" Sam's words caused Alexis' eyes to widen but not enough to scare her client off. *Not what I expected,* Alexis thought.

"No, I offer everything escorts offer." She smirked. "But I prefer this side of things."

"Good to know." Sam smiled but Alexis felt a pang of disappointment. "So, I think I'm pretty much done here."

"Okay." Alexis smiled shyly. *Why are you behaving like this?* She warred with herself internally. "The night ends when you say it does."

"I'll just get the bill and then I'll...you know."

"Right, yes." She knew Sam was referring to payment, but in this moment, money was the last thing on her mind. Over the two years she'd worked as an escort, she had never felt a connection with any of them. At least, not like this. There had been one other who she felt was testing the boundaries of their relationship, but this, how she felt this evening? It had never happened before. Sam, though...something was different about her. While Alexis knew absolutely nothing about her, she felt drawn. A pull she'd never experienced in this line of work before.

She watched on as Sam paid the bill, her slight fingers holding the card machine so delightfully. Her deep brown eyes focused fully on the digits on the keypad. How her hair fell down the side of her face exquisitely. Sam, to Alexis, was a high-class woman. But she was also someone who had a past. Alexis could see that. Her only hope after tonight ended, was that Sam would one day contact her again.

"All done."

"Great." Alexis blushed, knowing she'd been caught staring. "Shall we walk out?"

"I'd like that." Sam smiled. She'd felt Alexis' piercing gaze on her, but she knew what it meant. If she wasn't careful, one thing could quickly lead to another with this woman.

Alexis stood, waiting for Sam to do the same. Now that they'd gotten better acquainted, Alexis struggled to keep her eyes from trailing her client's body. Curves in all the right places and legs that had clearly seen the gym multiple times this week left her own knees feeling weak. She placed her hand on the small of Sam's back as they left the restaurant side by side, pleasantly surprised when she didn't back away. She fully expected her to, given the unease she'd sensed at times during their arrangement, but Sam had evidently relaxed as the night wore on, leaving Alexis more perplexed than she was moments ago.

"Can I call you a cab?" Sam asked as they reached the dock wall. "I'm only ten minutes from here."

"I can walk." Alexis smiled, her eyes taking in Sam's beautiful features. The tiny freckle above her right eyebrow, her flawless jawline. Everything about Sam was the opposite of Alexis' usual attraction in women, but she couldn't deny the feeling of wanting to kiss this woman. "Which way are you?" Alexis pulled herself from the thoughts she was battling with. "I'm off Portland."

"Oh, I'm the same way." Sam busied herself inside her purse. "Do you prefer cash or cheque?"

I'd prefer you. Alexis cleared her throat, keeping her arousal in check.

"The agency state that cash transactions are required, but whatever is easier for you." Alexis had done this hundreds of time, so why did she suddenly feel awful for taking Sam's money?

"Cash it is then."

"Thank you."

"Oh, seems I don't quite have enough on me." Sam smiled, an embarrassment in her eyes evident. "You said you live off Portland Street?"

"I do."

"Then we could walk home together," Sam suggested. "I live on Birchall."

"Okay..." Alexis drawled out.

"I'll run up and get the rest. Won't take a second." Sam could happily kick herself for not being better prepared, but she hadn't expected to stay at the restaurant for so long. Especially not since it was her first meeting with an escort. A drink, perhaps two, then she'd planned to leave. Now, knowing that she'd spent some four hours with a woman she didn't know...it left her feeling confused.

"Works for me." Alexis shrugged as they slowly made their way off the dock and towards the city's main road.

"I didn't think I'd spend so long with you, I'm sorry."

"I didn't think you'd stay," Alexis admitted. "You looked like you wanted to be anywhere but with me when I first met you."

"This is just...new to me." Sam side-glanced at Alexis. "I never thought I'd contact you."

"Why *did* you contact me?" Alexis asked, the humid evening air causing a slight perspiration to settle on her forehead.

"Company."

"Well, we established that earlier this evening..."

"What you're asking is, why the company of an escort?" Sam's eyebrow rose. "When I have a wife, why am I contacting you?"

"Like I said earlier, Sam... Whether you have a wife or not is none of my business."

"Still...you must wonder why you have clients who are married, no?"

"I'm paid to make my clients feel good. Not know the ins and outs of their lives." Alexis hated being so formal about their evening, but her desire to take this further was becoming too much, and far too soon. *I have to remain distant.*

"Right." Sam managed a smile but Alexis saw through it.

"That doesn't mean I don't take an interest, so please don't think that's what I meant."

"No, you're right." Sam held up her hand. "This is an arrangement. This is your job."

Alexis felt a guilt settle deep in her belly. She hadn't meant to appear so nonchalant about Sam and her life, but as an escort, she distanced herself from getting to know people too well. After all, the end result was still the same as every other arrangement she had. She still went home alone. She still woke up alone. Her everyday life was very much alone. Though she felt something for Sam, as ridiculous as it seemed, Alexis knew nothing could ever possibly escalate. Sam was married and this was an arrangement.

"So, this is me." Sam cleared her throat as she took her keys from her bag. "Give me a second, okay?"

"If this is too much for you..."

"I've had a great evening." Sam offered Alexis a sweet smile. "Now you get paid."

Alexis watched Sam disappear into her apartment block, the heavy glass door closing behind her. Whenever she was with a client in such close proximity to their home, it usually ended differently. She certainly couldn't recall a time that she was left standing outside, but Sam had made it clear that their arrangement was dinner and conversation. Now that was over, her client was sticking to her word. Alexis pushed her blonde hair from her face as a breeze whipped around her, sighing as she leaned back against the wall of the building.

Why am I attracted to her?

She closed her eyes, pushing Sam from her mind and the way she made her feel. Alexis had *always* been in control of her evenings with clients, and while she didn't particularly feel that she wasn't in control tonight, nothing felt how it should. In reality, she should go home this evening and wait for another booking with Sam, but right now, she wanted to ask her to dinner on her own terms. Without the escort façade. Without the payment at the end of the night. Without...this.

The door clicked and Alexis turned to find Sam staring at her. "Thank you for waiting."

"Thank you for choosing me to spend your evening with." Alexis' hand brushed Sam's as she took the envelope from her.

"How much of this do you give to the agency?"

"Oh, I can't say..." Alexis smiled faintly.

"Then there is a cheque in there for you, too," Sam stated. "Separate from the cost of tonight."

"Sam, that's not necessary." Alexis shook her head. "Please, take it back."

"Goodnight, Alexis." Sam leaned in, but hesitated.

"Goodnight." Alexis took the lead, pressing a kiss to Sam's cheek. "Perhaps I'll see you again."

CHAPTER FIVE

Sam made her way up the garden path, steeling herself for an evening with her mother. She'd somehow managed to avoid a family dinner for the last couple of months, but Lindsay insisted that tonight was the night when they could all catch up together. Their father wouldn't be there, but Sam had become accustomed to that over the years. William Priestly worked his fingers to the bone, even at the age of sixty-seven. Sam curled her hand into a fist, knocking on her parents' door. On the way here, she discovered that her set of keys had been misplaced, unable to remember the last time she had used them.

"Sam!" The door flew open. "I thought you'd cancel *again*."

"Not now, Mum." Sam pulled her mum into a hug. "I'm here, aren't I?"

"You are, sweetheart." Susan pulled back, looking at her daughter. "You look tired."

"Thanks." Sam blew out a deep breath as she crossed the threshold. "Can I at least get inside before the insults begin?"

"It wasn't an insult, my love. It was an observation."

"Yeah, dress it up however you like." Sam dropped her bag to the floor, moving through her parents' home. "Lindsay home?"

"She has a photo shoot." Sam noted how her mum's eyes lit up at the mention of Lindsay working. "I think it's a big one, too."

"That's great." *She didn't tell me about it.*

"You know how she likes to be out there and doing what she loves." *Evidently, we are talking about two different people.*

"So, why haven't I seen you in so long? Are you eating? Sleeping okay?"

"This is why, Mum." Sam cocked her head. "I don't need a million questions from you. I can take care of myself."

"Judging by the weight you've lost, I beg to differ."

"What weight?" Sam let out an exasperated sigh. She loved her mother dearly, but the worry and the questions really had prevented her from visiting. It was a never-ending theme.

"You look sick, Sam." Susan pulled her daughter into the conservatory. "Why don't you come home for a while?"

"Because I have a home."

"Which one?" Her mother raised an eyebrow. "The beautiful one in the countryside, or that bloody flat you live in?"

"It's an apartment and it does me perfectly fine."

"Your father wants us to come and visit you," Susan said. "He's home this weekend."

"And I'm probably going to be busy."

"As always..."

"Mum, please." Sam dropped her face into her hands. "Can I not just come here for dinner and hear about how your day has been? Any plans you have? Why does it all have to revolve around me and the miserable life you *believe* I lead?"

"You work too much. You're going to kill yourself!" her mother shrieked. "I don't want to wake up one day to news that my daughter is dead."

"Um, a little dramatic...don't you think?"

"No! No, I bloody well don't." Susan stood, pacing the floor. "Come home, Sam. Come and stay here. Take a break."

"I own a business, Mum. I don't have the option of taking a break."

"You lost your wife and you didn't take a single day off. That's not healthy. It's not right."

"I'm leaving." Sam shook her head. "I'm not sitting here listening to the same thing I've listened to for two years."

"Something is going on with you." Susan narrowed her eyes. "You and Lindsay. You're behaving very suspiciously, and I don't like it."

"Suspiciously?" Sam snorted. "And what do you think it is that we're up to?"

"I don't know because neither of you will speak to me!"

"And can you blame us?" Sam asked. "You're always worrying, Mum. Let it go. We're both fine."

"I'M HOME!" Lindsay's voice bellowed through the lower level of Sam's childhood home.

"Then you should come in here before Mum has us both sectioned!" Sam yelled. "Now!"

"What?" Lindsay appeared. "Sectioned? Why?"

"She thinks we're being secretive—"

"I said suspicious," Susan interrupted.

"Uh, I've been working so I have no idea what's going on." Lindsay set her camera bag down.

"You working *is* suspicious." Sam smirked. "How did it go?"

"Fine, yeah." Lindsay shrugged as she disappeared into the living room.

Sam knew something was off with her sister, but she wouldn't bring it up here. Not when their mother was already on the warpath. Sam knew well enough to wait until she was alone with Lindsay, especially if she had any chance of getting out of here in one piece tonight. Her mum...she was relentless when it came to discussions.

"Go and sit with your sister. I'll make dinner."

"Yes, Mother." Sam rolled her eyes, leaving her mum standing in the middle of the conservatory.

Sam joined Lindsay in her parents' outdated living room. Wrinkling her nose as her eyes landed on the distressed leather couch, she took a seat and eyed her sister.

"What's going on?"

"Huh? With who?" Lindsay side-glanced at Sam.

"*You*. Smart arse."

"Nothing, why?" Lindsay kicked her feet up onto the coffee table. "Have you been in touch with Alexis again?"

"No. Stop deflecting." Sam lowered her voice. "Work...where was it?"

"In town."

"Where?" Sam asked.

"F-For some company."

"Name of the company?" Sam leaned in closer. "Address of the company?"

"What?" Lindsay's forehead creased. "What the hell is wrong with you?"

"I want to know where you've been working!"

"A new bistro. They wanted me to do some food shoots for them. Someone recommended me to them."

"You don't do shoots unless you need the money."

"I needed the money." Lindsay shrugged. "Obviously."

"Are you putting that shit up your nose again?" Sam gritted her teeth.

"N-No." Lindsay's voice broke.

"So why do you need the money?" Sam clenched her fists. "Do you owe someone? A dealer?"

"Fuck off, Sam." Lindsay pulled her knees up to her chest.

"Mum said you're being suspicious. Now you're working when you don't usually. What the fucking hell is going on?"

"I thought you knew me better than that!" Lindsay shot off the couch. "I thought you knew I wouldn't ever do that again.

Fuck you!" Lindsay disappeared, her heavy footsteps up the stairs ending with a slammed door.

"Fuck!" Sam dug her nails into her palms. "Mum, I have to go!" she yelled as she snuck out of the living room and towards the front door.

"Go where?" Susan stood in the kitchen doorway.

"Something came up at the office. I'm sorry." Before Susan had the chance to respond, Sam was rushing out of the door and down the garden path.

"Lindsay, please call me." Sam spoke to Lindsay's voicemail for the sixth time in thirty minutes. Her evening had barely begun with Alexis, but her escort was the last thing on her mind at the moment. As much as she wanted to enjoy another summer's evening on the dock with the incredible blonde, Sam found herself standing at the dock wall, desperately seeking some kind of contact with her sister.

"Is everything okay?" Alexis asked as Sam walked towards her, her hand gripping her phone.

"Yeah, just trying to call my sister."

"Oh, okay." Alexis had noticed Sam's lack of conversation since she arrived, but she couldn't really comment on it. Not when it had nothing to do with her. She would sit and wait, hoping Sam would find at least five minutes to converse with her before their time was up for the evening.

"I'm sorry. I know I should be fully here with you, but we fell out earlier and now I can't contact her."

"Nothing serious, I hope?"

"Could be, I don't know." Sam sighed, sitting down next to Alexis. "Gorgeous night, huh?"

"Perfect." Alexis' eyes trailed Sam's profile. "Should I order us more drinks?"

"Yeah, we should definitely do that." Sam stared out at the calm water, the sound of laughter and music playing around her. "Surprise me." Her hand settled on Alexis' thigh briefly, pulling away when she realised what was happening. "Sorry."

"Don't." Alexis smirked as she stood up and leaned down. "Someone like you touching me?" she whispered. "Any time, Sam."

Sam swallowed hard, watching her escort walk inside the bar.

Don't, Sam. Just don't!

She calmed herself, taking deep breaths and trying to remove the feel of Alexis' muscular thighs from her memory. Sam hadn't touched another woman since the day she met Lucia, but just that brief moment with Alexis had ignited something inside her. Something she wasn't sure she could control.

"They're bringing them out to us." Alexis' breath washed over Sam's ear, causing the hairs on the back of her neck to stand on end. "Shouldn't be too long."

"O-Okay."

"Anything from your sister yet?" Alexis returned to her seat, shifting that little bit closer to Sam.

"No, I haven't tried again."

"Maybe she just needs some time to herself?"

"That's what I'm worried about," Sam said. "She used to have a cocaine habit."

"Oh, I'm sorry." Alexis placed her hand over Sam's, their connection undeniable. "If you need to leave, I wouldn't be offended."

"That's the problem." Sam smiled, her eyes distant. "I don't want to leave."

"No?" Alexis squeezed Sam's hand, bringing her back to the moment.

"What?"

"You said you don't want to leave…"

"Right, yeah." Sam blushed. "It's a beautiful night and I'm sitting here with you. Why would I want to leave?"

"Well, Sam." Alexis took her bottom lip between her teeth. "When you say things like that..."

Watching Alexis bite her lip was doing everything imaginable to Sam's body. "Don't finish that sentence."

Just stop talking. Sam ached inside. Alexis and her words...her voice, the cause.

Interrupted by the waiter, Sam was thankful for the reprieve. As much as she felt the need to let off a little steam right now, Alexis couldn't become that woman. Whether that was what she was here for or not, Sam couldn't take her home. She wanted to—she was just about done with putting herself last—but it would be for the wrong reasons. Sam believed that sex wasn't just a casual thing. If it went that far, it had to mean something more.

"We should take this conversation back to your place..."

"Oh, we shouldn't." Sam shook her head, a wave of heat coursing through her body. "We can't."

"Sorry, I don't know where that came from." Alexis held up her hand, embarrassed that she could even insinuate doing such a thing with someone like Sam. Her client had never been anything other than respectful from the moment they met, so offering something more seemed wrong on every level. *Wow, it comes to something when an escort feels bad for offering her services.* Alexis put on her best fake smile. "Dinner and conversation. Got it."

"I thought you preferred this side of things?" Sam asked, her eyes finding Alexis'.

"I do...but what does that tell you?" Alexis inwardly chastised herself. However hard she tried, she couldn't help the flirtatious comments.

"I don't know." Sam smiled. "What does it tell me?"

Sam's phone buzzed on the table, Lindsay's name flashing on the screen.

"Hello? Linds?"

"Sorry, I was sleeping."

"Why?" Sam glanced at her watch. "It's only seven."

"Because I have a shift at the bar tonight," Lindsay said. "So, no...it's not because I plan to do an all-nighter in a drug house."

"I'm sorry about earlier." Sam sighed as she turned away from Alexis. "Look, if you're stuck for cash, you only have to ask."

"But I don't want to ask, Sam."

"I wish you would."

"Why? So you can forever hold it against me?" Lindsay laughed. "I have to go. Enjoy your night."

"Lindsay, wait!"

"What?"

"Come and stay with me tonight."

"I have to work remember..."

"I need to speak to you about something." Sam glanced over her shoulder, thankful to find Alexis looking the other way. "I need advice."

"I have a shift."

"Call in sick. You know I'll see that you're all right."

"Fine," Lindsay said. "But the first mention of drugs and I'm leaving."

"I promise you, it's not about that."

"Should I come over now?"

"I, uh...give me an hour." Sam ended her call with her sister and turned around to find Alexis responding to something on her own phone. "Everything okay with you?"

"Oh, yeah." Alexis beamed. "Just a client."

Sam's heart sank. The idea of Alexis seeing another client made her stomach churn. She understood this was just an arrangement, but tonight Sam felt as though she wanted more. Alexis had already offered more in her own way, but Sam being Sam, had to play hardball. Unable to think straight, Sam removed an envelope from her bag and slid it towards Alexis on the bench between them.

"I have to go." Sam's voice trembled. "Thank you for another wonderful evening."

"Go?" Alexis' eyebrows rose. "We haven't even been here an hour."

"Well, there is enough in the envelope to cover the entire evening." Sam smiled. "After last time, I didn't want to be caught short again."

Sam stood and pulled her bag up onto her shoulder. She could see Alexis' worry in her eyes, but this was about herself. Not the kind and sweet escort who made her feel like a million dollars.

"Sam?" Alexis followed her away from the table, the idea of overstepping weighing firmly on her mind. "Was it me? Did I do something I shouldn't have?"

"No, you've been great." Sam leaned in and kissed Alexis' cheek. "I'm assuming you have another client waiting so you should really go."

"I didn't accept their invitation. I was busy with you." After being here, Alexis couldn't bear the thought of meeting anyone else tonight. Last week, it wouldn't have been an issue, but Sam had gotten under her skin and honestly, she never wanted her to leave.

"And now you're not." Sam shrugged as she backed up. "Go. Have fun."

"I already was." Alexis' shoulders slumped. "You're more fun than you realise."

"I'm sure somebody else would be happy to rock your world tonight." *God, I wish it was me.* "Be safe."

Sam pushed her front door open to find Lindsay already waiting for her. Settled on the couch, her legs crossed, Lindsay glanced at her through hooded eyes. She didn't know where to begin with an apology, but she was thankful that her sister had shown up. After leaving Alexis and wandering the streets for the last thirty minutes, she really was unsure about her feelings towards her escort. At one point, she'd thought about cancelling with Lindsay and calling Alexis to her apartment. Then, common sense kicked in and ultimately prevailed. Sam didn't sleep around, she never had, so why did she feel different since meeting Alexis? Why did she stare at her lips at any given opportunity during their short but sweet arrangement tonight?

"You look like you need a drink." Lindsay's brow knitted. "And where have you been?"

"With Alexis."

"Why the hell aren't you still with her now?" Lindsay sat forward. "Get it while you can, Sam."

"Well, I guess it's useless asking you for advice now..." Sam kicked off her heels.

"Um, what are you doing? Put them back on and go find her!"

"It doesn't work like that, Linds." Sam laughed, falling back onto the couch. "She has another client."

"Ew!"

"Behave." Sam swatted her sister's leg. "What she does is her own business. I just pay her to talk to me."

"You know, you really should be paying her to do *anything* other than talk."

"Excuse you!"

Sam loved her sister more than anything in the world, but she wouldn't discuss her sex life with her. Not now, not ever.

"What? We all have sex, Sam!"

"I don't want to know." Sam held up her hand. "So long as you're careful, I don't need to know any more than that."

"Don't you miss it?" Lindsay made herself comfortable, lying back and clasping her hands behind her head. "Being with someone..."

"At times, yes."

"I know you don't want to, but you really don't think Alexis could help you out with that?"

"That's actually what I wanted to talk to you about." Sam glanced at her sister. "Tonight, it felt different."

"Different how?"

"She was flirtatious with me. I think I was close to doing the same thing..."

"And it felt good?"

"Weirdly normal," Sam said. "It felt like I didn't have to worry about it. You know?"

"You mean, you didn't feel guilty about it?"

"No, I didn't." Sam ran her fingers through her hair. "I just... I'm scared."

"You have nothing to be scared about. It's her job."

"That's the problem though. I think I'm attracted to her. In a way that I shouldn't be. She's my escort, Lindsay. You have to tell me this is wrong."

"Oh." Lindsay sat up, chewing her bottom lip. "Um..."

"Do you see my problem?" Sam asked. "Why I have to be careful about this..."

"Kind of, yeah." Lindsay nodded. "But what if she feels the same way?"

"She doesn't."

"But she could...one day." Lindsay beamed. "Why don't you take her away? Show her the real you?"

"What?" Sam scoffed. "Take her away?"

"Yeah. Book her for the entire week."

"I know it's your favourite film, but this is *not* a scene from Pretty Woman."

"God, it's such a classic." Lindsay sighed. "Maybe we should watch it tonight. Get a few pointers."

"You're out of your mind."

"And so are you." Lindsay winked. "You've got the hots for your escort, Sam. You either have to admit it or move on from her."

"That would mean not booking her again."

"I know."

"I don't think I could do that." Sam tugged the hem of her dress. "I like her company too much."

"Then you have some decisions to make."

Alexis lay back, her head on her pillow. She couldn't bring herself to see another client after leaving Sam, so she switched her business phone off and wound down for the night. She worked her way through a bottle of wine, followed by a scorching shower, but Sam remained on her mind. Her client. The woman she wasn't supposed to become attached to. Sam, the person she would fall asleep thinking about. Alexis figured their second meeting wouldn't be as intense as the first, now that she knew what to expect, but she'd been wrong. Very wrong. Nothing had changed for her, other than the fact that she wanted to kiss Sam more than she had when they first met.

I need to speak to someone about this.

Just thinking about Sam left Alexis feeling aroused. That arousal was like nothing she'd experienced before. A look from Sam, a slight touch of her skin, and Alexis' body was on fire. She had friends at the agency, women who'd been there a lot longer than she had, but she knew speaking to them would only leave her disappointed. They would tell her it was forbidden. They would offer to take Sam off her hands. Alexis didn't want that, she just wanted to figure out how she was feeling, hoping that Sam may someday want more. Alexis knew that was selfish, knew she was putting herself in a position that would ultimately end in her being hurt, but she believed Sam was worth it.

I don't know this woman.

Alexis was right, she didn't know Sam. That didn't deter her from lying here thinking about her though. It didn't stop her thoughts of what could be if she persisted with the flirtatious behaviour, the glances and the touches. Deep down, Alexis felt a connection to her client, a connection she presumed would only grow stronger the more time they spent together. Alexis glanced at the phone number sitting on her screen. Sam's. It was a mistake adding it to her personal contact list, but before Alexis could stop herself, she was opening a new message.

A: I hope I wasn't the one that made you run earlier.

Alexis held her breath, her anxiety rising as the three little dots beneath her message signalled that Sam had read it and, was in fact, texting her back.

S: Who is this?
A: Alexis.
S: Isn't this against policy?
A: Are you going to call the agency and tell them?
S: Of course not.
A: Then will you answer me one question?
S: Okay...

Alexis thought about the next message she would write. It could change everything, and it likely would, but she needed to ask Sam out to dinner. She needed to give herself the opportunity to find someone truly worthy of her time, rather than be someone's escort. Her thumbs tapped the screen, but she quickly hit the delete button.

A: Never mind. It's not important.
S: Seemed important enough for you to break policy.
A: See you around, Sam. Goodnight.
S: Goodnight.

Alexis threw her phone to the bed, groaning as she placed her hand over her face. How could she be so stupid to think that a woman like Sam would even contemplate agreeing to an actual date? Alexis knew she was easy on the eye and she knew she could charm anyone into bed, but Sam was *so* not that kind of woman. Sam...would never be *her* woman.

CHAPTER SIX

Sam woke to the sound of her phone buzzing on the bedside table. Her alarm hadn't yet gone off, so whoever was calling her at such an ungodly hour should have one hell of an excuse. With one eye opened, she reached for her phone and accepted the call.

"Sam, hello?"

"Lindsay, what the hell do you want at this time?"

"You didn't call me after I left last night…"

"And you thought it would be appropriate to call me at what…" Sam glanced at the alarm clock. "Five-thirty in the morning?"

"I was worried."

"You should be," Sam spat. "Because when I get my hands on you, you're dead."

"Sorry I woke you up, but I didn't hear from you. I've been awake all night wondering if she came over once I'd gone."

"Linds, I'm fine." Sam dropped back onto the mattress. "I didn't ask her to come over."

"Why?" Lindsay asked, her voice less panicked than it was moments ago. "I thought you wanted to see her again?"

Sam closed her eyes, a small smile curling on her lips as she thought about Alexis. As much as she wanted to spend time with her, Sam knew she had to distance herself. It may not last, but that was her plan as she climbed into bed last night. "I don't think I'll be seeing her again."

"Why not?"

"Because I don't think I can." Sam wasn't willing to offer any more than that for the time being. She was yet to process her own thoughts regarding last night. She hadn't expected Alexis to privately text her and the last thing she needed, was Lindsay influencing any decisions. "I would really like to get another hour. I'll call you when I'm at the office."

"Fine, okay," Lindsay said. "Bye, Sam."

"Bye."

Sam ended her call and dropped her phone down beside her. While she'd fallen asleep perfectly fine last night, Alexis had been on her mind. During their first dinner date, Sam was impressed by her. She wasn't the woman she imagined she would be and as the minutes passed, she found herself truly laughing for the first time in forever. It felt good to have that side of her slowly coming back to life. Nobody made her laugh like her wife once had, but Alexis was doing a good job of coming close second. That was why she arranged a second meeting so soon after the first. Yes, Sam cut it short, but that was for more than one reason. She couldn't concentrate while worrying about her sister, and Alexis' flirtation had thrown her. The thigh grab on her part, that was totally unexpected.

If she was being honest with herself, that worried her. How she could so easily enjoy the company of another woman with no thought for her wife or how she would feel about it? It didn't feel right, and the more she thought about it last night, the more it gnawed away at her inside. The more her guilt rose. Yes, Lucia wanted her to be happy...but don't people say that to lessen the blow when the time actually comes to leave? Don't they *pretend* that they wouldn't be hurt by their significant other moving on?

Sam sat up and shifted back, leaning against the headboard. She had the perfect view out of her windows, but she was beginning to suspect that nothing would calm her today. The moment Lindsay got wind of how she was feeling, Sam knew she would never hear the end of it. She knew that no amount of lying to her sister would work, not with something ground-breaking like this. To the outside world, it was nothing, but to Sam and everyone around her...it would be shocking news to find out that she may be potentially ready to move on with her life. A life *without* Lucia.

She turned her head, her eyes focusing on the picture beside the alarm clock. *God, you still take my breath away.* Sam slowly lifted the framed photograph and studied it. When she met Lucia, she had been a breath of fresh air in her life. Only months apart in age, Lucia brought an immense amount of joy to Sam. Mentally, physically, and sexually. Every moment she woke beside her wife gave her life a meaning, and Sam knew she would spend forever with Lucia. They got each other. They knew exactly what made the other tick. Sam would always be thankful for the moment Lucia walked into her life, but was this how it would be from now on? A constant guilt? A panic every time she even looked at another woman? Sam couldn't live that way, she knew that, but she struggled to let down her walls and let go of her past. A past that would never be anything more.

"So, this isn't like you." Shannon, a fellow escort, took a seat facing her at the coffee shop they'd agreed to meet at. "Since when do we meet for coffee?"

"Since I lost my fucking mind." Alexis sighed. "I needed to talk to you about something. I know you love this life, the things that go on, but I need you to be serious for a moment and give me some advice."

"Serious. Got it." Shannon straightened her back and smiled. "What's going on, Lex?"

"I have a new client." Alexis' mind wandered to Sam and her beautiful smile. "We've had two bookings."

"And I'm sure you'll have many more. You know the clients love you."

"Oh, I'm not so sure about that." Alexis shook her head as she brought her cappuccino to her lips. Delighting in the aroma, she gave herself a moment before continuing. "I haven't told anyone yet, because I was originally undecided, but I'm thinking of leaving the agency."

"You won't find better elsewhere. We're the top agency in the northwest."

"No, I don't plan to leave for another. I'm leaving all together."

"Oh." Shannon's dark eyebrows drew together. "Why?"

"It's just not working for me anymore. I have other commitments. Career commitments."

"Right, okay."

"But after taking on this new client, I'm torn." Alexis brought her hands together on the table in front of her, clasping them. "She's absolutely gorgeous. A wonderful person."

"A wonderful person?" Shannon laughed. "Where has Alexis gone?"

"What?"

"You're an escort, love." Shannon leaned in, lowering her voice. "We don't think about how *wonderful* someone is. We give them what we want and get paid."

"You, perhaps." Alexis narrowed her eyes. "But me? Not so much."

"I know you hate that side of things, and that's okay, but you're still an escort, Lex," Shannon said. "We don't really have the option of thinking about clients and how great they are."

"I know, and that's why I asked you to meet me." Alexis nodded. "You're the only one I feel I can trust with all of this."

"All of what?"

"I just—"

"You got attached." Shannon sighed. "You got attached to this new client, didn't you?"

"I'm trying not to." Alexis hung her head. "I'm trying so hard not to think about her, but I've already overstepped by texting her from my personal number."

"You know what happened last time, love." Shannon reached her hand across the table, squeezing Alexis'. "You know what happens when we let things carry away with themselves."

"She's different."

"They all are...until they're not."

"No." Alexis pulled her hands away. "She is. She's completely different to anyone I've ever met."

"Have you heard from the other one at all?" Alexis appreciated the fact that Shannon didn't use her ex-client's name; she knew how much it grated on her. "She's been gone a while."

"No, I've heard nothing and I'm praying it stays that way."

"Me too," Shannon agreed. "But, Lex...you have to step back from this. If you have to turn down her bookings, then so be it."

"I don't want to turn them down. I want there to be more of them."

"And that's exactly why you should stop taking her on as a client." Shannon relaxed back in her seat. "I know you have a huge heart, but this is business. Pleasure shouldn't be mixed with it."

"I know, I know." Alexis held up her hand. "I'll see how it goes, okay?"

"Mm." Shannon rolled her eyes. "I know exactly how it's going to go, and you'll be the one who gets hurt."

"No, it's not like that."

"If it's not like that, why are you here discussing it with me?"

"She just...she's married."

"Uh, a lot of our clients are married. Why is it suddenly a concern of yours?"

"Because the others didn't matter," Alexis said. "I've never been attracted to the others, so I was just doing my job. This... I feel like everyone could get hurt if I ask her out to dinner. It *would* be an affair."

"I understand what you're saying." Shannon nodded. "I completely understand."

"She ran out on me yesterday." Alexis closed her eyes momentarily. "I don't expect to see her again, so I don't know why I'm worried about it. I'm also positive that this is *all* one-sided."

"She ran out?"

"Said she had to leave." Alexis smiled weakly. "Something came up, but I was flirtatious with her and may have scared her off."

"You, scare someone off?" Shannon snorted. "You're gorgeous. Any woman would be lucky to have you."

"Uh, thanks." Alexis lowered her eyes to the table. "Thanks for listening. It was all I needed."

"Us girls stick together, Lex." Shannon smiled. "Plans for tonight?"

"It's my night off."

"Then you should relax and sleep well. Tomorrow is a new day."

"Yeah, it is." Alexis couldn't help but wonder if Sam was thinking about her as much as she thought about Sam. "When we both finally get a night off together, I'll make this up to you."

"You don't have to do that." Shannon waved Alexis off. "I wasn't busy, and we always make time for one another."

"Still, I really appreciate it."

As the day wore on, Sam found herself staring at her phone. Cheryl had been by once or twice to enquire about her plans during the week, but she had so far gotten nothing from her boss. Sam suspected Cheryl knew the truth, and while she wasn't ashamed of what she'd done twice in a matter of days, she wasn't ready to let other people know. She didn't feel prepared for the questions that may be asked, but more than anything, she couldn't bear the thought that perhaps Cheryl had spent the night with Alexis. Her assistant had always been very forthcoming with her sexuality and her sex life, but Sam didn't need to know anything about her days of booking escorts. Not if one of those escorts had been the woman Sam spent the evening with.

A tinge of jealousy reverberated through Sam, shocking her. How could she be jealous of her assistant and an escort? How could she for one moment think that she had any right to be jealous regardless of who it was? Sam knew what she needed, but the thought of taking a break from work and heading off to sunny climates meant that she wouldn't have a chance to book Alexis again if one night she felt the need. No, she didn't need a holiday. What she needed was to focus on her work.

You pay her for her time. Stop getting hung up on something that will never be.

A light knock on her door brought Sam out of her ridiculous mindset. "Come in."

"Mrs Phillips..."

"Sam." The word fell from her mouth unexpectedly. If she was ever going to potentially move forward, the first thing she could do was to lessen the use of her married name. It hurt, but it wasn't the end of the world.

"Pardon?" Cheryl's brow knitted. "You want me to call you Sam?"

"Yes, is that a problem?"

"Well, no." Cheryl stepped into her boss' office. "It's just not what I expected."

"Feeling like a change." Sam smiled, focusing briefly on Cheryl and the shock on her face. "Sit down, you're making me feel uncomfortable."

"It's just about tomorrow," Cheryl said. "I know Friday is drinks night, but I can't make it."

"Standing me up?"

"I have a date." Cheryl sighed. "I tried to change it to Saturday but my girl is out of town for the weekend and I really don't think I can wait until Tuesday to see her again."

"Then I will grab a nice bottle of wine on the way home tomorrow and enjoy it alone…"

"We could do Saturday instead?" Cheryl suggested. "I'm free all weekend."

"Can I get back to you?"

"Oh, you have plans?" Cheryl's smile widened. "That's fine. We can just skip this week."

"I don't have plans." The sudden surprise from Cheryl didn't sit well with Sam. "But even if I did, why is that such a shock to you?"

"It's not… I just—"

"What?"

"I saw you, okay?" Cheryl wrung her hands together in her lap. "A few nights ago. I saw you."

"Saw me where?" Sam narrowed her eyes, her heart free-falling into her stomach.

"At the restaurant. I was with my date."

"Must have been someone else." Sam shrugged, focusing on her work. "I have to leave at midday. I don't have anything else planned for today, do I?"

"No." Cheryl sighed. "She seemed nice. She made you laugh…"

"I've been home every night this week, Cheryl."

"Then you have a doppelganger." Cheryl snorted. "Or you have the ability to be in two places at once."

"Cheryl." Sam gave her assistant a stern look.

"Why don't you want to be happy, Sam?" Cheryl cocked her

head, confused by her boss' lack of life outside the office. "And I know it's none of my business, but I saw you. Don't deny it."

"What the hell do you want me to say?"

"I don't know. Anything."

"Fine. I was with an escort," Sam said, her tone harsh. "If that is all, I'd like to finish up here."

"Did you enjoy it?"

"Don't fucking push it!"

The sound of the TV played low in the background, Alexis' eyes glazing over rather than watching it. She'd been home for a couple of hours, but Shannon's advice hadn't appeared to help as much as she thought it would. Sam, once again, was on her mind. Right at the front. Centre. Alexis knew she was a fool to even consider thinking about Sam in any other capacity than as her client, but there was something about her that she couldn't put her finger on. Something that dragged Alexis down every time she tried to push away. She could dress and head out for the night, but even that was a non-starter. Alexis didn't have the energy. She didn't have the strength to look at any other women. This was an infatuation, she knew that, but it didn't deter her from thinking about Sam.

She lifted her phone from the arm of the couch and called her mum's number.

"Hi, love."

"Hi, Mum. You all okay?" Alexis sunk further down into the couch and lay back. "Dad doing okay?"

"He's out on a job. Helping Steve with some paving."

"He's good like that." Alexis smiled. "You know, I have the weekend off so I thought I'd come up early Sunday and spend the day with you."

"I'd love that." Jackie perked up. "Should I make Sunday dinner?"

"Mm, you should. Nobody makes roasties like you do."

"Will you be coming alone?"

"Um, why wouldn't I be?" Alexis laughed. "Did you want me to drag someone off the street?"

"You know what I mean, love." Jackie sighed. "What I'm asking, is if you've met anyone?"

"Since I spoke to you three nights ago? No, Mum. I haven't."

"That's a shame."

"I'm fine with how I am," Alexis said. "I'm too busy with work anyway."

"I know, but I hate knowing you're alone in that flat when you're not at the station."

If only you knew the truth, Alexis thought.

"When I'm not at the station, I'm sleeping. I don't have much time for anything else."

"Okay, I'll stop asking. I know you hate it."

"I know you want what's best, but I'm okay here in Liverpool. You also know that you can visit whenever you want to."

"Hard to plan it when your dad has the car all the time."

"I can come and pick you up. It's no problem."

"Give me a few weeks and I'll come and stay for the weekend. When you're available."

"That would be great, Mum." Alexis glanced at the screen of her business phone sitting on her coffee table, lit up. "Well, I have to go and get some laundry done," she lied. "Talk to you soon. Love you."

"Love you too. Bye, love."

As the call cut out, Alexis' hand trembled, reaching for her phone.

A booking.

From Sam.

While her heart leapt out of her chest, she still had a bad feeling about this. Of course she wanted to spend the evening with Sam, but it would only complicate things further. It would only stop

Alexis from forgetting this woman ever existed and getting on with her life.

"Oh, wow." Alexis' eyes widened. "She wants the girlfriend experience."

"The girlfriend experience..." Sam clicked on the link sitting at the top of Alexis' profile, intrigued by what that could possibly mean. "Okay, nothing too much." She nodded, scanning the description briefly. "A night in, basically."

An hour ago, Sam had once again found herself in a situation she couldn't control. As she drove through the city with Cheryl's comments playing on her mind, she made the decision to book Alexis again. She hadn't expected her to be available at such short notice, yet here she was, waiting for her escort's arrival. Knowing that she'd been seen in the city with a beautiful woman didn't feel right to Sam, so the girlfriend experience was what she chose for her night ahead. Another small fortune spent on a woman who was only here for her money. Deep down, Sam wanted to believe that Alexis wasn't only in it for the money, but she knew she was being naïve.

It's her job, for the love of God!

Sam's buzzer blared through her apartment, startling her. "Shit! I'm not ready."

She rushed to the intercom and granted Alexis access to the building. She'd already provided her with the apartment number when she contacted her earlier in the evening, but like last night, Sam was beginning to have second thoughts. While she didn't have any ties to her wife at this apartment, she still had her things. Pictures. Clothes. Anything she had struggled to let go of.

Sam glanced down her body, satisfied that her clothing for the night would be compatible with the girlfriend experience. After all, it was just a night in like any other. At least, that's what she assumed it to be. The website hadn't given her a great deal of information, but she knew Alexis would put her at ease the moment she walked through her door.

A knock on the door.

Sam froze.

Should I really have her in my home?

It was too late to back out now. Alexis was standing out in the corridor.

With shaky hands, Sam steeled herself and opened the door. "Hi," she breathed out. "Come in."

"Wow." Alexis glanced around, seemingly taken aback by Sam's apartment. "You have a beautiful home."

This will never be home.

"Thank you." Sam closed and locked the door, desperately praying that her sister wouldn't turn up uninvited. "Can I get you something to drink?"

"Yes, thank you." Alexis moved through Sam's open-plan space with ease, heading straight for the large window. Her eyes widened when she spotted the Welsh mountains in the distance, the view breathtaking.

"Is red okay for you?"

"Perfect." Alexis glanced over her shoulder, smiling. "How do you pull yourself away from this window? The view is incredible."

"I guess it loses its effect after a while." Sam watched Alexis, her tall, slender body resting against the wall. "But you're more than welcome to enjoy it for as long as you like."

She took in her escort's features from behind. How her form-fitting jeans hugged every inch of her lower body so beautifully. The deep blue blouse she wore complimented her golden hair, the transparent material leaving very little to the imagination. *Stop, Sam!*

"Have you lived here long?" Alexis turned to face Sam, a full smile sitting on her mouth as she took a glass of wine from her client.

"A couple of years." Sam returned to her seat, offering the opposite end of the couch to Alexis. "Moved into the city when my business really took off." It wasn't the truth, but it was all Alexis needed to know.

"It's beautiful."

"It does the job," Sam said, fully aware of how stunning her home was but having no interest in it. "It means my morning commute takes all of ten minutes."

"That sounds ideal." Alexis crossed her legs, her black heels catching Sam's eye.

"Are those Louboutin?"

"They are." Alexis gave Sam a slight nod of the head. "This season..."

"Impressive." Sam relaxed against the couch, sitting side on with her head resting in the palm of her hand. "And here I am sitting in my office clothes."

"You look great, I wouldn't worry." Alexis could spend the entire night admiring Sam, however wrong she knew it was.

Not what I expected, Sam thought, suddenly feeling a blush creep up her neck. Here she was, sitting with a twenty-five-year-old escort, and being complimented. This wasn't Sam's life. She made it a habit to refrain from this behaviour, but it felt good. It felt easy. She would be lying if she said she didn't appreciate Alexis' time and attention. After all, what woman doesn't want to be flattered?

"So, you didn't tell me what you do..."

"Me?" Sam's eyebrow rose. "Nothing you'd find exciting."

"Try me..."

"I'm a property developer," Sam said. "There is nothing glamorous about it but I love it."

"If you love it, that's what matters."

"Do you love your job?" Sam asked as Alexis' perfume wafted her way. Something about this woman left her feeling completely open and exposed, yet safe and calm at the same time.

"Which one?"

"Um..."

"Oh, you mean the escort job?" Alexis smiled. "I believe I've already answered that. Our first night together, if you remember."

"The other job?"

"It's very demanding and tiring," Alexis said. "But when I'm not working, this is the ideal way to unwind." Alexis glanced around before facing Sam again and raising her wine glass. "I'd just come off a twelve-hour night shift the day you contacted me about dinner."

"Well, I wouldn't have known." Sam cleared her throat. "You looked refreshed."

"I'm used to it now."

"Okay, so this other job...what is it?"

"Oh, I'm a firefighter."

Sam almost spat out the wine she had just sipped, her heart stopping dead in her chest.

Alexis laughed. "Not what you expected?" People usually ran a mile when she divulged information about her career. Alexis didn't know why she'd offered Sam that piece of information; she'd never told a client about her personal life.

"N-No." Sam shifted uncomfortably. "Not what I expected at all."

"Well, I'm full of surprises, Sam." Alexis winked as she took her wine glass between her lips. "Full of them."

"Yeah." Sam sighed, her heart hurting in her chest. "I guess you are."

Just as Sam was beginning to think about enjoying time with this woman sitting in front of her, everything told her not to. She couldn't. Involving herself with a woman like Alexis was a bad move in Sam's mind, and one move she wasn't prepared to make.

"I won't lie, I can pull off a mean fireman's lift."

Okay, is she flirting with me? Sam flushed. "How do you do it?"

"A fireman's lift?" Alexis sat forward, placing her wine glass down. "Stand up and I'll show you."

"No, the job." Sam held up her hand, staring intently at Alexis. "How do you put yourself in that position? Running towards fire?"

"Because I'm the kind of person who wants to help people," Alexis said. "I know there are other ways of doing that, but since I was a kid...it's all I wanted to do. Watching London's Burning on repeat didn't help. I found my mum's old tape recordings in a box in the loft. It all went downhill from there."

"You watched London's Burning?"

"Not when it aired, obviously."

"Christ, I think I used to watch it before a night out." Sam suddenly felt ridiculously old. "Now I'm showing my age."

"Mm, I did wonder about that." Alexis licked the wine residue from her lips, her deep blue eyes never leaving Sam's. "You're what? Thirty?"

"That's sweet." Sam blushed. "But you're a terrible liar."

"Thirty-one?"

"Try again." Sam rolled her eyes. "But once I tell you, I won't mind if you choose to leave."

"Your age makes no difference to me, Sam. It's my job to come here and give you whatever it is that you want." Alexis winced. Once again, she had reverted to the cold-hearted escort who didn't care about people's feelings. Deep down, she wanted to know everything about Sam, but she saw that flash in her eyes when she told her about her career. That unease. An unease that told her Sam would never want to be caught up in a relationship with someone who worked unsociable hours. The usual look she received.

"I'm thirty-seven," Sam said. "Thirty-eight in a few weeks."

"Well, life has treated you *very* well."

"Thank you for coming tonight at such short notice." Sam chose to avoid the comments Alexis was making. As much as she liked hearing it, she couldn't become attached. It was one thing to get involved with an escort, but to get involved with a firefighter was an entirely different world she couldn't be a part of.

"You wanted the girlfriend experience, and here I am." Alexis held out her arms. "At your service."

"I like your confidence." Sam narrowed her eyes. "It's invigorating."

"You've no idea what the girlfriend experience means, have you?"

"Nope."

"I thought as much." Alexis shifted closer, settling her hand on Sam's that rested on the back of the couch. "You wanted dinner and conversation."

"I-I do."

"This, what you've asked for, is *not* dinner and conversation." As much as Alexis wanted to provide her client with what she'd booked, she knew Sam had no idea what it truly entailed.

"Alexis..."

"Do you want more?" Alexis asked, praying that the answer would be 'yes'. "Without asking me, do you want more?"

"I-I can't." Sam pulled her hand away. "I just wanted company."

"Okay." Alexis backed away a little, noting a fear in Sam's eyes.

"Your cash...it's in the envelope on the kitchen counter."

"This was my night off." Alexis lifted her wine glass and relaxed back into her previous position.

"And you're here with me?" Sam's forehead creased. "You should be at home relaxing. Not sitting here with me."

Like the times before, Alexis found herself unable to control her thoughts...or her words. "Perhaps I want to be sitting here with you."

Alexis washed her hands in the huge sink basin, her eyes focused on herself through the infinity mirror attached to the wall in front of her. She'd been at Sam's place for near on two hours and the longer she spent with her, the less she could figure her out. While this was simply an arrangement, Alexis got the impression that Sam had no idea what she wanted. Sitting beside her, watching her and sharing her space, Alexis was also unsure of her own needs. This line of work was so far from what she did professionally, but it was a welcome break from the smoke and fire. Being alone in a beautiful apartment with a beautiful woman was worlds apart from sitting at the station with the lads. The men. As she had anticipated, Alexis was the only woman at their watch, but it didn't concern her. Fighting fire wasn't for the weak or for those who just wanted a nine-to-five job. It required grit and determination, and she had that in bucket loads.

Why do I feel my determination lacking when I'm around Sam? Alexis questioned herself, the answers nowhere to be found. She wanted to go back out into the living space Sam was residing in and ask her out on a date. She wanted to, but she couldn't. No, she *shouldn't*. She didn't know Sam. She didn't know her situation. Yes, she knew she had a wife, but where was she? Working away? Had they separated? Alexis wanted to know the answers to all of the questions and thoughts running through her mind, but what right did she have? Sam was no different to any other client she chose to spend the evening with.

Except she is. She's different in every way imaginable.

Sam didn't look at Alexis like a piece of meat. She didn't spend their time together wondering how long it would be before she stripped her naked. Sam...she was kind and sophisticated. She was a newness in Alexis' life. But this wasn't real life, and this wasn't Alexis. At least, not the *true* her. How could she build a relationship with a woman that to most is based on secrets and lies? Affairs? Anything other than genuine attention?

Drying her hands on the small towel hanging from the rail,

Alexis fixed her blouse on her shoulders and straightened herself out. She knew the evening would be coming to an end soon, so the less time she spent in the bathroom avoiding her client, the better. *She's not my client tonight.* Alexis had already made the decision to decline Sam's cash payment for her being here, but she wasn't sure how Sam would take it. While Sam likely didn't feel anything for her, Alexis had lain awake for the entire night thinking about her. It was hard not to when Sam gazed at you from across the table, that gaze representing respect rather than lust, but Alexis had something she needed to say to her client, and she believed that tonight was the night when she should. She wanted nothing more than to continue this arrangement, but it wouldn't work. She needed more.

Alexis gripped the door handle and pulled it open, stepping out into the small corridor. The walls were adorned by some beautiful artwork, but that wasn't Alexis' forte. She didn't know the first thing about paintings or what they represented, so she chose not to mention them for fear of sounding like a complete idiot if Sam questioned her opinion on them.

Barefoot, Alexis slowly entered the open space. The silence at times tonight had been deafening, but peaceful too. Sam sat with her back to the corridor entrance, her silky dark hair pulled up into a bun, her caramel highlights weaving through it perfectly. Alexis admired Sam's neck, exposed for the first time since they'd met. She didn't make it a habit to check out her clients, but with Sam, she struggled. She struggled more than she would ever care to admit. Her dark eyes held a trust Alexis hadn't expected, but they also told her to be wary. Of what, she didn't know, but she wouldn't press Sam. It wasn't her place to do so.

"Your bathroom is bigger than my entire flat."

Sam jumped a little, unaware that Alexis was behind her. "Sorry, what?"

"Your bathroom...it's huge."

"Yes, quite ridiculous really." Sam half-smiled. "I thought you'd snuck out for a moment."

"On you?" Alexis arched an eyebrow. "Not likely."

"Do you have plans tomorrow?" Sam asked, her eyes never leaving Alexis' body as she rounded the couch and returned to her seat.

"I have a client." Alexis offered Sam a small smile. She hated admitting to seeing other people, but it was her job, and Sam didn't care anyway. "It's my last booking before I have to be at the station all weekend."

"Oh."

Alexis sensed a disappointment in Sam's tone which surprised her. Given half the chance, she would happily cancel her plans and take this gorgeous woman to dinner instead.

"Well, we should probably call it a night." Sam sat forward, arching her back as she stretched. "I have to be at the office earlier tomorrow. Conference call."

"Sounds exciting."

"It would be, but I like my sleep and I'll be getting less of it tonight."

If only you were getting less sleep for other reasons. Alexis' mind wandered.

"Tonight has been great, Sam." Alexis slipped her heels on and lifted her bag from the floor beside her. "Enjoy your weekend, okay?"

"You'll be careful?" A fear flashed in Sam's eyes. One Alexis didn't expect or understand.

"Careful?"

"At work. At the weekend..."

Oh, she's concerned about my safety. Alexis was surprised by Sam's worry, but understood at the same time. Sam was a woman that clearly cared and respected people.

"Always." Alexis cocked her head, her heart bursting. "Are you okay?"

"Me? Yes." Sam climbed to her feet and approached the kitchen counter, taking the white envelope from beside the coffee machine. "For you."

"No, I don't want it." Alexis held up her hand. "I told you, tonight was my night off from the agency."

"I contacted you. You came."

"Because I wanted to, not because I had to." Alexis pushed the envelope back towards Sam, her hand settling on the older woman's wrist. "Please, don't offer it to me again."

Alexis couldn't do this. She couldn't take money from a woman who she didn't see as a client. The moment she checked her out, the moment she found herself wanting to kiss Sam, she'd crossed the boundary. As she looked into those deep brown eyes, she realised she also couldn't be here any longer. She couldn't see Sam anymore.

"Please?"

"I had something I needed to tell you." Alexis cleared her throat. "The afternoon you contacted me... I'd promised myself that this would be my last month as an escort."

"O-Okay..."

"I was dwindling down my clients. Work is a little more full-on with the government cutbacks, and I don't really have the time for anything else."

"But you accepted my request to join me for dinner."

"Because you're gorgeous." Alexis' fingertips ghosted over Sam's hand.

Sam blushed, it not going unnoticed by Alexis. "Well, thank you for giving me the opportunity to know you." Sam's eyes lowered. "I guess it was fun while it lasted."

God, this woman is devastating. All it would take was a simple kiss, but Alexis couldn't bring herself to do it.

She leaned in, her lips pressing against Sam's cheek. "I want to know more of you, but I know you're involved." She stepped back. "You have a wife, and this... I can't be here anymore."

"I-I..."

"Sam, I don't know the first thing about you. I don't know who you are, but I know that I want to kiss you...so I have to leave. I have to go and become invisible to you."

"It was just dinner and conversation." Sam spoke barely above a whisper. "How can you feel this way when it was just dinner and conversation?"

Alexis got the impression that Sam was asking herself that question, however ridiculous it may seem. This woman could never be attracted to Alexis, she knew that, but the idea that it was a possibility still sat firmly in her mind. Alexis decided to be bold, regardless of the fact that it was a waste of time.

"To me, it was so much more."

Alexis stepped around Sam, heading straight for her apartment door. Without looking back, she slipped out into the corridor, holding back the emotion she could feel churning inside of her. She knew everything she had just said would only complicate things, but she wouldn't have an affair with a married woman. Whether she was an escort or not, Sam was married...and she would be partaking in the relationship for all the wrong reasons. She was used to meeting women who wanted sex and nothing more, but if Alexis continued this, and things did go further, emotions would be involved and everyone would get hurt. Alexis. Sam. And her wife.

CHAPTER SEVEN

Sam found herself tossing and turning again. For seven nights, she'd lay awake thinking about the moment Alexis effectively cancelled their arrangement. For seven days, she wandered around the office aimlessly, her own emotions bubbling to the surface as each day passed. She hadn't expected those words from her escort. She hadn't expected someone so young or beautiful to even acknowledge her existence. Alexis had though, and it only complicated Sam's life. She needed someone to talk to, but she didn't know where to turn. Her friends were all mere acquaintances through business, and her assistant had been giving Sam a wide berth since she mentioned the fact that she'd seen her boss out in town. A week later, nothing made sense.

Lindsay continued to call her repeatedly, demanding answers and details about her original night out with Alexis, but Sam couldn't bring herself to talk about it. Not only did she feel embarrassed for ever contacting the escort agency, she felt worse knowing her escort had kicked her to the kerb. *I must really be the life and soul of the party if an escort doesn't want to stick around.* Sam climbed from her bed, tears welling in her eyes as she thought about how lonely the last week had been. She hadn't realised how much Alexis' company had impacted her life in those few short days but being without her was really beginning to take its toll on Sam and her everyday life.

She knew she needed to take back her life, whatever that meant, but she didn't know where to start. Lindsay had invited her to a bar this evening but Sam wasn't sure it was a good idea. Once she'd taken her first sip of wine, she would bare all...leaving Lindsay with her head in a spin. She knew the outcome of their conversation wouldn't make things any easier, so Sam avoided contact with her sister. In her mind, it was the best option. It was the coward's way out, but since Lucia's death, Sam had made it a habit to become cowardly in her personal life.

She tied her ivory silk robe around her body and moved barefoot down the corridor to her kitchen.

"Thought you'd never rise!"

"Fucking hell." Sam placed her hand over her chest. "You really are intent on killing me!"

"Calm down." Lindsay laughed, perched on a kitchen stool. "I made you some coffee."

"Thank you, but you're still not in my good books."

"Ooh, the horror." Lindsay wiggled her eyebrows. "You're not working today..."

"Ten points for your observation." Sam sighed, taking a coffee cup from the counter. "Is that why you're here? Playing the concerned sister?"

"What do you mean...playing?" Lindsay asked, hurt by her sister's nonchalance. "I *am* concerned."

"You have no reason to be. I'm entitled to take a day off like everyone else."

"Of course you are," Lindsay agreed. "But that doesn't mean you usually do take a day off."

"I don't feel very well." Sam shrugged, moving into the living room and dropping down on the couch. "You should leave; I could be contagious."

"Hilarious."

"Linds, please," Sam whined. "I'm not in the mood."

"Tonight, you and I are going out," Lindsay stated. "Like originally planned."

"I just told you I'm sick!"

"Wrong." Lindsay held up her hand as she climbed down from her stool. "You lied to me, and I saw through it. There is nothing wrong with you, Sam. At least, nothing health related."

"Don't you have somewhere else to be? Like, pissing somebody else off..."

"You never told me if you met up with the escort again..."

"Because it's not your concern."

"Her name *was* Alexis, right?" Lindsay snuggled up beside her sister on the couch. "Cheryl says she's great."

"Cheryl?" Sam's heart sunk as her eyes landed on her sister. "How would Cheryl know?"

"Well, I'll give you one little tiny guess..."

"She's been to dinner with her." Sam's admission was hard to say, her voice wavering. "Should have known."

"Oh, dinner was first on the agenda." Lindsay winked. "I think you know how their night ended."

"Why are you telling me this?" Sam's eyes closed, her head resting back. "I don't need to know the personal lives of my staff."

Sam aimed to be as blasé as she possibly could, but her voice was determined to betray her. If Lindsay continued to talk, tears would fall. It was inevitable.

"I just wanted you to know that Cheryl thought she was great."

"Yeah, well Cheryl is welcome to her." Sam climbed to her feet, approaching the window. "We haven't had contact in the last week."

"Why?"

"Because, the twenty-five-year-old escort doesn't want me around anymore."

"Fucking hell, Sam." Lindsay scoffed. "How the hell did you manage to push the escort away? It's her job, for the love of God."

"This." Sam turned to face her sister. "All of this...this is what I am now. Alone. Miserable. Fucking out of my mind for booking an escort in the first place."

"That's not true." Lindsay dropped her gaze, her voice trembling. "You have so much to give."

"She couldn't see me anymore. That's what she said as she walked out the door."

"Okay, but she must have had an explanation."

"She did." Sam's lips curled slightly. "She wanted to see me outside of the agency."

"Are they allowed to do that? Isn't it against policy or something?"

"I don't know," Sam breathed out, leaning back against the window. "She's leaving the agency."

"Wait!" Lindsay's forehead creased. "Are you telling me she wanted to see you...like, date you?"

"I-I think so." Sam blushed. "She said she wanted to see more of me but I have a wife."

"Did you explain?"

"No, I couldn't." Sam shook her head as her body relaxed. "I was too shocked by what she was saying to me. She's twenty-five, Linds."

"Age ain't nothing but a number, sister."

"There was something else, too." Sam chewed her bottom lip, her anxiety beginning to appear. "She has another job."

"That's great."

"She's a firefighter."

"Wow, that's hot." Lindsay fanned herself. "Can you imagine her body? Phew."

"How can I date a firefighter?" Sam focused on her issue rather than Lindsay's comment. She had, in fact, thought about Alexis' body on more than one occasion. She would never admit to that, but as she climbed in bed last night, her thoughts drifted to what lay beneath Alexis' clothing.

"Well, I think you're a fool to turn down such an opportunity," Lindsay said. "A woman who wants you, with that kind of background? You're out of your mind."

"Just think about it. How in the world could I date someone like that?"

"Like what?"

"Someone who runs into burning buildings. Someone who may never come home."

"Not everyone is Lucia, Sam." Lindsay offered her sister a sympathetic smile. "And I know, I know how awful this must all feel, but you have to give it a chance."

"I can't." Sam shook her head. "I can't sit here every moment of the day wondering if she's alive."

"It's her job. It's not the same thing." Lindsay held out her hand, ushering her sister closer. "Come here. Sit with me."

"Why do you think it's taken me so long to even think about dating someone else?" Sam wiped a tear that had escaped down her face. "I still see it now. Most nights. And I can't do anything to save her."

"Look at me..." Lindsay gripped her sister's jaw. "What happened to Lucia was a terrible accident."

"No, it could have been prevented."

"And I agree, it could have." Lindsay nodded. "But you couldn't have done anything to save her. We both know that. Alexis, what she does...she's trained for those situations. Do you think she would do something like that without having a sound knowledge of every inch of the building?"

"People can be careless..."

"Please, for yourself, call her. Contact her." Lindsay squeezed her sister's hands. "Please?"

"I-I tried." Sam smiled weakly. "There is no trace of her on the site. She sent me a message the night you left last week, and I foolishly deleted it. I booked her the night after through the site and that was the last I saw of her."

"Right, okay." Lindsay dropped her hand from Sam's face. "Today is Friday. We are going out and we're going to talk this through properly. If we can't figure out how to contact her, I'll speak to Cheryl. She won't have to know it's for you."

"Why are you and Cheryl so friendly?" Sam eyed her sister intently.

"She's been your assistant for three years. I have to listen to her drawl on every time you ignore your mobile and I have to call the office. Why not use that to my advantage?"

"You and I...we're two very different people." Sam laughed, pulling her sister into a bone-crushing hug. "But I wouldn't have you any other way."

"I know."

Sam approached the club she was meeting Lindsay at, her forehead creasing as the sound of heavy bass blared through the open doors. Why Lindsay would choose a place like this, Sam would never know, but she would have one drink and then suggest they move on. She was too old and too experienced to spend her night at a club, but Lindsay was offering a shoulder, so Sam would have to accept her choice of establishment. She flashed the doorman a smile as she fixed her royal blue dress on her thighs, squeezing past his gut to get inside.

Lindsay was already here, that evident as she waved Sam over to a space at the bar. Sam moved through the crowd, the humidity inside already too much to bear. Back in her younger days, this would have been her typical Friday night, but those days were long gone. Judging by the cringeworthy look on Sam's face, she was happy about that.

"What are you drinking?"

"Huh?" Sam strained to hear her sister.

"I said...what are you drinking?"

"Oh, gin and tonic," Sam replied, her eyes scrunching at the corners as she tried to attempt conversation with her sister. "Why are we here?"

"What?"

"Here? Why?"

"It's new. Thought we could try it out together." Lindsay smiled. "I got us a booth at the back. VIP."

"I hope they have soundproofing back there!"

"You're so fucking old." Lindsay laughed, rolling her eyes playfully. "Come on!" She manoeuvred through the crowd with their drinks, Sam holding onto the back of her sister's jacket.

Once they had finally moved away from the horrendous bass, Sam released a deep breath, dropping down into the leather-interior booth. Lindsay bopped her head to the music, sliding a drink to the side of her for Sam, and relaxed.

"What do you think?"

"Of what?" Sam asked. "This place?"

"Yeah."

"I fucking hate it!"

"Just a couple here and then we'll go somewhere quieter," Lindsay said. "Did you manage to get in touch with Alexis?"

"No." Sam sighed. "I don't think I'll see her again but maybe that's for the best."

"Why do you say that?" Lindsay turned side on, a questioning look on her face. "You don't want to see her again?"

"I do, in some way, but she made it clear that she couldn't see me anymore. I have to respect that."

"To me, it sounds like she was backing out for your sake rather than hers."

"Because..."

"Because she said she wanted to see more of you," Lindsay stated, matter-of-factly. "Correct?"

"Correct." Sam sipped her gin and tonic, nodding. "But the fact still remains…she's way too young for me."

"You didn't think that when you booked her."

"No, but I had no intentions of feeling something more for her, either." Sam looked at her sister pointedly. "And I wouldn't say it's anything too extreme, but I didn't think I'd look at her the way I have at times."

"And how *have* you looked at her?"

"Do we really have to do this, Linds?" Sam sunk down into her seat. "I know you want to help, but I'm not sure this is helping anyone."

"Sam… I need you to be honest with yourself."

Sam nodded slightly, staring at her hands in her lap. "I've lay awake since last Thursday thinking about her." She swallowed hard. "She made me laugh, Linds. For the first time since I lost Lucia, she made me laugh. I actually enjoyed being in her company."

"Any woman who can do that to my sister deserves a chance."

"It would last five minutes…" Sam ran her fingers through her dark, curled hair. "She would see the differences in us, our ages, and it would be over before it started."

"I think you underestimate her," Lindsay said.

"No, I don't." Sam's heart fluttered just thinking about Alexis. "She's mature. I believe she knows exactly what she wants…but I'm not sure I could be enough."

"Sam…"

"Just hear me out." Sam toyed with the glass on the table in front of her. "I want to date, okay? I want someone who I can spend my time with. I also don't want to rush into anything."

"She's gone, Sam." Lindsay took her sister's hand. "It's been two years."

"I know how long it's been." Sam could never forget the time that had passed since Lucia died. "What if I go into another relationship and fail? Lucia got me. She was my one true love. How can I try to give someone my all when she is the only woman to ever really know me? Isn't that cruel? To give yourself to someone else...but not fully be there?"

"You don't know what's going to happen, Sam."

"I don't follow."

"You may meet someone one day and fall head over heels in love with them. That wouldn't mean you never loved Lucia, and it also wouldn't mean you no longer did...it would just mean that a part of your heart was ready for someone else."

"You're going to make me cry."

"I'm sorry." Lindsay offered a sympathetic smile. "But I don't want to see you grow old with nobody in your life. I don't want my big sister to forever wonder 'what if'. We all want you to be happy, Sam. Every single one of us."

"I want to be happy, too." Sam smiled. "And I thought I was. Alone. Then she showed up and made me feel like myself again. In some way, she has turned my world upside down."

"We have to find a way to contact her." Lindsay suddenly looked like a woman on a mission, her back straightening as she squared her shoulders. "There is no way I'm letting you mess this up."

"I-I didn't do anything to mess it up." Sam frowned. "*She* is the one who walked out on me."

"She thought she was doing the right thing," Lindsay said. "Don't forget, she thinks you're married."

"I *am* married!"

"In a way, yes," Lindsay agreed. "But not in the way Alexis thinks."

"I need to use the bathroom." Sam gritted her teeth. "You're relentless."

Sam climbed over her sister and out of the booth, heading in the direction of the toilets. This place wasn't as bad as she thought it would be; so far, her feet hadn't stuck to the floor. Thankful that the VIP area was quieter than the rest of the club, Sam breathed a sigh of relief as she pushed the door open, only a small line of people waiting.

But then she heard that laugh.

A laugh she couldn't forget.

A laugh that made her smile harder than she had in too long.

Alexis. *Fuck!* Sam glanced up and looked to her right to find Alexis against the sink with another woman standing between her legs. She wanted the floor to swallow her whole. This couldn't be happening. Whoever this woman was, she wasn't a client. Alexis wasn't dressed in her usual pricey clothing. She didn't look like she was in any mode other than herself.

Their eyes met and Sam froze, swallowing the lump she could feel rising up her throat. Rather than glaring in a bitchy jealous rage, Sam simply smiled at Alexis and moved down the line. She needed to escape before they met again, but the problem was, she had nowhere to go.

Alexis dropped back into her seat, glancing around the VIP area for any signs of Sam. Once she'd watched her ex-client slip into a cubicle, she rushed out of the toilets with her date and moved swiftly to the dance floor. That was twenty minutes ago, and now she was sat alone while her date ordered more drinks at the bar. She hadn't expected this to be the outcome of her evening, but in the last week, she'd left the agency and done anything she could to get Sam off her mind.

Alexis didn't get hung up on anyone, ever. She didn't pine after a woman she didn't know or had only met a few times. She was supposed to be a life-saver, a member of the emergency services. Yet, here she was…looking for the woman who had kept her awake at night. The woman she had thought about yesterday as she ran into a warehouse fire, Sam's concern for her safety on her mind. How could she think about someone she was supposed to *just* keep company? Alexis knew exactly why. Sam...she was so far from the clients she usually accepted on her books. Nothing about her screamed that she wanted sex and a good time. She just wanted someone to notice her, to see her. Alexis wanted to be that person for Sam, she really did, but after just a couple of hours with her, she knew she was falling in deeper than she ever should. How her eyes held Alexis'. How her hands held her wine glass like a delicate rose. How her scent was subtle but intriguing. Sam was nothing like the others before her, and that was the only downfall Alexis could think of. *She was supposed to be just another client.* Alexis knew that was a lie. She accepted Sam's offer because she saw how breathtaking she was. This, now, was all her own doing. Alexis just refused to accept it.

As she glanced around again, she found a woman she'd never seen before staring back at her. Alexis raised her eyebrows and the woman turned away. She wasn't alone, but Alexis couldn't see who her companion was. As the stranger sat back and took her glass between her lips, she caught sight of Sam. Her gorgeous royal blue dress hugging her body. Her breasts sitting exquisitely in place. Her smile, non-existent. Alexis groaned, her head falling back against her own booth.

"Why me?" She looked up at the ceiling. "Why. Fucking. Me!"

"Why you what?" Her date, Steph, appeared with fresh drinks.

"Oh, nothing." Alexis laughed, waving off Steph's question. "Just had a call from one of the lads. They want me to cover tomorrow's shift," she lied. "Couldn't really say no. He always covers for me."

"So, I'm going home alone tonight then?"

"Looks that way. I'm sorry." Alexis offered an apologetic smile. "I have to go in."

"Yeah, I know. Local hero and all that." Steph winked, leaning in and kissing Alexis. "I need to pee. Be back in two."

Steph disappeared through the crowd, but she was the least of Alexis' concerns. As she turned her attention back to Sam's booth, she watched her stand and hug the friend beside her. Pulling her bag up onto her shoulder, Sam headed towards Alexis. "Sam." She stood, moving towards her. "Hi, I just—"

"Goodnight, Alexis." Sam smiled. "You look great. It was nice seeing you again."

Alexis' mouth fell open as she watched Sam leave the club. She wanted to run after her, she wanted to kiss her, but something prevented her. She no longer had to worry about receiving payments for Sam's time, but she was still a married woman. That's exactly what was stopping Alexis.

"Excuse me?" An unfamiliar voice broke her from her stare. "You're Alexis, right?"

"Depends who's asking..." Alexis snarled slightly.

"Me. That's who." Lindsay stood toe to toe with the escort. "Lose the attitude."

"I don't know you." Alexis stood taller than Lindsay, by a few inches at least. "Whatever that woman told you, you have nothing to worry about."

"Come again?"

"The woman you were with, was that your wife?"

"Sam?" Lindsay laughed. "That's my sister."

"Oh, I'm so sorry." Alexis grimaced, shoving her hands in the pockets of her jeans. "Hi, what can I do for you?"

"Follow her," Lindsay said. "Please, just follow her."

"I can't." Alexis shook her head. "I really can't."

"That stuff you said to her...did you mean any of it?"

"Depends what she told you." Alexis shrugged.

"Look, I know about you two. I know what you were to her." Lindsay pulled Alexis away from her booth and out of sight of everyone else. "You don't realise how big this is. Sam doesn't date. She can't bring herself to do it."

"I should think not. She's married, for fuck sake."

"Everything isn't what you think," Lindsay said. "I can't tell you any more than that, but I know she's just gone home after seeing you and I know by now, she will be almost home and probably upset."

"Why would she be upset seeing me?" Alexis was lost. She had no idea what Sam's sister was talking about. As far as Alexis was aware, this feeling was totally one-sided. "I need you to give me a little more to go on before I go running after her..."

"This isn't my business and she will kill me tomorrow when she finds out I've spoken to you. I've just promised her I wouldn't but I'm sorry... I had to."

"I'm glad you did, I think." Alexis lowered her eyes momentarily, scuffing her feet across the floor. "Does she like me?" Her voice held an element of nervousness.

"She does." Lindsay smiled fully. "She really does."

"So, her marriage? Is she separated?"

"You could have caught up with her by now."

"I know, but you've completely thrown me, so I don't know what the hell is going on."

Lindsay groaned, rolling her head on her shoulders. "It's complicated, but Sam is very much *not* involved."

"Wow, okay..."

"Will you leave with me now?" Lindsay asked, knowing Alexis had a date with her tonight. "I know you're busy, and it's okay if you don't want to see Sam tonight, but I'd really like you to be the one who comforts her. She will only back off if I show up."

"I, uh..." Alexis looked around the club for Steph, catching her attention and waving her over. "Give me one minute." Alexis approached Steph. "Hey, so something came up and I need to leave. I'm so sorry."

"Will you make it up to me some other time?"

I hope I won't have the chance to.

"If I can, yes," Alexis agreed, squeezing Steph's hand. "I really have to go."

"Okay, call me?"

"Sure, yeah." Alexis took her jacket from the far corner of the booth and tipped her head towards the door, signalling for Lindsay to follow her.

Once they reached the pavement, away from the deafening noise inside, Alexis turned to face Lindsay. She couldn't fathom how she'd come to be here with Sam's sister, but she was, and she had all the time in the world for both of them.

"What now?" Alexis asked.

"I'll let you into the block. Then, you're on your own."

"What? That's ridiculous." Alexis laughed, her anxiety fast approaching. "You can't just expect me to show up at her door alone."

"It's what she needs."

"I'm not so sure about that..."

CHAPTER EIGHT

Sam threw her purse to the floor, kicking her heels off as she slammed her apartment door shut. *How could I have been so stupid?* Not only was the woman at the club all over Alexis, she had to be at least ten years younger than Sam. She couldn't compete with that, not in a million years, but that wasn't the only thing that was bothering her. The idea of pouring her heart out to Lindsay had been a moment of weakness for her and that was what she regretted more than anything else. Alexis...she was free to do who and what she pleased, but Sam? Sam could have handled it better. She could have stayed home tonight and wallowed in her own self-pity. She didn't need to see Alexis. Of course she wanted to...but wanting and needing were two different things.

She lifted her dress from her body and moved into her bedroom, slipping a pair of comfortable sweatpants on. She knew she should shower and head off to bed, but her mind was working overtime. She needed a few more drinks before she could even think about turning in for the night, so she took a T-shirt from her wardrobe and moved back into the open space. The cool air felt good against her naked upper body, just her bra covering what needed to be covered.

Hearing a knock at the door, Sam rolled her eyes and removed a bottle of red wine from its place on the rack. "Lindsay, I'm not interested in anything you have to say."

Another knock.

"Seriously, when will you fucking listen to me!" Sam opened the bottle and set it down on the worktop. "Alexis is not my concern. I never should have contacted her. She was a mistake. Go home."

Another knock sounded out around Sam's apartment, and *that* was the straw that broke the camel's back. "Lindsay, I swear to God! If you don't back o—" Sam froze as she opened the door. "Oh."

"I'm sorry I was a mistake." Alexis lowered her eyes. "And I never meant to be your concern, but if I could just have a few minutes, I'd be really grateful."

"Alexis, I'm sorry...just my sister is very persistent."

"No, she's an angel." Alexis smiled faintly. "Did, uh...?" She cleared her throat as her eyes landed on Sam's chest. "Maybe cover up?"

"Oh, shit!" Sam turned around, pulling the T-shirt in her hand over her head. "Sorry."

"Don't ever apologise for showing your gorgeous body off."

Sam felt a blush creep up her neck, Alexis' words leaving her weak at the knees.

"So, can I come in?"

Something about Alexis seemed different. She wasn't the confident woman Sam had first come across, but this shy side pleased her. "Yes, come on in."

"Thanks." Alexis closed the door behind her, a guilt settling in her stomach for being with another woman at the club. "I'm sorry about what happened back at the club."

"Why?" Sam asked. "You had a date; there is nothing to be sorry for."

"I just... I didn't know you were even remotely interested in me." Alexis tugged her earlobe, shaking her head. "Why would you be?"

"First of all, I'm going to murder my sister before this night is over. Secondly, why *wouldn't* I be?" *Okay, that was brave of you.* Sam may not have meant to say those words, but it felt good doing so.

"Was it the escort in me that you were attracted to?" Alexis' crystal blue eyes penetrated Sam as she looked up. "I'd understand if that's what it was..."

"I can't say I was or wasn't attracted to that side of you. I'd tried to push it down whenever we met, so I didn't have the chance to truly feel anything for you." Although Sam was unsure, seeing Alexis like this...casually dressed, it sent her mind and body wild with want.

"Right." Alexis nodded. "So..."

"So?"

"Do you think maybe we could talk?" Alexis leaned back against the kitchen counter. "Your sister said I should come over and see you."

"Oh, she did now?" Sam's eyebrow rose, causing a smile to form on Alexis' mouth. "And did she have anything else she couldn't keep to herself?"

"No, she actually told me I had to come here and find out for myself."

"I don't know what she wants me to tell you." Sam sighed. "I don't even know what to tell myself."

"I quit the agency."

"I thought so, but why?"

"As you know, I'd already planned to leave. I just decided to do it sooner."

"I wish you hadn't," Sam admitted. "I would have liked to see you again..."

"I don't want to see you as an escort, Sam." Alexis pushed off the counter, closing the distance between them. "I don't want to see you, only to be paid at the end of the night."

"But that's how it works..."

"You're not my client," Alexis said softly, her hand settling on the side of Sam's face. "You're so much more than that. You deserve more."

Sam's eyes closed, her brain unable to form any words.

"I want to see you as me. Just me. Not Alexis. Not through the agency. But as myself."

Sam's forehead creased. "Not Alexis?"

"No," she said. "That's my escort name."

"God, I don't even know you." Sam dropped her head, feeling defeated. "I don't even know your name."

"Luciana."

"What?" Sam stepped away, stumbling back against the kitchen island. "What did you just say?"

"My name...is Luciana Foster."

"You have to leave." Sam's voice broke. "I don't know who is playing fucking games, but you have to leave right now."

"Sam."

"Don't." Sam shook her head, her emotions taking over. "Don't say my name. Don't come here again. You have to leave."

"I don't understand." Luciana clenched her jaw. "She told me to come here. Your sister..."

"Did she put you up to this?" Sam asked, feeling as though she was losing her mind. "Did she think it would be funny to mess with my fucking life!"

"Okay, calm down." Luciana stepped towards Sam but she continued to back away. "Please, can we sit down?"

"No, get out!" Sam cradled her head with her hands. "Please, get out."

Panicked, Luciana picked up Sam's phone, praying it didn't have a passcode on it. Relieved when it opened, she scrolled to L and found her sister's number. Waiting for the call to connect, she glanced back at Sam who was now sitting on the kitchen floor, her knees up to her chest.

"Sam?"

"No, it's me. Luc-Alexis."

"Oh, hi." Lindsay perked up. "How's it going?"

"You need to come over right now."

"Why?" Lindsay laughed. "I'm sure you don't need me there to hold your hand. It can't be that bad."

"Lindsay, I'm serious. She's freaking out."

"What did you do?"

"I didn't do anything. I just told her my name and she told me to get out."

"Um, why would she do that?" Lindsay asked, confused.

"I told her I couldn't see her as Alexis, as her escort. But I was willing to date her as me. Luciana."

"Whoa!" Lindsay gasped. "You have to leave."

"That's what she said." Luciana stood in the middle of Sam's apartment, with no idea what was going on. "You know what, I'll just go. She can't be as into me as you said she was."

"Her wife. She's dead."

"I'm sorry to hear that." Luciana sighed. "But I don't know what that has to do with me."

"Her name was Lucia."

"No..." Luciana looked up at Sam, her heart breaking for the woman sobbing on the floor. "You should come over right away. I'll leave. Let her calm down."

"I'm on my way."

Luciana ended the call and approached Sam, getting down to her knees. "I'm so sorry. I had no idea." She wasn't entirely sure what she was apologising for. After all, her name was her name.

Nothing.

Silence.

"I can be whoever you want me to be, Sam." She leaned in and pressed a kiss to her hair, her eyes closing as the scent of Sam's shampoo reached her nose. "If you ever want to talk, call me. I'll leave my private number on the kitchen worktop."

"I'm sorry." Sam shook her head, crying.

Luciana jotted down her number and moved towards the door. "I don't expect to hear from you, but I really am sorry."

Sam climbed to her feet ten minutes after Luciana had left her apartment. Tonight, she'd had every intention of talking to her escort when she showed up at her door, but now? Now, she was truly thrown. How could it be that the woman she was tempted to date was so similar to her wife? Was it a sign that someone somewhere was laughing at her, or was it a sign that she should push forward, an eerie blessing being sent from her wife? Sam had never believed in blessings or an afterlife, but when Lucia died, something changed for her. She felt her wife's presence. She felt their connection once she received the news that Lucia was dead. That time for Sam had been terrifying, not knowing if her wife would ever walk through the door again, but deep down, she knew. She felt one connection end the moment she turned on the TV, but another form as the news was confirmed.

Here she was, alone in her apartment, feeling as though someone was playing games. She knew it was nonsense and she knew nobody would do that to her, but this was a lot to take in. *Luciana.* Sam braced herself against the kitchen counter, the idea of Alexis' name being something different to what she had once known. *I can't do this. I can't date a woman called Luciana.* Sam felt as though everyone would stare. Everyone would talk. Perhaps she was looking for the next best thing. Sam knew that was utter rubbish, but people still judged. How would it be down the line when she introduced her to family and friends? Would they make a comment? Sam knew they would. Still, she wasn't sure she could let a name deter her from potentially finding happiness. She was beginning to think that it could be a sign. A good sign.

"Sam?" The apartment door flew open. "Are you okay?"

"No, I feel like a complete idiot." Sam laughed, the reminder of her behaviour now at the forefront of her mind. "I looked like a fucking lunatic!"

"I'm glad you find it funny. I've just met her downstairs crying."

"Say her name."

"What?" Lindsay's face dropped.

"Say *her* name."

"Sam..."

"Say it, Lindsay."

"Luciana."

Sam's eyes closed, a slight smile forming on her face. "Say it again."

"Luciana."

"Call her. Ask her to come back." Sam's eyes opened, the softness in them evident. "If she doesn't think I'm completely crazy, I'd like her to come back."

"Yeah?" Lindsay beamed. "You really scared her, you know."

"I told you this would fall apart before it began."

"I'll call her. She was leaving when I came up here." Lindsay eyed the paper on the counter and dialled Luciana's number.

Sam waited impatiently for the call to connect, unable to find any reason for her behaviour just moments ago. It was the shock. It was the disbelief that Alexis was, in fact, called Luciana.

"Hi, it's Lindsay."

Sam breathed a sigh of relief when she heard Luciana's voice filter through the phone.

"Yes, she's okay." Sam noted the smile from Lindsay. "Sam was wondering if you could come back?"

Sam waited with bated breath.

"No, I understand that." Lindsay nodded. "Of course, yeah. No... I know you didn't expect it."

"Give me the phone." Sam held out her hand. "Please?"

Lindsay knew she'd already overstepped tonight and decided against pissing her sister off any more than she already had.

"Hey, it's me." Sam moved into the living room. "I'm so sorry about before. If you'd be willing to come back up, I can explain. I'll tell you everything."

"Sam, I'd love to... I really would."

"But you can't." Sam closed her eyes, knowing she'd messed up. "That's okay."

"I just..."

"You don't have to explain." Sam shook her head. "Thank you for coming over tonight. It was good seeing you again."

"Maybe in a few days..." Luciana said, her voice tired and unsure. "Give you some time, you know?"

"That won't be necessary." Sam felt her embarrassment come back tenfold. "Be safe, okay?"

"I'm always safe, Sam."

"Still... I need you to just be safe."

"Always."

Sam ended the call before Luciana could say anything else. There was no more to be said, but she got the impression that their conversation could potentially continue for the sake of it. Neither of them wanting to end the call for fear of it being the final time.

"Is she coming back?" Lindsay asked, but Sam knew she already had her answer.

"No," Sam said nonchalantly, setting Lindsay's phone down in front of her. "You can go home. I need some sleep."

"I can stay..."

"I don't need you to stay." Sam glanced up at her sister, frowning. "Just text me when you're home so I know you got back okay."

"I'm sorry she didn't want to come back." Lindsay lifted her phone and slid it into her pocket. "Call you tomorrow?"

"Not too early," Sam said. "I plan on having a lie in."

"Sounds like the perfect Saturday morning."

"Your norm, you mean?"

"Same thing." Lindsay kissed her sister's cheek before leaving the apartment. "Love you, Sam."

"Love you, too."

Sam watched her sister leave, the door closing and signalling another night with her own thoughts. The difference with tonight was that she actually had something to think about. A new name with a familiar face. A woman who thirty minutes ago wanted to date her…only for it to fall apart because of Sam's inability to block out her past. She turned out the light and moved into her bedroom, taking Luciana's phone number with her. Keying it into her contact list, she saved the number, beginning a new message.

S: Thank you for coming here and being honest with me tonight. X

Sam stripped off, discarding her clothes and underwear. She slipped an oversized T-shirt over her head and pulled on a pair of boxer shorts, ready to settle down for what she hoped to be a peaceful night's sleep.

Her phone buzzed.

L: I'm outside the block. Couldn't go home. Can I come up? X

Sam's heart beat harder, the thought of Luciana being in her home again sending her thoughts wild.

S: Come up. One minute. X

She rushed out of her bedroom and reached for the intercom, granting Luciana access. She waited, her hand on the door handle of the apartment door, her breathing calm. If she didn't control the little things like her breathing, Sam knew she would end up in a heap on the floor. Anxiety. Apprehension. Memories of her wife. All coupled together could create a mean cocktail of emotions and she wasn't prepared for that again. Not tonight. Not any time in the near future.

"Sam?" a voice whispered behind her door. "You there?"

Sam unlocked the door, smiling. "I'm here."

"That's better." Luciana stepped into the darkened apartment. "I like seeing your smile..."

Sam reddened, thankful for the darkness. "Come in."

"You're sure it's okay for me to be here?"

"Yeah, I'm not crazy. I promise."

"Aren't we all a bit crazy from time to time?" Luciana took Sam's hand as she attempted to move further into the dark space. "Hey?"

"I think I've used up all my crazy."

"You looked gorgeous tonight," Luciana whispered, leaning in. "And I know you've been through a lot this evening, but I need you to know something."

"What's that?" Sam's eyes closed, Luciana's scent overpowering her senses.

"I don't care what you call me...so long as you *do* call me." It would be the easiest movement in the world to kiss Sam, but Luciana refrained from doing so. She was thankful to be here, and that, right now, would be enough.

"Luciana will be fine," Sam replied.

"Sounds good hearing my name fall from your lips." Luciana chanced her luck, locking the door. "I'd like to stay a while if you didn't have any plans?"

"None," Sam whispered, the proximity of Luciana making her dizzy. "None whatsoever."

CHAPTER NINE

Luciana leant against the window frame, looking out at the dots of light on the river in the distance. Sam hadn't said much since she'd agreed to allow her to stay a while, but Luciana wasn't concerned. There was no rush, and honestly, she didn't want to push Sam to talk if she didn't want to. She could see the tiredness in her eyes, the heaviness in her shoulders. All she wanted was for Sam to feel safe with her, trusted. Those moments when she had to watch Sam fall apart in front of her had been hard, so she couldn't imagine how Sam herself was feeling. She was likely to be embarrassed, but Luciana understood. It wasn't every day that you met someone whose wife had died, her name far too similar to your own. It also wasn't every day that she met a client who had such an impact on her life. Sam, when she was ready, could talk. Until then, just being here was good enough for Luciana.

"Can I get you anything?" Luciana broke the silence. "Anything at all?"

"You could pour me a glass of wine and then join me over here if you wanted to?"

"I'd like that." Luciana smiled, pushing off the window frame and heading into the kitchen. "You mind if I help myself to a glass?"

"A glass of wine is the least I can offer after my outburst before."

"Not an outburst." Luciana shook her head. "Just...a moment. One that you're more than entitled to."

"So, you're Italian?" Sam watched Luciana moved around the kitchen. A hint of a smile played on her lips.

"My dad, yes. My mum was born and bred here in the northwest. Manchester."

"I just didn't expect it," Sam said, running her fingers through her hair. "Still, I shouldn't have reacted like that."

"I was worried about you."

"That's really very sweet but I'm okay. I promise."

"I saw it in your eyes," Luciana said, handing Sam a glass of wine. "The fear."

"It was a moment of weakness. I don't have many of them, but it does happen rarely."

"You really don't have to explain yourself to me..."

"I know that." Sam patted the seat beside her. "Sit with me?"

"Of course." Luciana sat down, sipping her wine before setting it down on the glass coffee table. "Seriously, are you okay?"

"I'm fine." Sam took Luciana's hand. "Thanks for coming back."

"I needed to see for myself that you were okay. I didn't want you to ask me back here because you felt bad."

"I do feel bad, but that's not why I asked you back here."

"Then why did you?" Luciana asked the question, but she wasn't sure she'd like the answer.

"Because I need you to know that I've really enjoyed spending time with you. More than I thought I would."

"Why do I get the impression that this is a final goodbye from you?" Luciana's forehead creased, her hand trembling as she settled it in her lap. This wasn't supposed to end like this, not when she'd just been made aware of Sam's feelings for her. "Sam?"

"You know I think you're beautiful. I find it hard to take my eyes off you."

"But?" Luciana's voice wavered.

"But this...us, it would never work."

"How can you know that? Nobody knows what the future holds." Luciana gripped Sam's hand tighter, their fingers laced together.

"And I know that better than most." Sam nodded. "The woman you were with tonight? Your date..."

"Hardly, but yeah." Luciana snorted.

"You looked good together." Sam smiled. "You looked like you should be together."

"I don't even know what that means..." Luciana frowned.

"I'm turning thirty-eight in a few weeks. You're twenty-five, Luciana."

"So, you're telling me that we can't date because I'm too young for you?"

"I'm telling you we can't date because I'm realistic." Sam squeezed Luciana's hand. "I'm not prepared to get into something with you, only to hurt you down the line."

"That's bullshit."

"To you, perhaps." Sam sighed. "But to me, it's inevitable."

"I'm sorry you feel that way." Luciana wiped her hands down her jeans. "Really sorry."

"Hey!" Sam's hand clung to Luciana's knee. "You're great. Stunning. I'm shocked you ever agreed to take me on as a client, let alone all of this."

"But it's not enough for you." Luciana dropped her head on her shoulders. "That kinda hurts."

"I'm sorry."

"I don't even know you and it hurts." Luciana laughed. "I don't do this. I don't fall for women I shouldn't."

"I'm sure you haven't fallen." Sam squeezed her knee.

"And I'm sure that given half the chance... I would have."

"Luce..." Sam grimaced.

"There's not even a chance I can prove myself to you? Take you out to dinner?"

"You have *nothing* to prove. Trust me."

"I think I should leave." Luciana climbed to her feet, Sam's hand dropping from her knee. "If you ever want to grab a drink or you need some company, you know?"

"I'd love to... I want to, but it's not a good idea."

Luciana glanced down at Sam. Everything about this woman was what she never imagined she needed, but she did. She needed more. It was evident how torn Sam was, stuck between wanting to say yes and believing it couldn't be, but Luciana didn't know how to change her mind. She didn't know how to show Sam that she could be whatever she needed. A friend. A lover. Everything.

"It was great getting to know you, Sam." Luciana leaned down, pressing a kiss below Sam's ear. "Really great." Her lips lingered. "I'm sorry I couldn't be what you need."

"You're everything I need," Sam whispered. "But I can't accept this. You."

"Why?" Luciana's lips continued to hover around Sam's ear. "Would it really be the worst idea in the world?"

"For you, yes..."

"All I've wanted to do since I met you is kiss you..." Luciana's eyes closed, that faint hint of Sam's perfume still present. "So much..."

"I know that feeling." Sam leaned into the sensation created by Luciana's breath. "But you should go now."

"If that's what you want..."

"I don't know what I want." Sam pulled back, meeting blue eyes once more. "You spend your life running towards danger."

"I think about you all the time."

"And I'd forever wonder if you were alive."

"For you, I'd fight."

"I don't want you to have to fight. I just want you to live a full, incredible life."

"And what about you?"

"I had it and lost it."

Luciana's heart shattered in her chest as Sam's admission reached her ears. She could never be what Sam wanted and needed in her life, that much was clear from her words, but she wished things could be different. How could Luciana ever compare to the wife Sam lost? She knew, in this moment, that she would be second best. As much as she wanted Sam, Luciana knew she couldn't spend her life being second best. When she fell in love, she wanted it to be completely. Wholeheartedly. Forever.

"Goodbye, Sam." Luciana offered a half-hearted smile. "Take care, okay?"

"Yeah, always do." Sam stood up, moving across the open space towards the door. "I lost her. I can't lose someone else I care about."

"I don't plan on going anywhere." Luciana smiled as she stepped out into the corridor. "Not anytime soon."

"She told me the very same thing." A tear slipped from Sam's eye, caught by Luciana's thumb. "You run into fire. She tried to escape the very same thing."

"O-Oh." Luciana lowered her eyes. "I didn't know..."

"Neither did she until she was engulfed by it and the ceiling collapsed on her."

"Sam...if you ever need to talk." Luciana's heart weighed heavy in her chest. "As a professional or as a friend. Any time, okay?"

"Thank you." Sam nodded, closing the door. "I'm going to miss you..."

"Yeah, me too."

Sam found herself lying awake at six am, Luciana and her words playing over on repeat in her mind. She knew she shouldn't think too hard, it never did her any favours, but that voice...her breath, everything felt like it should in the moments before she left. Sam never wanted to ask her to leave, knowing how much she wanted something more, but doing so was the right thing for them both. She knew it deep down, and one day, Luciana would realise it too. At least, that was what she hoped to be the outcome. She would go to the office today and Luciana would forget she ever existed. It couldn't be that hard, right?

Rolling from her bed and slipping her robe on, Sam moved into the kitchen, a desperate need for caffeine relief required this morning. As she turned the coffee machine on, the beans automatically grinding, she felt a sense of sadness settle in the pit of her stomach. Luciana's scent remained, her impossibly blue eyes, too. Whenever she closed her own, blue was the first image. Followed by that, impeccable, honey-coloured hair. As the moments passed throughout the night, Sam wondered if she'd made a mistake in asking Luciana to leave, but in the cold light of day, she still thought it was the right decision. Their ages still remained... Sam's worry about Luciana's job. The only reason she had not to ask her to leave, was selfishness. That connection. Intimacy. The thought that perhaps she could feel another woman's hands on her skin for the first time in two years. As much as Sam wanted to feel that once again, terror tore through her.

Thinking about calling Lindsay and getting her own back on the recent early morning calls from her sister, she lifted her phone from the counter, smirking. When she unlocked the screen, she found something she hadn't expected.

L: I'm lying in bed thinking about you. Sleep well.

Time stamped 4:54 am. Sam glanced at the clock.

S: We shouldn't do this. Don't put yourself through it. I'm not worth it.

Sam busied herself in the kitchen as she slid her phone into her robe pocket, preparing a cup of coffee and moving into the living room.

Her phone buzzed, surprisingly.

L: I've lay awake this entire night. Don't tell me what I should or shouldn't do. If I want to spend my time thinking about you, I will.

S: But what good is it doing?

L: More than you think.

S: I'm sorry.

L: Stop apologising. It loses its meaning after so long...

Sam locked her phone and set it down beside her. She didn't have the mental capacity for this today, she knew that much, but she'd also spent the night thinking about Luciana. Whatever she decided, she couldn't win.

S: Do you want to meet for lunch?

L: I can't. I have to be at the station in two hours.

S: Oh.

L: You may think I'm going to die, but I'm really not. I have plans. Big plans.

S: Well, I hope for your sake, that works out for you.

L: Could have worked out for the both of us. I'm just a kid though so I don't suppose you take anything I say seriously.

S: Luciana ...

L: Yea?

S: Stop!!!

L: You are so fucking gorgeous. I hope you know that! Pull them in and then tear them apart...

S: You're the first woman I've looked at in two years. That's not fair.

L: Then you should meet me tonight when my shift finishes.

S: We shouldn't.

L: We should.

Sam smiled at the persistency of this woman. Not only was it refreshing, but it made her feel good too.

S: I have a lot of work on. What time do you finish?
L: I'm on an 8-8.
S: Come over when you finish.
L: Yeah? You really mean that?
S: I don't say anything I don't mean...
L: So, you still mean everything you said last night?

Sam pondered their previous conversation, her heart breaking in her chest. To an extent, she meant it all. That didn't mean she didn't want to see Luciana again though. She may have said she didn't, but this woman had an effect on her that she'd never expected. Would it really be such a bad idea to just go with it, and see what the outcome was?

S: Just come over. I'll have dinner ready for you since you'll be working a bitch of a shift.
L: I make the fire my bitch, baby!

Okay, that's hot. Sam released a deep breath, typing out a response.

S: I'm sure you do. I don't doubt it.
L: Better believe it. X

Sam smiled, her gaze following the early morning clouds as they rolled in off the river. Another sun-filled day was beginning outside, and the temperature was rising in her life for the first time in two years. Could it be that Luciana was the one to bring something out in her? An intensity for life that she hadn't felt since Lucia took her last breath? As the seconds passed, Sam was beginning to wish she'd never asked her to leave last night. Her emotions got the better of her, her fears for the future too, but now...as she watched the morning flourish outside her window, she felt an energy for life. A potential love for everything it brought. Lucia would always remain in her heart, but Sam knew her friends and family were right. She had to move forward.

S: I'm sorry I asked you to leave last night. X

Sam toyed with her phone, praying Luciana wouldn't leave her hanging for a response all day.

Her phone buzzed, sending her heart rate through the roof.

L: It's okay. I'll let you make it up to me. X

What the hell have I got myself into?

Draining the contents of her coffee cup as she moved through her apartment, Sam refilled and disappeared into her bedroom. *I'm a thirty-seven-year-old woman who is thinking about a twenty-five year old. I've lost my fucking mind.* Sam laughed. *Who cares. I lost my mind a long time ago.*

The buzzer of her apartment sounded, causing Sam to freeze.

Surely not...

It couldn't be. Could it?

She rushed through into the kitchen and lifted the receiver. "Hello?"

"Hi," a soft voice said, lulling her into another world. "Are you busy?"

"N-No," Sam said, her voice low. "Why?"

"Are you hungry?"

For you, yes. "I could eat." Sam smiled.

"Me too." Luciana's voice was like syrup.

"So..."

"So, let me up," Luciana whispered. "I'll make it worth your while..."

Sam braced herself against the kitchen counter as she unlocked the apartment block door. She stood in nothing but her robe, the inability to move from her position leaving very little time to change. Should she? It was barely morning, so she had every right to be standing in the bare minimum, right?

A light knock jolted her from the thoughts running through her mind, her feet taking Sam to the door immediately. Unlocking it, she prepared herself for the vision she was about to be met with.

Oh, wow. Her hand gripped the door as her eyes trailed Luciana's body. A tight, navy-blue T-shirt tucked into her tight, navy-blue combat pants was finished with a black belt and a pair of black heavy work boots. "H-Hi." Sam's voice betrayed her. "Come in." She opened the door fully, breathing in Luciana's scent as she brushed past her. "I didn't expect you to come by right now."

"I'd offer to leave but I really don't intend to." Luciana turned to face her, her blonde hair pulled into a tight, low bun at the back of her head.

I never thought I'd be attracted to a woman like this. Sam's entire body throbbed for something more than what it was currently receiving.

"I made breakfast at home and decided to bring you some."

"That's sweet." Sam's face flushed, her eyes closing momentarily as she attempted to remove her aroused thoughts from her mind.

"Are you just going to stand at the door until I leave?"

"What? No!" Sam closed the door, flicking the lock. "Just... surprised to see you here."

"A good surprise, or?"

"A very good surprise," Sam admitted. "So, what's for breakfast?"

"Food...and me." Luciana winked, placing the paper bag down on the kitchen worktop. "My company."

And if I wanted more? "The, uh..." Sam calmed her nerves, trying again. "The plates are in the cabinet above the dishwasher. I'll be back in a few."

"Wait!" Luciana gripped Sam's wrist. "Where are you going?"

Sam glanced down her body. "To change."

"Don't." Luciana took her bottom lip between her teeth. "I'm the one who showed up here unannounced. Stay as you are. This is your down time."

God, she's too much.

"It will take me two minutes..."

"And that's two minutes less with you before I have to leave for work..."

"Okay." Sam smiled. "If you insist."

"I do." Luciana released Sam's wrist. "I really do…"

"This really was a nice surprise."

"I wasn't even supposed to be working today." Luciana groaned. "I made the mistake of lying to my date last night…then one of the lads called me when I got home."

"Lied?"

"It was just easier than explaining how I was feeling." Luciana held up her hand. "I don't make it a habit to lie."

"No, you don't seem like you do." Sam took Luciana's hand, guiding her further into the kitchen. "So, what did you bring me for breakfast?"

"Bagels. Fruit." Sam turned, leaning against the worktop, pulling Luciana against her. "Why don't you just open the bag and see?" Blue eyes focused on Sam, darkening as the moments passed. "I don't even remember what I brought."

"A forgetful firefighter?" Sam teased, arching an eyebrow. "Doesn't bode well…"

"Not forgetful." Luciana tucked Sam's hair behind her ear, smiling. "Preoccupied."

Sam closed her eyes, the sensation of Luciana's fingertips on her skin setting her on fire. This woman may be significantly younger than her, but it felt right. In this moment, Sam could get used to having her around. *How the hell did I ask her to leave last night?*

"B-Breakfast," Sam said. "We should have breakfast…"

"Mm, I suppose we should."

CHAPTER TEN

"Foster!"

Luciana turned to find her captain standing behind her, his moustache twitching as he smiled at her.

"Boss." She dropped the rope in her hand and approached him. "Did you need something?"

"Good job today." Dave Harper has been the man around the station since long before Luciana joined, but he was very much a father figure to the brigade. When he complimented someone, he meant it. "Is everything okay?"

"Of course, why?"

"You seemed a little...distant." Dave ushered Luciana towards his office. "On your game, but distant."

"I'm sorry, boss. I wasn't aware of that."

"It's not a criticism. I just wanted to check in with you." He stepped inside his office, closing the door behind Luciana. "I know you've been taking extra shifts and helping Craig out when he's had to take June to the hospital...but if it's too much...?"

"It's not. I'm here to help out wherever I can."

"You're not due back here until when? Tuesday?"

"Yes, Tuesday." The thought of two days off seemed like the perfect end to a hectic week for Luciana. "Tuesday, late shift."

"Then I don't expect to see you until then."

"Sounds good enough to me." She smiled. "How is Craig's wife?"

"Stage four." Dave sat down. "He's keeping it together, but I don't expect him to be here full time until he has more information."

"That's awful." Luciana dropped her head on her shoulders, saddened by her colleague's news. "If there's anything I can do around here to help out, just let me know."

"Tuesday, Foster. Not a moment before." Dave looked at her pointedly. "You need to rest. Take a couple of days to relax."

Luciana sighed. "Tuesday. Got it."

"Now, get out of here. You're already over on your hours."

"Goodnight, boss." Luciana smiled as she left his office.

Distant? I've been distant?

Perhaps it was knowing she could have been doing other things this evening. Perhaps it was Sam on her mind. Whatever the reason, Luciana wouldn't think about it too much tonight. She was already thirty minutes late for dinner with Sam, but she knew she would understand. Today had been a whirlwind for the both of them. The last thing Luciana had expected from Sam was a response to her text message in the night. While she had gone home with every intention of letting Sam go, Luciana's mind had other plans. Yes, she may never be the love of Sam's life and yes, this would likely end sooner rather than later, but Luciana was prepared for that. Who said she couldn't have a little fun with a gorgeous older woman?

Don't fall in love with her, Luce.

She removed her phone from her back pocket as she made her way towards her locker.

L: Finished late. Should I go home?

As much as she wanted Sam to respond with the perfect

answer, she had been left to think about their morning. Luciana hadn't been given that opportunity with work the only thing on her mind, but whatever Sam's response, she would respect it.

S: Dinner is ready if you are...
L: Okay, that's amazing!

Luciana's smile beamed as she grabbed her belongings, shoving her rucksack up on her shoulder. As the day wore on, she wondered if Sam regretted any of their morning together. No money had been exchanged, only glances at one another, the heat rising between them.

S: What time should I expect you?
L: Give me fifteen and I'll be there. X
S: Perfect. X

"Drinks tonight, Foster?"

"Oh." Luciana turned around. "Not tonight. I've got plans."

"You? Plans?" her colleague, Jack Bridges, said. "That's not like you."

"Yeah, well." She shrugged. "Found someone who holds my interest."

"Christ, they must be special." He patted her on the shoulder and winked. "Enjoy your night off, Foster. See you next week."

"Thanks, Jack."

Luciana had never divulged her escort job to any of the brigade —it wasn't their business—but Jack was right. Luciana never had plans, none that were worth mentioning anyway. This, telling her colleagues at work, was huge. For her and the team.

Sam busied herself in the kitchen, waiting for the moment when Luciana would arrive. As her day progressed, she decided that it wouldn't be necessary to head into the office, her mind currently on *other* aspects of her life. The differences she felt just having Luciana here had come as a shock to Sam, but she was trying to embrace the changes she was anticipating. She never imagined anything would run smoothly, not all the time, but the ease she felt this morning when her guest arrived at the door had given her a sense of contentment. Whether it took a week or a year to fully open up to Luciana, she wasn't worried. Nothing seemed forced, and Sam knew that this newfound relationship with a younger woman could truly bring herself back out again. There was no pressure. No expectation. Just two women, enjoying one another's company.

God, I want to do so much more than enjoy her company.

Sam sighed, a smile playing at the corner of her lips. Luciana looked at her as though she was the only woman in the universe. That meant more to Sam than anything else. Her featherlight touches, those soft blue eyes, it turned Sam into a woman she didn't recognise anymore. A woman she believed was dead and buried, along with her wife. Although Sam never imagined she would be happy again, not in a relationship, she was prepared to take it one day at a time. Nothing would happen overnight, she knew that.

Her phone buzzed on the counter, her stomach fluttering.

L: I'm outside. X

S: Buzzing you up now. X

L: Perfect. X

Sam went through her usual routine of checking everything within her apartment was where it should be, while fixing her own clothes better on her body, hoping she looked good enough to Luciana. She'd always taken pride in her appearance, but over the last two years, that was merely for herself. Now that someone was here, with an attraction for her, she wanted to give the best impression she possibly could. While she was a businesswoman, she was also a human being. So tonight, Sam opted for a comfortable pair of jeans and a white tank top. Barefoot, she opened the front door as she buzzed Luciana into the building.

Returning to the kitchen, soft music playing throughout the

sound system, Sam relaxed her shoulders and finished preparing a salad.

"Hello?"

The door creaked open.

"Sam?"

"Come in," Sam called out, glancing over her shoulder. "Everything okay?"

"Yeah." Sam noted the tiredness in Luciana's eyes, her shoulders sagging as she turned her back and closed the door. "How was your day?"

"Actually, it was quite enjoyable."

"Good, that's good." Luciana stifled a yawn but Sam caught her in the act.

"You look like you could sleep for a week." Sam stepped away from the salad bowl she was filling, taking Luciana's hand. "I won't be offended if you want to go home."

"I really don't."

"You're sure?" Sam arched an eyebrow. "We can have dinner another time."

"I've been wanting dinner with you like this since the moment I met you, Sam." Luciana's lips curled. "There is no way I'm about to miss that opportunity."

"Sit down." Sam guided her to the couch, removing Luciana's rucksack from her shoulder. "I'll leave this in the kitchen, okay?"

"Thanks." Luciana sat awkwardly on the couch, staring up at Sam.

"What?"

"Nothing."

"No. What is it?" Sam asked, dropping the rucksack and sitting beside Luciana. "If something is on your mind, I'd rather you told me than kept it in."

"You look gorgeous."

"Oh." The tips of Sam's ears heated, her eyes smiling. "Thank you."

"Really gorgeous." Luciana reached out, running her thumb across Sam's cheek. "You asked me to leave last night...but I'm sitting here, Sam." Sam's breath caught as a soft thumb slipped to her bottom lip. "This is real, right?"

"Y-Yes," Sam whimpered. "This is real."

Luciana leant in, her breath tickling Sam's lips. Without a second thought, her lips pressed gently against Sam's, stealing every ounce of oxygen her body held. As their lips parted slightly, Luciana slid her tongue against Sam's, moaning in delight.

Luciana tasted delicious. Her soft lips captivating Sam's every sense. Nothing in this moment mattered. Not her worries or her apprehension. Their ages...non-existent. Luciana was breathing life back into Sam, at a rate faster than she anticipated.

"O-Oh." Sam's eyes remained closed as Luciana's lips disappeared from her own. "Shit."

"God, I've wanted to do that for too long." Heat pooled between Luciana's thighs, the very thought of this woman against her body ignited every nerve ending.

"Yeah..."

"I'm not worried, Sam." The distance between them minimal, Luciana's eyes bored into Sam's soul. She felt it returned. That piercing gaze. The heat. The intensity. "I'm not worried about any of this."

"This. Us. I need to adjust." Sam pressed her fingertips to her own lips, her eyes closing momentarily. "I need to take it slow."

"I've got all the time in the world." Luciana beamed a full, wide smile. "Please, trust me when I tell you that."

"I do." Sam nodded, Luciana's taste lingering on her lips. "Slowly, okay..."

Luciana gently gripped Sam's jaw, taking her own bottom lip between her teeth. She nodded, her eyes flickering a lighter shade of blue. "Slowly."

CHAPTER ELEVEN

Sunday flashed by like a blur. For the first time in a while, Sam took the day off completely, only showering and changing into comfortable clothes once it reached midday. It wouldn't become a common occurrence, not by any stretch, but she had enjoyed lounging around, doing nothing. Her only issue had been the lack of contact with Luciana. With plans already in place for her to leave the city and visit her parents, Sam was left wandering around her apartment with no idea as to what she should do. She could shop, she could visit Lindsay, but her sister hadn't contacted her in two days, and Sam was beginning to wonder if her outburst at her parent's house had caused a rift between them. It may be true, but Sam would always be concerned about her younger sister. After all, she was the one who had to pick her up out of the gutter when she hit rock bottom, a hefty drug bill attached to her name. Sam wouldn't allow her to spiral again, not when life was good for them both.

S: Call me. I miss you.
L: You? Miss me? On what planet?
S: Are you mad at me?
L: Why would I be mad at you?

She's right, why would she be mad at me? We've been out together since Mum's.

S: Never mind. Are you busy?
L: I'm not. Are you at the office?
S: Just like I am every Monday.
L: Nothing from Luciana?
S: Actually, yes.

Sam's phone buzzed in her hand, Lindsay's name flashing on the screen.

"Might have known you'd call instead." Sam laughed.

"I can't believe you didn't call to tell me you've contacted her."

"She spent the evening with me on Saturday."

"Sam! It's Monday." Lindsay scoffed. "Why didn't you tell me?"

"Because I thought you'd be sick of hearing about it by now." Sam wasn't sure why she hadn't called her sister to update her on her personal life, but she couldn't change it now. "I'm sorry."

"So you should be." Lindsay sighed. "I've spent all my time trying to make you understand that you need to move on, and then this happens and you don't even send me a text?"

"Linds, I'm really sorry." Sam sat back in her office chair, staring out at the vast river in front of her. "What can I do to make it up to you?"

"Just promise to never do it again..."

"Okay." Sam tugged her bottom lip. "I, uh..."

"You what?"

"Nothing."

"Sam," Lindsay said, her tone tinged with worry. "What's going on?"

"I just... I miss her."

"You do?" Lindsay's voice softened. "Oh, sis."

"That's stupid, right?" Sam asked. "How can I miss her? Just a couple of days ago I told her I couldn't let it go any further."

"You did? When... I mean, why?"

"Friday, after you left..." Sam cleared her throat as she crossed her legs. "She came back. I told her it was a bad idea, that I couldn't spend my life worrying about her. About us."

"And?"

"And she left."

"God, you're an idiot sometimes." Lindsay groaned. "You really are."

"I woke up to a text from her, Linds. To say that she was thinking about me."

"That's cute." Sam knew her sister was smiling; she could feel it.

"The next thing I knew, I was texting her back and telling her I'd have dinner ready for her once her shift finished. I don't know what the hell I'm doing, but it feels good."

"So let it, Sam. Just let it feel good."

"Yeah, I'm trying." Sam closed her eyes, her head resting back against her leather office chair. "I hoped I'd spend the day with her yesterday but she had plans."

"Have you called her today?"

"No. I don't know what to say to her..."

"Ask her to come over."

"I'm going to be at the office late," Sam said. "Maybe she could come here...what do you think?"

"I think there is no harm in asking. She seems like an honest person. If she wants to come to the office, I'm sure she will agree."

"Yeah, right." Sam sat forward. "I'll call her."

"Let me know if you have plans this evening. If not, I'll be over to hear all about this."

"Love you." Sam smiled.

"Love you, too."

Ending the call, Sam brought up Luciana's contact details and waited for her call to connect. If she chose not to spend time with Sam today, she wouldn't be too upset, but she would be miserable. How could one person change how you feel so suddenly? How could *anyone* break down the walls Sam had tried so hard to maintain?

"Hey." Luciana's voice filtered through the earpiece of Sam's phone.

"H-Hi."

"Everything okay?"

"Yeah, of course. I just… I wondered if you were busy?"

"When? Now?" Luciana asked. "If you consider binge-watching TV busy, then yes… I'm up to my eyeballs."

An image flashed through Sam's mind of Luciana spread out on the couch, relaxing.

"I thought maybe you could come by the office and have lunch with me?"

"I'd like that." Luciana sighed. "You're sure it's okay?"

"Okay with who?" Sam laughed. "I own the place. I say what goes."

"That's hot."

Sam blushed, her lips curling at the corners.

"What time do you want me there?" Luciana asked, her tone raspy.

"An hour ago would have been ideal, but whenever you're ready will suffice."

"Babe, I'm on my way."

Luciana cut the call as Sam's heart fluttered in her chest. A term of endearment had been missing from Sam's life for a long time, but hearing it…wow. Giving herself a moment to process what was happening, Sam climbed to her feet and approached the window. She leant against the frame, wrapping her arms around herself, and smiled. This undeniable feeling of enjoyment should be a lot for her to take in, but in this moment, everything was perfect. If nothing came of the relationship she could feel approaching, Sam would be saddened, but the potential of what it could bring drowned out that worry. She gripped the sapphire necklace sitting on her chest and brought it up to her lips.

You know I'll always love you, but it's time to move on.

Luciana glanced down at her phone in her hand and checked the address Sam had given her for the office. Impressed by what stood in front of her, her eyes trailed the tall, glass building, the sun bouncing off the windows. *Why are you standing out here looking at this when you could be in there looking at her?* She fixed the open blue shirt hanging from her shoulders, checking her shoes were still the pristine white they'd been when she left her flat twenty minutes ago. Satisfied that she looked good enough, Luciana stepped towards the glass doors, a whooshing sound signalling the opening of them. Inside, the area seemed quiet, and as she spied a woman sitting at a desk, Luciana made a beeline in her direction.

"Hi, excuse me..." She stopped at the desk. "I'm here to see Sam."

"Do you have an appointment?" The woman didn't look up from the paperwork on her desk. "Mrs Phillips doesn't do walk-ins."

"She, uh...she asked me come by." Luciana shifted uncomfortably, shoving her hands in the pockets of her jeans. "I spoke to her before."

The woman looked up, and Luciana's eyes widened. "C-Cheryl, hi."

"Alexis." Cheryl's eyebrows rose. "What are you doing here?"

"Sam asked me to join her at the office." She shrugged, aware that the woman in front of her had used her escort name. It didn't bother Luciana, she often kept her name private from anyone she'd done business with in the past. "Call her and check..."

"Are you sure? Mrs Phillips wouldn't just arrange anything without making me aware. I handle all of her day-to-day business."

"Well, I guess I'm not her day-to-day business."

Luciana chose not to think about the fact that Sam was still referred to as Mrs; it wasn't her business.

"Straight down the corridor. You'll see her office doors ahead of you."

"Thanks." Luciana smiled. "Good to see you again."

"Y-Yeah. You too."

Luciana pushed off and made her way down the corridor, the thought of seeing Sam at her business making her hot under the collar. She'd always had a thing for the older woman, but Sam...she was incredible in every sense of the word. Dinner on Saturday was amazing, both of them talking freely about anything that came to their minds, and as the end of the evening approached...the thought of leaving Sam alone in her apartment hurt Luciana's heart.

She knocked on the heavy wooden doors, waiting to be invited in.

"Come in," Sam's soft voice called out and Luciana turned the handle. Sam mouthed "one minute" as she continued on a call and Luciana simply nodded, closing the door behind her and leaning against it.

"Well, I'm glad you came to your senses, Roger." Sam rolled her eyes, smiling at Luciana. "You know you won't find a better quote than mine. At least, not without cutting corners."

Luciana's mouth salivated as she watched Sam stand from her seat and round her desk, her black, tailored suit fitting perfectly. *Sweet Jesus!*

"Okay, well I'll be in touch." Sam nodded. "I have business to tend to."

Sam cut the call, her eyes finding Luciana's as she placed her phone down on her desk. "Hi."

"H-Hi."

"Did you find the place okay?"

Luciana nodded, unable to form any words. Sam's dark hair fell down one side of her face, curling ever so slightly as it sat below her breasts. The white shirt beneath her blazer showed the ideal amount of cleavage, and Luciana struggled to keep her eyes where she knew they should be.

"Hello?" Sam dipped her head. "You with me?"

"Mm?" Luciana's head shot up. "What?"

"I said it's great to see you."

"Likewise," Luciana squeaked. "H-Have you been here all morning?"

"I have. Since eight am."

I could have been here at 8:01.

Luciana swallowed hard as Sam rested back against her desk, crossing her legs at the ankles. Everything about this woman oozed class, so Luciana was now beginning to wonder what the hell she was doing receiving attention from Sam.

"Something's wrong." Sam narrowed her eyes. "You seem different."

"Me?" Luciana laughed. "I, um... I didn't expect this." She waved her hand in front of her, motioning up and down Sam's body. "Phew."

"What?" Sam's brow creased, following Luciana's line of sight. "The suit?"

"Mm."

"I know it's not very appealing but it's the businesswoman in me, I'm sorry."

"Not appealing?" Luciana arched an eyebrow. "Your arse, in those pants..." Luciana pinched the bridge of her nose, breathing through her arousal. "What I meant to say was...hi, how's your day been so far?"

"Good. Better now that you're here." Sam held out her hand. "Come here..."

Oh God. I don't think I can. Luciana's breath quickened.

She moved on shaky legs, clearing her throat as she approached Sam. Taking her hand, her body was pulled between Sam's legs, one hand settling on Luciana's hip. "I wanted to see you yesterday..."

"I wanted to see you, too." Luciana's eyes flickered between Sam's eyes and lips. "It was late when I got home. I'd already kept you awake and woke you early on Saturday."

"But if I said I liked being kept awake by you..."

"You told me you love your sleep." Luciana smiled. "And I don't want to get on the wrong side of you." She pushed a lock of Sam's hair from her face. "And then I lay in bed last night thinking about kissing you..."

"You did, huh?"

"Thought about it every minute of the day." Luciana's voice dropped, her every sense heightened.

"Well, I wouldn't want you to think about it for too long..."

"Babe, I'd spend my life thinking about it if that's what you wanted." Luciana searched Sam's face for any signs of discomfort. There was a look in her eyes she didn't recognise, but it certainly wasn't discomfort. "Too much?"

Sam gripped the back of Luciana's neck. "Not enough."

Their lips met, that perfect pressure, softness. Sam could spend her entire day kissing Luciana, never wanting it to end. Her lips felt safe. Calm. Trustworthy.

"Mrs Phillips?" A knock on the door pulled them apart and Sam sighed.

"I'm sorry." She offered Luciana a sad smile. "Give me one minute."

"Do your thing. I'm happy to sit here just watching you."

"Hold that thought." Sam winked. "Come in, Cheryl."

Luciana backed away, dropping down onto the black leather couch against the back wall of the office.

Cheryl appeared. "I'm going to lunch, Mrs Phillips. Are you coming?"

"I've told you to call me Sam."

"Oh, yes." Cheryl blushed. "Just hard when I've never known you as that inside the office."

"Well, learn it. Use it." Sam got the impression that Cheryl was attempting to hit a nerve, but she wouldn't rise to it. She wouldn't play the game.

"Right, yes." Cheryl nodded. "So, lunch?"

"I have something on right now." Sam glanced at Luciana momentarily. "You go on."

"Okay." Cheryl backed up. "Bye, Alexis."

Bitch. Luciana cringed, wanting to disappear into thin air hearing her escort name. She knew it was Cheryl's way of claiming they once had something, but she didn't need this right now. Not when she was trying to build something with Sam.

"Ah." Sam laughed as her office door closed. "I forgot you two knew each other."

"H-How did you know?" Luciana stuttered, sitting forward and running a hand through her hair.

"Cheryl can be very vocal when she wants to be." Sam shrugged, approaching Luciana sitting on the couch.

If she comes any closer, I'm going to struggle to keep my hands to myself.

Luciana sat back against the couch, shocked as Sam straddled her legs.

"Okay, this is a completely different side to you..."

"Problem?" Sam asked, daring to be bold.

"No problem here." Luciana's hands fell to Sam's thighs. "Fuck," she muttered, her eyes closing.

"So, you and Cheryl?"

"Business," Luciana said. "Completely business."

"Still...my assistant has seen you naked."

"And if you hadn't requested dinner and conversation...you would have too," Luciana countered. "Such a shame."

"But there's a difference, no?" Sam's hands pressed firmly

against the couch either side of Luciana's head. "At least, I believe there is."

"A huge difference."

"And what is that difference?" Sam asked, her lips inching closer.

"I want so much more with you." Pulling Sam impossibly close, their lips crushed into one another's, an urgency for something more. "And I know..." Luciana pulled back. "I know we're going slow, but fuck...you're something else, Sam."

"I'm not sure you realise just how good this feels." Sam smiled into another kiss. "That night when I asked you to leave...it hurt."

"I'm here now." Luciana took Sam's bottom lip between her teeth. "I'm here and I hope to be for a long time."

"Come over tonight," Sam said, breathless.

"I'm already there, babe."

CHAPTER TWELVE

Sam manoeuvred into the parking space outside her apartment, cutting the engine of her Range Rover before sitting back in her seat and closing her eyes. Her afternoon at the office had been intense and nothing she'd expected, but her boldness had come from somewhere. She knew it was a hint of jealousy when Cheryl appeared at her office door, but it was also something more. Something she couldn't quite put her finger on. Luciana had shown up looking like a masterpiece in her casual clothing, and Sam felt that pull once again. The lack of time spent with her on Sunday meant that the moment she saw Luciana, Sam needed to kiss her. Yes, it may have been out of the blue for her and yes, it was Sam who had suggested they take things slow, but kissing never hurt anyone.

Sam exited her car, taking her bag from the passenger seat. Luciana was due at her apartment in the next ten minutes, so sitting in the car park and thinking about what had already happened was a waste of time. She wouldn't dwell on it, not when she enjoyed kissing Luciana as much as she did.

Sam took the lift up to her apartment, slipping her key into the lock and releasing a deep breath.

Okay, now what do I do with myself?

Sam glanced around her apartment, everything perfectly in place as it usually was. She needed to keep her hands busy and her mind free from any uncertainty. *What if she's expecting more tonight?* Sam wrung her hands together, the prospect of turning down anything intimate with Luciana weighing heavy in her chest. She didn't want to come across as the woman who'd grieved for two years, but she had. However she dressed it up, her entire world still revolved around her wife. *I'm going to mess this up with her, I know I am.* She sighed, lifting her long dark hair and tying it up. Tonight, Sam wanted relaxed. She wanted conversation and Luciana's soft voice. Her body may be telling her she needed more than just that, but Sam had always been good with self-control. At times, too good. *Just go with it.*

The buzzer sounded, signalling Luciana's arrival. A smile instantly settled on Sam's lips, and as she approached the intercom, her entire body relaxed. *I have nothing to worry about with this woman.*

"Hey, come on up..." Sam granted Luciana access to the building, unlocking her apartment door as she did. Moving through into the kitchen, she chose a bottle of wine for later and opened it. The sound of footsteps caused her stomach to flutter, and as she turned around, Sam found Luciana standing in the doorway.

"You know, you should really keep your door locked. Anyone could walk in here..."

Sam's heart slammed against her ribcage, Luciana's smile beaming.

"Just you." Sam cocked her head. "Still no plans for this evening?"

"Just you." Luciana closed the door, her rucksack slung over her shoulder. "This may be very forward of me, and you can tell me to piss off at any point, bu—"

"You plan on staying?" Sam cut in. "The night..."

"I know it's a ridiculous idea, and I'm not *that* lucky, but who knows?" Luciana shrugged.

She is expecting more. Sam's palms became clammy, her brain unable to form any words.

"I've had a great day with you, Sam. I guess I'm just not looking forward to it ending." The last thing Luciana wanted was to scare Sam off, but as the seconds passed, an awkwardness in the air, she suspected she was doing exactly that.

"Could you excuse me for twenty minutes?" Sam asked, keeping a slight distance between them. "I'd like to shower before we relax."

"Sure." Luciana narrowed her eyes as she watched Sam walk away, her back turned. "Hey, Sam?"

"Yeah?" She glanced over her shoulder.

Luciana felt an uncertainty building between them. "Should I just go?" She threw her thumb over her shoulder. "Wait to hear from you?"

"I'll be twenty minutes, okay?"

"Right, yeah."

Luciana sat perched on the edge of Sam's super king-sized bed, a framed photo in her hands. She smiled, studying every pixel of the image. Though she loved seeing Sam happy when they spent time together, the happiness she was seeing as Sam stood beside her wife was unmistakable. It wasn't jealously brewing inside Luciana, not at all, but she would be lying if she said she didn't wish Sam looked at her the way she looked at her late wife. That look in Sam's eyes was complete heart-stopping love. A love Luciana never imagined she would find in her lifetime. It hurt to know that Sam would never feel that way about her, but it was understandable. At one point this afternoon, Luciana had thought about a potential future with Sam, but now, sitting here...something felt off inside her.

"I thought you'd left." Sam's soft voice filled the space around Luciana. "I didn't expect to find you in here."

"I'm sorry." She set the picture down and climbed to her feet, smiling as she took in Sam's comfortable appearance. Her grey yoga pants hugged her hips like a glove, while a white jumper hung from her shoulders, her hair dragged up into a comfortable bun on top of her head. "I didn't know what to do with myself and I just ended up here..."

"It's okay." Sam gripped her wrist, aware that Luciana was bearing the weight of something she couldn't quite put her finger on. "It's not as though I have anything to hide."

"No, that's not what I thought." Luciana shook her head. "Sam, I think I should go."

Sam hesitated. "Okay..."

"It's not you." She took Sam's hand, squeezing it. "It's me. I don't feel so good."

"Are you sick?" Worry flashed in Sam's deep brown eyes.

"No." Luciana smiled faintly, appreciative of Sam's concern. "I'm not sick."

"Then what is it?" Sam asked. "Something must have happened in the time I've been away. You came here with the intention of staying the night...but now you're leaving."

"Just...got some stuff on my mind." Luciana lifted Sam's hand, pressing a kiss to her knuckles. "I'll call you, okay?"

"Sure." Sam pulled her hand from Luciana's, backing up out of her bedroom. "I don't expect a call, but whatever you want to do."

"Sam..."

"I don't know what's changed, but I find you in my bedroom and now you're just about ready to run out the door."

"Your wife..." Luciana smiled. "Absolutely gorgeous."

"Yet, she's still dead." Sam laughed. "You really don't have to worry about her coming in here and demanding me back."

"I'm just worried that I won't live up to what you'd expect of me." Luciana couldn't believe what she was saying. She was young, confident. Where had this insecurity come from? *I just don't want to mess this up with her,* she sighed.

"All I expect..." Sam faced Luciana fully. "Is your honesty and your respect."

"You have that one hundred percent." Luciana nodded. "But you said it yourself the night you asked me to leave. You told me you'd had the incredible life."

"I did," Sam agreed.

"So, what could I possibly give you that would even come close to what you had?" Luciana asked. "How could I make you happy when your wife is your everything?"

"I haven't kissed another woman since the first date I had with Lucia thirteen years ago." Sam dropped down onto the couch, running her fingers through her hair. "I've never had another woman in my home, or my office, or in my life." Luciana's heart fluttered. "I don't know what I want out of this with you because until last week, I hadn't even looked at anyone else."

"May I sit?" Luciana decided that it wasn't time to run out on Sam. Not when she was opening up to her. They had to be mature about this. It wouldn't work otherwise.

Sam nodded. "If you want the absolute truth, I'm simply enjoying my time with you and waiting for it to crash and burn."

"What?"

"Oh, come on." Sam laughed. "It's only a matter of time before someone else catches your attention. Someone younger. Someone who wants to see the world and enjoy festivals. Clubs. Whatever it is twenty-something women do these days."

"That's not me."

"Maybe not, but I still expect you to walk away from this someday. I expect it and I'm okay with it."

"You are?" Luciana's eyebrow rose. "Because I'm not."

"I'm nearing forty." Sam gave Luciana a knowing look. "I'm a businesswoman who comes home to an empty apartment every night and doesn't bother to contact her friends anymore."

"I don't like knowing you're alone."

Sam shrugged, her eyes focused on her hands in her lap.

"I don't like knowing you're feeling any of this."

"What I'm saying, is that I want to enjoy this time with you. Explore the woman I used to be..."

"I want that too."

Sam glanced up. "But you've just said you needed to leave."

"A moment of insecurity." Luciana offered Sam a sad smile. "Forgive me?"

"Did you really want to stay the night?" Sam's eyebrows drew together.

"What can I say?" Luciana smirked. "I like to chance my luck."

"You're too much." Sam laughed, tugging the cuff of her sweater. "Maybe we could just see how the night goes?"

"Sounds like the perfect evening to me." Luciana settled her hand over Sam's. "Just so you know, I don't plan on having my head turned by anyone else."

"Day by day." Sam leaned in, kissing Luciana softly. "Day by day is how I'm taking this."

I really wish she would give me more credit.

Sam felt Luciana's eyes on her, an intensity growing between them as the moments passed. Deep down, she wanted her to be the woman she spent her nights with, but Sam had been around long enough to know that it likely wouldn't happen. She also recognised just how beautiful the younger woman was, with the option of having the pick of the women in the city. Yet here she was, sitting beside Sam and seemingly content with doing so. Her hand hadn't left Sam's since they sat down together after dinner, and her touch, light as a feather, was soothing. If she could enjoy this feeling for more than a brief moment, it would be all she could ask for. Luciana had noticed her, had become attracted to her, so she knew she still had something to give down the line. Not with Luciana—she wasn't that lucky—but there was apparently life left in her yet.

"What happened?" Luciana asked, her fingertips trailing Sam's hand, moving towards her wrist.

"When?"

"Lucia." The younger woman offered Sam a sad smile. "We don't have to talk about it..."

"She was out of the country on a business trip. Lucia was an architect."

"She looked like an architect." Luciana smiled.

"She was supposed to come home the night before but her flight was cancelled. Bad weather. She decided to just stay another night rather than sit around the airport for hours on end. Well, I suggested it."

"Okay..."

"The hotel...they didn't have the relevant precautions in place. The sprinkler system was dud."

"Shit." Luciana's gaze fell to their hands. "I'm sorry."

"She was on the thirty-fifth floor." Sam sighed. "An electrical fault caused the fire, and she couldn't get out."

"Sam..."

"If the sprinkler system worked, she would still be here."

Sam glanced up at Luciana, her bottom lip trembling. She appreciated her sympathy, her emotion too, but it wasn't necessary.

"Hey, it's okay." She squeezed Luciana's hand. "It's been two years. I'm okay."

"You said there was a collapse?"

"Yeah. An hour into the fire, as I watched it unfold on TV, the news reporter said there had been a collapse inside."

"Nobody should be in that situation." Luciana gritted her teeth, appalled by what she was hearing. "I spend my days instructing people on how to be safe, how to prevent fires, and nobody should be in that fucking situation."

"The company was fined millions," Sam said. "It doesn't bring her back, but they're no longer functioning so they can't hurt anyone else."

"Where did it happen?"

"France. She was designing a new building. She'd gone to confirm the final plans, check everything was in order. Lucia was big on safety."

"And the lack of it killed her…" Luciana sighed, trying to keep her anger in check. Deep down, she wanted to rip the company a new one, but the damage was done long ago. Long before she showed up in Sam's life. "I'm so sorry you went through what you did. Because of incompetency and a lack of care, your world fell apart."

"I try not to think about it," Sam admitted, a lump rising in her throat. "It keeps me awake if I do."

"Nightmares?"

"At times…"

"Have you thought about speaking to someone?" Luciana asked. "It may help."

"I'm talking to you right now." Sam squeezed Luciana's hand, shifting and leaning against her. "I feel safe talking to you."

"Then I want you to do it more often." Luciana kissed the top of her head, sending Sam's heart rate through the roof. "Whenever you need to."

"I really don't want it to become a part of this." Sam tilted her head back, finding Luciana's deep blue eyes staring back at her. "This…it's new for me. I want to feel it as I should."

"I appreciate that." Luciana smiled. "But I also don't want you to feel like you can't have days when you think about her. About what you had. I won't be offended, Sam."

"I know."

"I'm not here to replace anything you had."

Sam's entire body fluttered. She sat up, turned to face Luciana, and climbed into her lap.

"I'm here to make you happy, but not replace your wife."

"You." Sam smiled, leaning in and caressing Luciana's cheek. "You really are something special."

Sam knew Luciana wasn't like most women in the city. For a twenty-five-year-old, she was mature. She had likely seen things nobody should see in her line of work, her career, and it was in this moment that Sam realised Luciana wasn't just a young woman who wanted fun. As she looked into her eyes, Sam saw honesty and trust.

"I could say the same about you." Luciana leaned into Sam's touch, her eyes closing. "You were just supposed to be a client, Sam."

"I know." Sam's breath washed over Luciana's lips. "And you were just supposed to be dinner and conversation. An arrangement."

"Are you sure that's not what you want anymore? Are you sure you want me for me?"

"I don't think I've been sure about anything in a long time." Sam's bottom lip collided with Luciana's. "But you?" She pulled back, staring directly into blue pools. "I'm sure about you."

"I could get used to this." Luciana gripped the back of Sam's neck, pulling her in close. "Evenings. Weekends. Whenever I can get you alone."

Sam smiled into a kiss. "Perhaps that will happen."

CHAPTER THIRTEEN

The silence of the morning slowly brought Sam from her deep sleep, a smile playing at the corners of her lips as she sat up and glanced out of the window. *Another gorgeous day.* Giving herself a moment to think, to feel, Sam remained in her spot as she ran her fingers through her hair. Last night played over in her mind like a dream, her only regret being that Luciana wasn't lying next to her in bed. She'd thought about it...about inviting her in, but something stopped her. Perhaps it was the idea of taking things slowly, potentially the worry of being blown off, or it could have been the fact that Luciana was almost sleeping last night before Sam decided that it was time to head off to bed. Her only hope this morning was that Luciana would still be here.

Thankfully, she hadn't decided to go home last night, giving Sam the opportunity to offer her the spare room, but as the sun approached, beaming through her bedroom window...the prospect of not sharing her morning with Luciana sent a wave of sadness through Sam. Her time spent with her last night had been thrilling and incredibly satisfying. Not only had they discussed what they both expected, Sam had relaxed in another woman's arms. A woman who didn't want or expect the world and a woman who understood her need to process this before going too far. That, to Sam, was everything.

If she was being honest with herself, hearing Luciana talk about not being good enough for her hurt. Sam wasn't that kind of person. She didn't compare. Of course, she never thought anyone could compare to her wife, but as the days passed since meeting Luciana, she was slowly beginning to realise that it wasn't about comparing. It wasn't about expecting the things her wife once gave her. Ultimately, it was about being happy and fulfilled in a relationship. Lucia was gone, Sam was more than aware of that fact, so now she could choose to push away a woman who genuinely cared about her or grab it with both hands. As the day began outside her window, Sam chose the latter.

Standing, she lifted her arms above her head, stretching from side to side. Her sleep had gone uninterrupted and, in this moment, she wanted to cancel all plans at the office and spend the day with Luciana. It wasn't possible since Luciana was due at the station tonight, but Sam could change meetings around at the office and grab every moment she possibly could today with the beautiful blonde outside her bedroom door. *God, I hope she's still here.*

Sam left her bedroom, her breath quickening as she watched a tall, slender body move through her kitchen with an ease she, herself, didn't possess in this apartment. *Oh, wow.* Sam held back, leaning against the wall at the end of the small corridor leading from her bedroom. Watching, delighted, Sam wrapped her arms around herself and smiled. *She looks so good here.* Brown eyes trailed a sculpted body, a Buddha tattoo covering the expanse of the back of Luciana's right thigh, catching her attention. The younger woman stood in Sam's kitchen wearing nothing but a tank top and a pair of boxer briefs. Every fibre within Sam screamed to move closer, to touch the body she was admiring from the other side of the kitchen, but her bare feet remained glued to their spot.

THE ARRANGEMENT

Though she ached to touch Luciana's soft, silk-like skin, she couldn't. *Damn it!*

Luciana hummed along to the radio as it played low on the central island, her hips gyrating as she did. Sam couldn't help but bite her lip, pleased by her morning so far. Her morning *and* the woman sharing it with her. Knowing she couldn't stand around silently for much longer, Sam cleared her throat and moved into the open space.

"Oh." Luciana jumped, glancing over her shoulder. "Good morning."

"Morning." Sam smiled shyly, approaching the coffee machine. "Can I get you some?"

"I'd love some." Luciana smiled. "I tried to figure out how to work it but thought it was best to leave it alone."

"It's really not that hard." Sam shook her head. "Come here, I'll show you."

Luciana leapt towards her, the proximity of her body sending Sam's heart rate soaring. "I'm watching." A strong hand settled on Sam's hip, Luciana's chin resting on her shoulder from behind. *She's trying, I'll give her that.* "Hit me with it."

"What did you want?" Sam tapped the tablet beside the coffee machine.

"Just uh... Americano?" Luciana tried to remove the image of Sam's bare legs from her mind. The silk robe, it did everything to her body.

"Strength?"

"I'm easy." Luciana squeezed Sam's hip, smiling. "Whatever you usually have... I'll have the same."

"Coming up." Sam calmed her breathing as she tried to keep the biggest smile from forming on her mouth. She prepared coffee for them both, Luciana's body still pressing against hers.

"You know..." Luciana wrapped her arms around Sam's waist, pulling her body back against her. "...you look beautiful in the morning."

"Thank you."

"You look beautiful every minute of the day, but morning?" Luciana turned her head and pressed a kiss to Sam's neck. "Perfect."

"Okay, you really have to stop that." Sam released a deep breath, her hands settling on Luciana's. "As much as I love hearing you say those things... I have to shower." Ultimately, Sam wanted to drag Luciana down the hallway and worship her forevermore, but she couldn't. Not only had she insisted on taking things slowly, but she also didn't have enough time to truly give her the attention she deserved.

"Shame." Luciana untangled herself, sighing. "Thought we could share breakfast."

"We can." Sam turned to find a dejected look on Luciana's face. "Sorry, I didn't—"

"You don't have to explain." Luciana held up her hand as she leaned back against the counter. "Enjoy your shower. I'll dress and wait here for you."

"Luce—"

"Go and shower, Sam. Breakfast will be ready when you are." Luciana turned, busying herself in the kitchen. Sam wanted to apologise, wanted to run her hands all over the body in front of her, but she wasn't sure she could let Luciana go once she did. Her job, her career, the brigade, would be on hold for the rest of the week if Sam had her way.

"I'd like to share breakfast with you first..." Sam chanced, unsure of the mood Luciana was in. "If you don't have to rush off?"

"I have somewhere to be at midday, but other than that... I'm all yours."

I wish that was true.

"Great." Sam ran her fingers through her hair. "So, what's for breakfast?"

"Whatever you have in." Luciana laughed. "I may be able to rustle up a breakfast, but I still need ingredients to do so..."

"Right, yeah." Something about Luciana's attitude seemed to shift, her flirtatious nature from only moments ago disintegrating into thin air. Sam knew it was her reluctance to enjoy the attention she was receiving that had caused the shift in the room, but she wasn't used to this life anymore. She wasn't accustomed to having someone in her home, telling her everything she wanted to hear and cooking breakfast. "So...toast?" Sam arched an eyebrow. "I'm not sure I have anything else in..."

"Whatever works for you." Luciana nodded, her back once again to Sam. "I'll have a bigger lunch later."

"What time are you at the station?" Sam asked, genuinely interested as she climbed up onto a kitchen stool.

"Eight."

"Long shift?"

"Usual twelve-hour shift." Luciana was aware of the fact she was being short with Sam, but she couldn't for the life of her figure this woman out. One minute, she was doing and saying whatever the hell she pleased...but in the next, she was pulling away. Backing off. Doing anything other than what Luciana wanted her to be doing. It wasn't sex, that wasn't what she wanted, but she did want to have the opportunity to hold Sam when she woke this morning. To whisper in her ear. To make her feel good. When Sam stiffened a little during their coffee preparation, it only threw her more.

"Luciana." Sam sighed. "Is everything okay?"

"Sure, yeah." She glanced over her shoulder, half-smiling. "Fine."

"Something tells me that's not true."

"I just... I'm scared to make the wrong move with you." Luciana braced herself against the counter, her shoulders slumping and her head dropping. "I don't want to push anything, but I also want to enjoy my time with you."

"I want that too." Sam furrowed her brow. "You wouldn't be here this morning if I didn't."

"I'm not one of those women who keeps her distance, Sam." Luciana turned, her eyes holding unshed tears. If anything was ever going to move forward, she knew she had to be honest with Sam. "Kisses. Cuddles. Holding you. That's what I'm into."

Oh, God. Sam scolded herself internally for not explaining herself.

"I'm sorry," Sam said. "If I hadn't stopped you…just before… I'm not sure I'd ever stop."

"I don't understand."

"Look at you." Sam's eyes took in the incredible body before her. "You're in my kitchen at seven am wearing barely anything at all. Do you really think I don't want those things, too?"

"Sometimes I wonder." Luciana shrugged. "I'm trying to do the right thing, but it's hard."

Sam stared, wondering why she constantly pushed this woman away. Not necessarily literally, but something always prevented her from doing what she really wanted to do.

"It's hard to keep my hands to myself when I'm so into you."

"Come here." Sam stood, closing the distance between them. "I never meant to make you feel that way."

"It's okay." Luciana said, her worry lessening a little.

"You have to work tonight." Sam cupped Luciana's face. "And honestly, I don't think I could let you go if this went any further right now."

"Fair enough." Luciana sighed. "I'm beginning to regret not seeing you Sunday now."

"We have all the time in the world…" Sam leaned in, kissing Luciana softly. She had to keep control of this moment. If she had any chance of living a normal life today, she *really* had to control this. "Let me shower and then we'll go out for breakfast."

"Sounds good." Luciana's eyes closed as she leaned into Sam's touch, her thumb grazing her cheek. "Go and do your thing. I'm not going anywhere."

Luciana rushed down the street from her own apartment, heading towards the city centre. She was late, and she hated being late. It was unheard of in her job and while she usually kept to her arrangements, today she was a mess. She had a meeting at midday, and the time currently stood at ten minutes past. She took her phone from her pocket and unlocked the screen.

L: Sorry I'm running late. Be there in five.
J: Don't worry. I've just ordered us lunch. Don't rush. X
L: You're a lifesaver.
J: I believe that would be you, Alexis. Not me. X
L: See you in five minutes.

Luciana didn't really want to meet with an ex-client today, not after she'd spent the night at Sam's apartment, but she would have to meet with Janet at some point so why not do it sooner rather than later? It didn't mean anything, and it certainly wasn't a paid visit, so why did she feel so bad about meeting her? Why did she feel like she was doing something wrong?

Turning the corner, Luciana steeled herself, preparing to meet a woman she crossed the line with. Yes, it was a long time ago, and yes, it was way back when she first joined the agency, but Janet had always had a way with words...and ultimately, a strange hold over Luciana. Today, she would explain that she had left the agency, her business number no longer in use. Janet often contacted Luciana when she least expected it, and that extended to her personal phone number too, so it was time to put their arrangement to an end, no matter how fleeting it had become over the last year or so.

As the coffee shop came into view, Luciana released a deep breath and quickened her pace. She had plans for the rest of the afternoon, and those plans wouldn't be pleasant if she didn't get this over with once and for all. She pushed the door open and found Janet sitting at their usual table.

As she took in Janet's appearance, Luciana felt a complete lack of emotion for the woman now standing. Her black hair flowed down her back, hair as black as her heart. As always, Janet had that mature look about her, regardless of the fact that she was only four years older than Luciana. The woman had clearly experienced a hard life in terms of her ageing, but Luciana wasn't here to judge her appearance or her shitty personality; she was here to end everything with Janet.

"Alexis." She waved her over. "You look...different."

"Yeah." Luciana smiled weakly. "This is how I look when I'm not being paid for company." She glanced down at her choice of skinny jeans and pumps, accompanied by a black shirt.

"Mm, I'm not sure I like it." Janet tapped her chin, her dull, dark eyes adding to Luciana's discomfort as they trained on her. "Anyway, I haven't contacted you for a while so I suppose I only have myself to blame."

"Oh, this isn't that kind of meeting..."

"I beg to differ." Janet cocked her head, motioning for Luciana to sit down. "I thought we could enjoy some lunch and then go back to my place."

"I have to work tonight."

"That's okay." Janet smiled. "I'll give you enough time to go home and prepare for work."

"No, I don't think you understand." Luciana sighed. "The agency... I left."

"I'm aware of that. I looked you up online. No sign." Janet sipped her coffee. "So, who are you with now? An agency I know of?"

"No, I don't escort anymore."

"Since when?" Janet looked at Luciana, shocked.

This woman may have once been a big part of Luciana's life, but she didn't even know her real name. Sam...she was different.

Luciana wanted to share everything with her. Janet was too controlling. Too demanding. Too self-centred. Luciana recognised that some months into their arrangement, and to this day, had never divulged anything personal. Janet only knew about her profession because she saw her leaving the station one night. Had that never happened, Janet would be none the wiser.

"A few days ago..."

"Because?"

"I'm swamped at the station," Luciana said. "My career is more important."

Don't mention, Sam. She will only fuck it up for you.

"I don't know why you need that job. The agency pays much better."

"It's my life. My profession."

"Still, you could make double if you took on more clients."

Luciana had heard this all before. At one time, Janet had begged her to leave the brigade, assuring her that she would send clients her way. It wasn't the life Luciana saw in her future though. Escorting was simply a way of relaxing once her shifts for the week had ended. It offered her the chance to meet women without any strings. Not many would willingly fall in love with a firefighter, insisting that the demands of the job were too much for them, so she believed escorting on the side was ideal for her. Now, it was no longer required. She'd found the woman she wanted her attention on, and Janet wouldn't stand in the way of that.

"Call in sick," Janet stated. "We'll spend the night together. Catch up."

"I can't call in sick." Luciana had never taken a sick day unless absolutely necessary, and she wasn't about to do that now. "I have commitments."

"Alexis," Janet said, her tone warning. "We've been through this before." Janet slid her hand across the table, gripping Luciana's. "Don't fuck about with me. I contacted you because I wanted you. You know I'll get my way."

"I'm not doing this." Luciana pulled her hand away as the bell above the door jingled. "I'll have lunch with you, catch up, but then I have to leave."

"Bullshit!" Janet gritted her teeth, that familiar anxiety settling in the pit of Luciana's stomach. *Please, don't ruin this for me.* "Call the station."

"I can't." Luciana stood firm. "I have duties. A team who rely on me. I haven't heard from you in what? Four months! You can't just demand my attention. It doesn't work like that!"

"I know I've neglected you, baby." Janet shifted in her seat, moving closer to Luciana. "I'm sorry. Let me make it up to you." She leaned in, pressing her lips against Luciana's ear.

"You don't have to do that." Luciana shook her head, a shiver rolling down her spine. "I agreed to meet you because I had some things I needed to say to you."

"What *things*?"

"This. Us. Whatever the hell this is...it stops. Now."

"No."

"Janet, I barely see you. What we had those years ago, it was nice. It was fun. I'm a different person now." Luciana chose not to speak about the months they spent together before Janet stopped calling. She abhorred that behaviour. The control and demand from the other woman.

"I promise to keep in touch more often. Work has been full-on. I'm sorry."

"Janet?"

Luciana's heart stopped, her mouth dry. She recognised that voice. A voice that sounded so beautiful just this morning.

"Sam!" Janet stood, pulling Sam into an embrace. "Good to see you."

"It's been what? A year?"

Luciana glanced up to find Sam's jaw clenched, a look of confusion in her eyes.

"I know I promised to stay in touch. I've been out of the country for months. Before that, I had other projects on."

"Don't worry." Sam waved off the apology, shifting uncomfortably in her spot. She didn't need this right now. Seeing Luciana with another woman... it hurt more than she thought it would. *I'm sure it means nothing.* Sam silently prayed.

"I'm sorry, forgive my rudeness." Janet glanced down at Luciana. "This is Alexis, my girlfriend."

"N-Nice to meet you." A wave of devastation coursed through Sam momentarily. A devastation she knew was mirrored in her eyes. "Sam Philips." So, this was another client. Sam couldn't believe what she was hearing. Just this morning, Luciana had been offended when she stopped things from going further, but in this moment, Sam was glad she had.

"I, uh..." Luciana felt bile rising in her throat. "I'm sorry, but I have to go."

"Honey." Janet laughed, squeezing Luciana's shoulder a little tighter than she would like. "This is Sam. I work with her on the interior design of her developments. Say hello and don't be so rude."

"Yeah, great. H-Hi." Luciana wanted the floor to swallow her up, but this was happening now. Sam's eyes held an element of hate...but more hurt than anything else. "I'm sure your work is great."

"Mm, it is." Sam narrowed her eyes, choosing to be cold rather than upset. She wouldn't give Luciana *or* Janet Mason the satisfaction of seeing her hurt. Not today. Not ever. "Anyway, I should go. I was just collecting lunch."

"Drinks soon?" Janet offered Sam a sad smile. "I should really meet with you more often."

"I have so much on at the minute, but yes. Drinks soon." Sam threw a wave over her shoulder as she walked away. She had no intention of meeting with one of her old contacts. Not if she was dating Luciana. Sam couldn't do that. She couldn't watch what she thought was hers, in another woman's arms. "Bye."

Sinking back down into her seat, Luciana brushed a tear from her jawline. "Why the hell did you introduce me as your girlfriend?"

"Keeping up appearances." She patted Luciana's hand. "Sam lost her wife. Terrible story. She's also competition occasionally, so you know? A little jealousy never hurt anyone..." Janet smirked as she relaxed. "I saw how she looked at you. She was most definitely jealous."

"You're a bitch." Luciana's chair screeched back, almost toppling over. "Don't contact me again. Just...fuck off!"

Luciana rushed out of the coffee shop, desperately seeking any signs of Sam.

Nothing. She'd gone.

She pulled her phone out and frantically tapped the screen.

L: That wasn't what it looked like.

S: Looked self-explanatory to me. Delete my number. I'm too old for games.

L: Babe, please?

S: Don't. Don't you dare!

L: She's nothing to me. She never was.

S: Be safe at work. Goodbye, Alexis!

Luciana leaned back against the sandstone wall behind her, sinking down to the floor. How could something feel so good, so perfect...yet completely shitted up at the same time? This. This was why she didn't get involved with clients. Because of Janet. That woman, at one time, was close to ruining her. Her career. Her life. When she thought that Janet distancing herself had worked out for her, Luciana seemed to now be in for the shock of her life.

Sam sat at her desk, tapping her pen against a stack of papers incessantly. Nothing made sense. Just this morning, Luciana had told her how much she wanted to move forward with whatever they were getting involved in. But now, now she was sitting alone, feeling void deep inside. All that time when she spent her hours thinking about Luciana, she was sleeping with another woman. In a *relationship* with another woman. It hurt, but Sam would move forward. After all, Lucia was the only one for her. She tried to change her own mind, and she tried to move forward, but her assumptions had been correct all along. Nobody could fill the place of her wife. In all honesty, Sam was beginning to wonder why she ever bothered.

Luciana really was something else. Sam bit back a sob, the unshed tears in her eyes blurring her vision. She couldn't do this, not at work. She couldn't cry at her desk, she needed to be alone for that.

"Sam?" Cheryl knocked on her boss' open door. "Someone is here to see you."

"Who?"

"The same person you had here last week." Cheryl shifted uncomfortably. "A-Alexis."

"I'm busy." Sam cleared her throat. "Tell her to make an appointment."

"Right, yeah." Cheryl nodded. "Sorry to bother you."

"You're my assistant." Sam smiled genuinely. "And I know I've been a bit hit and miss lately, but never apologise for interrupting me."

"Did you want to talk about it?" Cheryl lowered her voice, wanting to be a friend to her boss. "Something is going on..."

"No, I'll be fine." Sam glanced up at her assistant. "Tell Alexis I'm busy."

"Okay." Cheryl's shoulders slumped. "She's nice, you know..."

"She's also involved." Sam laughed. "Anything comes in for me, let me know. Other than that, this conversation is over."

Sam sat back in her seat as Cheryl disappeared, releasing a breath she didn't realise she'd been holding. Yes, Luciana did appear to be nice, honest and genuine, but Sam was quickly learning that she couldn't just trust anyone. Life wasn't that simple, whether she perceived it to be or not.

Sam's phone pinged on her desk.

L: I'm not leaving until you speak to me.

S: Then you will be waiting a long time.

L: Fine by me. I'll wait in reception.

S: Didn't I tell you to delete my number? Do it or I'll block yours myself.

L: At least come out and talk to me before you do that...

S: I'm a businesswoman who has enough going on. I don't need someone like you upending everything for me. Please, leave my building.

L: Someone like me?

Sam pinched the bridge of her nose as she clenched her jaw.

S: Someone young who doesn't know what they want in life.

She regretted the message as soon as it popped up as delivered but she couldn't take it back. It was out there and whether Luciana was hurt or not, Sam was angry with her.

L: You meant more to me than what you believe, Sam. I'm sorry I'm too young and indecisive for you, but really... I think you're the one who needs to take a look at yourself.

Sam set her phone to silent and placed it back down on the desk. She wouldn't allow someone to come into her business and create a mess. The last thing she needed was to be known as the woman who was having an affair with Janet Mason's girlfriend. As much as she wished Luciana would choose her over Janet, Sam was done talking to her. She was done entertaining her. Luciana wasn't hers.

Sam found herself lying on the couch, a glass of wine sitting untouched on the coffee table in front of her. She'd spent the day working harder than she had in a long time, and now she felt alone again. *I have to stop this. She was just a thing. IT was just a thing.* Her bottom lip trembled as she thought back to this morning when Luciana pranced around her kitchen in very little. How she kissed her neck while she made coffee. She may have chosen to stop things there, but that moment was breathtaking for Sam. Everything she hadn't known she needed. How was it that she found herself lying here like this? How was it that Luciana was already taken?

If someone had told her some two weeks ago that she would meet an escort who meant more to her than anyone had since her wife, Sam would have laughed. She would have told them they were out of their mind. Though she felt awful for saying what she did earlier about Luciana and her age, she couldn't get the thought out of her head that she'd been well and truly played. Did Luciana want a fling with a successful businesswoman? Had she seen the vulnerability in Sam...sinking her teeth into it while she had the chance? Sam didn't believe that was the woman she knew, but Janet Mason had referred to Luciana as her girlfriend, so whatever she *believed* she knew no longer mattered. *She also called her Alexis.* Sam knew that it was just an escort/client arrangement, but it didn't matter. She couldn't be with someone who still had a job sleeping with women. It may work for some, but not for Sam. She wanted Luciana to herself. *Just* hers.

She sat up, swinging her legs over the couch, and took her phone from the coffee table. *I'll call Lindsay. She'll tell me what to do.* Sam didn't particularly want to vent to her sister, but she was going out of her mind worrying about the day she'd just had. Why, she didn't know, but Sam didn't know why her mind worked how it did at times.

Startled when a knock on the door reverberated through her apartment, Sam furrowed her brow and smiled. Lindsay always did have some kind of sixth sense when she needed help, and it seemed now, once again, her sister was about to come through for her. She sighed as she stood up, crossing the short distance to the front door.

She opened it and her heart plummeted.

"What do you want?" Sam spat. "And how the hell did you get into my building?"

"T-The door was open," Luciana cried out. "The door, it was open."

"Well, it shouldn't be." Sam folded her arms across her chest. "I have nothing to say to you. Leave." Sam attempted to close the door, but Luciana shoved her foot in the gap. "Don't!"

"Please, I need to speak to you," Luciana begged, tears falling freely down her face. "This. It's not what you think."

"Please don't insult me, Luciana." Sam shook her head. "And don't come here with tears, expecting me to give you a second of my time."

"When I kissed you..." Luciana's dull blue eyes found Sam's. "...when I kissed you, you can't say you didn't feel it too."

"It doesn't matter what I felt." Sam laughed. "Everything that happened between us was a lie."

"No. No, it wasn't." Luciana wrapped her arms around her body, her shoulders shaking. "Nothing I've had with you was a lie. Why don't you believe that?"

"Because I watched you share a table with Janet Mason today." Sam tilted her head. "I watched you cosy up to a woman I've worked with for a long time...after you'd spent the morning with me."

"S-She, I—"

"I'm not interested in you and her." Sam held up a hand, scoffing. "I'm really not."

"Five minutes. That's all I want." Luciana stepped closer to Sam. "Please, Sam."

"You should go." She glanced at the clock in the kitchen. "You have a shift in an hour."

"I called in sick," Luciana said. "I've never let the brigade down. Never. But for you, I had to."

"Then I'm sorry, but you wasted your time." Sam's shoulders slumped. "You don't need to be here, you don't need to worry about me. I'm just happy I found it out before I was in too deep."

"We had a thing...it started two years ago." Luciana's eyes closed. "It was stop-start, but it was always her way."

"Luciana..."

"Please, if you're going to cut me from your life, at least hear me out first."

Sam looked at the woman in front of her, broken and hurting. Opening the door wider, she motioned for Luciana to come inside and closed the door.

"I woke up to a message from her this morning. She wanted to meet me. I hadn't seen her in a long time."

"Just..." Sam sighed, unable to form any words. "Go on."

"She was one of my first clients when I joined the agency. She seemed really nice. Sweet. We had dinner *a lot*. Before I knew it, I was staying over at her place. Waking at her place most mornings. There was always a wad of cash left for me on the bedside table, but I felt like there was something more between us."

"Clearly, since she introduced you as her girlfriend."

"That shouldn't have happened." Luciana shook her head. "Before today, I hadn't heard from her in at least four months. She disappeared. I was thankful for that."

"Mm."

"I was." Luciana looked pointedly at Sam. "I know you have no reason to believe a word I say, and I don't really give a crap about Janet while I'm here with you, but I mean it, Sam. You...it's you, okay?"

"It's not me." Sam offered a sympathetic smile. "I was just a thing too, wasn't I?"

"You? A thing?" Luciana arched a brow. "Not in a million years."

Luciana approached Sam, holding out her hand.

"She tries to control me. Dominate me. I told her today that I'd left the agency and she told me to cancel my shift." Luciana held back tears. "She always threatened to expose me to the fire service, and I couldn't risk it, so I appeased her." Luciana placed her hand against the side of Sam's face. "But after meeting you, being here with you, I was done with caring."

"She threatened you?" Sam couldn't believe she was listening to this. She didn't fully believe Luciana, but Janet Mason was a force. A force she'd encountered on more than one occasion. "Why?"

"Because she didn't want to let me go."

I can see why... Sam studied Luciana's face, genuine hurt radiated from her tired eyes.

Sam remained silent, willing to hear Luciana out.

"Things became too much. I avoided her calls. Turned down her requests."

"And then?"

"She disappeared."

"But now she's back?" Sam asked. "Here. For you?"

"I don't believe she is. I think she's just chancing her luck."

"I know Janet and I know she doesn't chance anything she doesn't want." Sam sighed, her eyes closing as Luciana caressed her face. "Why did she call you her girlfriend?"

"She said there was nothing wrong with a little jealousy..."

"I wasn't jealous." Sam stepped back. "I was hurt. I *am* hurt."

"Babe, you have nothing to worry about." Luciana moved closer once again. "Janet is nothing. You... You are who I care about."

"I want to believe you..."

"But?"

"Seeing you with her...it really hurt me."

"If I could go back and refuse to meet her, I would," Luciana said. "I only met with her so I could end it all officially. After the morning I'd shared with you, I didn't see anyone else in my future, Sam. God, I want so much to continue this with you."

Luciana slid her hand to the back of Sam's neck, gripping a fistful of hair as her breath tickled her lips.

"I know you don't think I'm all in, and I know you don't think I'm good enough for you, but I'm going to prove myself, Sam. I'm going to sweep you off your fucking feet." Luciana's lips crushed against Sam's, a moan rumbling in her throat. "I'm not here to hurt you. I'm here to make you happy."

"Luciana..." Sam's tears fell hard and fast. "I-I don't know if I can do this."

"Do what?" Luciana's voice broke. "Sam?"

"Let you go..." Sam gripped her body, pulling her closer. "I don't know what happened today, and I'm not done discussing it, but I can't let you go tonight."

"I don't want you to let me go," Luciana said, her forehead pressing against Sam's. "Please, don't."

"S-Stay," Sam whispered, her lips ghosting across Luciana's. "Stay with me tonight."

"Yes."

"And not out here. Not in the spare room." Sam took Luciana's bottom lip between her teeth. "With me. *Really* with me." Sam's heart pounded at the prospect of spending the night with this woman, but it wasn't fear. It wasn't apprehension. It was excitement.

Luciana's hands trailed up and under Sam's shirt, smoothing over her soft, taut stomach. "Lead the way..."

"Oh, God." Sam whimpered as Luciana's hand trailed higher. "This is happening..."

"If it's what you want, yes...it's happening." Luciana smiled against Sam's lips. "Whatever you want, babe."

When Luciana said things like that, it was a no-brainer. Her relationship with Janet still needed to be explained, there was no doubt about that, but it could wait until the morning. Right now, she needed to feel this woman against her. Her hands. Her lips. Her breath. Luciana *was* the woman she knew, but it took this moment for her to realise it. Instead of disappearing, Luciana fought. That meant the world to Sam.

Sam tugged Luciana's hand, guiding her towards the bedroom. Nothing about this was nerve-racking as she thought it would be; instead, Sam's entire body felt calm. Aroused, but calm. With one final glance, Sam pulled Luciana through her bedroom door, kicking it shut with her foot.

CHAPTER FOURTEEN

Luciana stood frozen, unable to take her eyes off the beauty standing before her. Sam, in this moment, had an incredible sense of vulnerability about her, one that only encouraged Luciana to move closer. To place her fingertips on the body she'd craved to touch since the moment they'd met. Reaching forward, she took Sam's hand in hers, a gentle smile forming on her lips.

"May I?" Luciana asked, her voice thick with desire as her fingers slowly made their way to the buttons on Sam's white, silk blouse, still tucked into her navy-blue, form-fitting pants. "Sam?"

Sam stared, her heart slamming against her ribcage. She needed this, the connection, but she was struggling to let go. Her past flashed before her eyes, memories of her wife passing by fleetingly, before her pulse settled and her heart slowed. "Yes." Her deep brown eyes darkened as she focused fully on Luciana. "Please." Sam knew it was time to move forward. This woman, her touch, it sent her every emotion wild. Nothing had made sense over the last few weeks, but this? This made *perfect* sense.

Luciana took the lead, her hands steady and sure. Each button popped, leaving Sam standing in front of her with the silk material hanging from the olive skin of her shoulders. A vision. Heaven.

"Wow," she breathed out, her eyes closing momentarily. She slipped the blouse from Sam's body, her heart skipping a beat as ample breasts sat perfectly in white lace. The image alone sent Luciana's mind into a frenzy. *So close, yet so far.*

A gentle hand sat on Sam's hip as Luciana leaned in, her lips pressing against her lover's. "If you need to stop…" Her breath washed over Sam's mouth as her words hung in the air between them.

"No." Sam lifted her hand, pressing a finger against Luciana's full lips. "Shush."

Luciana smiled, Sam's body trembling as her fingertips trailed up the side of her stomach. The air around them thick and intense with a want they both felt, she guided Sam back towards the plush mattress behind her. Luciana had dreamt of this moment. The moment when their bodies would mould into one, a yearning for one another impossible to deny.

Sam's knees connected with the edge of the bed, and as she sat down, her fingers curled around the belt Luciana wore. Sam pulled her between her legs, her hand now splayed and travelling up a toned, indulgent stomach. She couldn't recall the last time she felt this sure about anything, but Sam knew without a shadow of a doubt that she wanted this. The connection she felt was too hard to deny any longer.

Luciana shuddered, a whimper falling from her lips effortlessly. She had no intentions of holding back with this woman…none at all. Sam deserved to know how she felt, those feelings conveyed in the form of Luciana's touch. Her kiss. Her emotions in this moment. She cupped Sam's face with one hand, the other pushing her hair from her shoulder and exposing an exquisite neck. "You." Luciana moaned as Sam's hand moved higher, squeezing her breast. "Fuck."

"Me, what?" Sam's eyes glistened, those deep brown pools begging for something more.

"Just…everything." Luciana lifted her T-shirt over her head, throwing it to the floor behind her. In a move that surprised but delighted Sam, she found herself on her back with Luciana straddling her hips.

"Luce—"

"I've waited for this moment." She leaned down, kissing her way up Sam's neck until she reached her ear. "God, you've no idea how much I want you."

"Show me." Sam gasped as Luciana nibbled her earlobe, thrusting her hips up in a desperate attempt for relief. "I really need you to show me."

"Gladly." Luciana sat Sam up, reaching behind her and unhooking her bra. "Fuck." She took her bottom lip between her teeth as Sam's breasts spilled out, possibly drawing blood if she bit down any harder. Sam's back connected with the mattress as Luciana dipped her head, rolling her tongue over a hardened nipple. That simple move elicited a guttural moan from Sam, sending a wave of pleasure straight to Luciana's core.

"O-Oh." Sam gasped, taking a fistful of Luciana's hair in her hand and forcing her mouth against her. Sucking and nipping, Luciana released Sam's nipple with a pop, smiling against the swell of her breast before her tongue expertly lapped at the skin beneath it.

Resting back on her knees, Luciana popped the button on Sam's pants, the slightest hint of white lace evident. With a steady hand, she lowered the zipper and climbed off Sam, removing her pants in one swift move. She positioned herself at the foot of the bed, sinking to her knees and running her hands up Sam's smooth legs.

"Luciana..." Sam released a breathy moan, unable to form any other words. Feeling lips press against the skin of her thigh, Sam's eyes closed and her mouth fell open. "Oh, God." Her hand gripped the sheet beside her when Luciana's mouth landed on her lace-covered centre.

"These have to go." Luciana smiled, her teeth tugging at Sam's underwear. "Right now." Slipping them from Sam's legs, her eyes focused on glistening arousal, an intoxicating scent causing her mouth to salivate. Slowly but surely, she moved closer, licking her lips as Sam's legs spread wider. Everything about this woman appealed to her, but to be here with Sam laid bare in front of her, it was bliss. Pure hedonism. Separating velvety folds, an abundance of wetness coating her fingertips, Luciana dipped her head and blew gently.

"Oh." Sam's hips lifted, her entire body squirming, urgently requesting more.

"Beautiful," Luciana whispered, her tongue poking out and seeking to taste Sam. To probe deeper. To pleasure.

"Please," Sam pleaded, her hand finding Luciana's on her stomach. Their fingers laced together, Sam inhaled sharply when Luciana's strong tongue rolled over her clit. "Y-Yes!" She gripped her hand tighter, rocking herself against the mouth that was sending shockwaves of white-hot heat throughout her entire being.

"You taste..." Luciana's tongue traced the length of Sam's centre, drinking up her wetness. "Like a dream."

"Oh, fuck!" Sam's eyes slammed shut when a single finger dipped inside her. A second found its way to her entrance and everything within her shattered. This moment with Luciana was everything she imagined, only more. So much more.

Luciana curled her fingers, slipping in and out of Sam with ease. The sound of sex filled the air, Sam's breathlessness only spurring Luciana on. With every moan, she sank deeper. With every throb of Sam's walls as they pulsed around her fingers, Luciana applied a perfect pressure to the swollen clit beneath her lips.

"O-Oh, I-I..." Sam gripped Luciana's head. "Shit, I—"

With a final thrust of her fingers, Sam fell apart beneath Luciana. Writhing, shaking, her name tore from Sam's throat, sending the younger woman closer to her own release. Slowing, drawing out the pleasure they both felt, Luciana climbed up Sam's body and found her lips. Smiling into a kiss, Sam cupped her face, gliding her tongue against her lover's.

"Thank you." Luciana pulled back, looking directly into Sam's eyes. "For letting me in. For trusting me."

Sam was lost for words. How could it be that someone like Luciana was here with her? Wanting her? Deciding that those thoughts could wait for another time, Sam smiled and flipped Luciana onto her back.

"I believe *you* are wearing too many clothes…"

Luciana cracked one eye open, the realisation of where she was hitting her unexpectedly. Sam was sleeping beside her, her bare back displayed like a private show for her eyes only. Naked and feeling incredibly spent, Luciana lifted her head and checked the clock. For the second time this week, she had woken here, but this morning…it felt different. Everything had changed. Last night went on until the early morning and Luciana was thankful she'd called in sick at work. Sam may be older than her, but that woman knew exactly how to rock Luciana's world. Five times, to be exact.

She turned on her side, peering over Sam's shoulder and smiling. Gently running her fingertips over her bare skin, she was about to give Sam the wakeup call she deserved but stopped, abruptly. *Oh!* Her eyes found the picture on the bedside table, Sam's wife staring back at the naked woman in her bed. Instead of the kiss she had planned for her, Luciana slowly climbed from the bed and grabbed her clothes from the floor. She scurried out of the bedroom and into the corridor, disappearing into the bathroom with her T-shirt and jeans balled in her arms. Was this inappropriate? Luciana knew she shouldn't second guess what happened last night—it felt too natural—but it was hard not to when Sam's dead wife glared back at her. She would admit that it felt strange seeing the picture, but it wasn't enough to make her run out of the apartment. No, Luciana was one-hundred percent in.

Once dressed, Luciana found herself in the kitchen, preparing coffee and worrying that Sam may regret last night. They still had to discuss Janet Mason fully, but that was a conversation Luciana would never be prepared for. As much as she wanted Janet out of her life, the interior designer was persistent. Frightening, too. She filled a coffee cup, sweetening the caffeine relief and moving towards the gigantic windows in the living room. The sun was rising but deep clouds rolled in off the river, mirroring the day Luciana felt she was going to have. While she felt completely satisfied, something uneasy tugged at her. Deep in the pit of her stomach.

"Hey."

Startled, Luciana turned around. "Hi."

"I hope you weren't planning to leave without saying goodbye."

"Of course not." Luciana lowered her eyes to the coffee cup in her hands. "Can I get you one?"

"That's okay." Sam smiled half-heartedly. "You look like you're about to run, so I won't keep you."

"No, I wasn't." Luciana shook her head. "I just…"

Silence.

Uncertainty.

"You regret last night, don't you?" Sam chose to break the painful silence, leaning back against the counter, just her silk robe covering her body. Her heart sank when Luciana didn't respond. "I thought it was what you wanted?"

"It is." Luciana's head shot up. "I do. You. Us. It is what I want."

"I'd like to believe that." Sam's fingers trailed her hair. "But I'm not sure even *you* believe it."

"Last night…" Luciana set her cup down and approached Sam. "It was incredible. *You* are incredible."

"But?"

"I guess I'm just processing."

Processing what? Sam thought. She understood that last night had been a whirlwind for both of them, but even she didn't feel the need to process what happened. This morning, Sam woke feeling the happiest she'd been in as long as she could remember.

"Do you need some time?" Sam asked nervously. "It's okay if you've changed your mind about me."

"No, I don't need time." Luciana took her hand, pressing her body against Sam's. "Not from you and not from this." She kissed Sam softly. *Stop worrying and just go with it.* She was out of her mind for ever leaving Sam alone in bed this morning, but she knew she didn't need time. She was in Sam's life now and no amount of guilt when she looked at Sam's wedding picture on the bedside table could change that. "Do you?"

"Do I look like I need time?" Sam's eyebrow rose as her hand slid beneath Luciana's T-shirt.

"N-No." Blue eyes flickered a shade darker. Luciana wrapped her hands around Sam's thighs and lifted her onto the counter. "We need to talk, but right now... I need to feel you."

"That can be arranged." Sam narrowed her eyes as she wrapped her legs around Luciana's waist. "This talk..." she asked breathlessly, Luciana's lips trailing her neck. "W-What about?"

"Talking comes later," Luciana whispered. "First, I need to take care of my lady."

Sam sat comfortably on the couch while Luciana took the opposite end and sprawled out. Their morning had been unexpected for Sam, but she wasn't complaining. She would *never* complain when Luciana was in bed with her, saying and doing all the right things. But now the time had come for them to talk and Sam had an anxiety building inside her. It couldn't be that bad, she knew that, but when someone told her they needed to talk, it didn't usually end well. This morning, she made it her mission to listen to whatever Luciana had to say...calmly.

"So?" Sam blew out a deep breath.

"What time do you have to be at the office?" Luciana toyed with the hem of her T-shirt.

"I have time." She settled her hand on Luciana's foot. "If you need to talk, I have all the time in the world."

"I don't want to interrupt your business."

"One thing you should know about me...is that I don't make time for just anybody." Sam smiled. "So, I'm here and I'm listening."

"About this morning..."

"It was something else." Sam smirked.

"No, before that." Luciana cleared her throat, blushing. "I don't want you to think that I regretted a moment of last night. Having to come here to apologise, yes. But everything that followed...never."

"Okay." Sam felt her heart settle a little with Luciana's words.

"I'm scared. I don't want to be, but I am, Sam. I'm terrified."

"About what?" Sam shifted, moving closer to the woman who looked like she was about to break down.

"Janet." She sighed. "When she finds out about us, she will go fucking crazy."

"You think I give a single shit about Janet Mason?" Sam laughed. "Without me, she wouldn't have the career she has today."

"I appreciate that, but you don't know how controlling she is over me."

Okay, she's really not playing around here. Sam sighed, taking Luciana's hand. "Leave Janet to me."

"N-No." Luciana's eyes widened. "She can't know." The idea of Janet knowing that Sam was in Luciana's life terrified her. She knew what the other woman was capable of, and to an extent, Sam did too, but this wouldn't just go away overnight. Janet Mason would soon be back, Luciana could feel it.

"You're hiding us from her?" Sam arched a brow. "That isn't going to work for me."

"I don't *want* to hide us. I want nothing more than to be seen with you...but the moment she finds out, she is going to ruin it. Us."

"Baby..." Sam smiled as she climbed into Luciana's lap, her term of endearment unexpectedly falling from her mouth. "Sorry."

"No, don't be." Luciana wrapped her arm around Sam's waist. "Don't ever be sorry."

"Okay." Sam nodded. "Do you honestly think I'd let anyone ruin this? When I've waited so long...refused to meet anyone?"

"No, I don't."

"Then there are no issues here." Sam shrugged. "Unless you have something you need to tell me that would require her being pissed off with you."

"She thinks I belong to her," Luciana spat, a venom in her voice Sam had never heard before. "That I'm *hers*."

"How can you be hers when you're mine?" Sam caressed Luciana's cheek with her thumb. "There's nothing going on between you two, right?"

"Nothing. Not that I was aware of anyway."

"Then I'll schedule a meeting with her. Explain that it's time for her to let you be."

"She won't," Luciana disagreed. "I know her and I know she is going to hit the roof."

"Hey!" Sam gripped Luciana's jaw gently. "Janet Mason may *think* she has it better, but I can assure you, she does not. She is a bully, and one that I will not stand for in the industry."

"That's hot." Luciana took her bottom lip between her teeth. "Really hot."

"Focus." Sam looked pointedly. "I *do* have to go to the office before the day is over and if you say things like that...it will never happen."

"You're gorgeous." Luciana sighed, tilting her head and smiling. "Really gorgeous."

"I guess I'm going to lose you to the job tonight?" Sam asked, refraining from partaking in Luciana's flirtation. "What time?"

"I called in sick, remember?"

"You did, but you can't remain sick forever."

"God, I wish I could." Luciana rested her head back, shifting until Sam was lay down beside her. "If it meant I could be here with you every night, I really would."

Sam remained silent, enjoying this moment.

"I think I'll take another day or two, though."

"Yeah?" Sam propped herself up with her elbow. "Really?"

"If you want to spend some time together, why not?"

"I don't want you to do what she expected of you. I'm not her and I understand you have a job and commitments."

Luciana laughed. "Fuck! You're really not her."

Sam sighed, smiling as she relaxed in her lover's arms. "Never will be."

CHAPTER FIFTEEN

"I'm about to walk into my flat now." Luciana smiled, the sound of Sam's voice calming her as she pushed her front door open. "You know, I was thinking maybe you could come over here tonight?"

"Sounds like a nice evening," Sam said. "What time do you want me there?"

"Whenever you're finished at work?" Luciana suggested. "You should know that my place is nothing like yours, though."

"I don't even know what that means..."

"It's not fancy." Luciana winced as the words slipped from her mouth. "I mean, it's not a shithole, but it's not your kind of place."

"Will you be there?" Sam asked. "And will there be food?"

"Yes, and yes."

"Then it *is* my kind of place."

"Thanks." Luciana felt settled by Sam's reassurance. "So, I'll see you in a few hours then?"

"You will." Sam sighed. "Will there be somewhere to park?"

"Yeah, you can use the spot next to mine." Luciana

approached her window and glanced down at the car park. "It's never usually taken anyway."

"Okay, then I will see you around six. I have a meeting in ten minutes so I should really prepare for it."

"Go and be amazing." Luciana leaned against the window frame. "I'll try and do something with this place before you get here."

"Stop worrying. I'm not a monster."

"No. No, you're not."

"Goodbye, Luciana."

"Bye, babe."

Luciana pushed off the window frame, throwing her phone onto the couch as she made her way into the kitchen. She loved her flat, it was her safety, but being at Sam's for the last two nights left her feeling different about the space she'd enjoyed for the last four years. Since she moved away from Manchester where her parents still lived, Luciana felt completely free some thirty-five miles down the road in Liverpool. She loved her parents, they meant the world to her, but once she qualified with the brigade, her mother's panic and worry for her safety made it impossible to return home daily. Her begging to change careers had pushed Luciana away to some degree, but as the years passed, her mum realised that her daughter knew what she was doing…and that she was safe at her job.

Luciana dropped down onto her couch, deciding that a shower could wait another ten minutes. She had so much to do before Sam arrived, but she wouldn't try too hard. Sam knew her well enough by now to figure out that they were both from completely different worlds, but she hadn't run or backed off, so Luciana was doing something right. What that was, she had no idea, but after this morning, she wasn't willing to overthink this. It felt too good, too heavenly. If Sam was happy to have her in her life, then Luciana wouldn't argue with that.

A knock at the door triggered a frown; she wasn't expecting anyone here for at least a few hours. It couldn't possibly be Sam, as she had work to finish at the office, but whoever was waiting on the other side of the door was knocking again.

"Alright! I'm coming!" Luciana yelled, yanking the door open. "Oh, uh...how did you get in here?"

"It's nice to see you, too." Janet slipped past Luciana. "Your neighbour on the fifth floor clearly doesn't take security seriously."

"Um..."

"He buzzed me up. I could have been anyone." Janet smirked. "You've been avoiding me."

"Good observation." Luciana smiled sarcastically. "I'm busy, so if you could leave, that would be great."

"You don't look busy." Janet's hand settled on her hip, a green flowing gown covering her body.

"How did you find out where I lived?" Luciana didn't like knowing that Janet was digging around for her personal information. This woman already made her feel uneasy without creeping her out, too.

"You forget that I know people." Janet set her purse down on the dining table. "Your friends at the agency will give anything up for a good fuck."

I don't need to know about her sex life. I really don't.

"So, what did you want?" Luciana shoved her hands in the pockets of her jeans.

"You ran out on me yesterday." Janet approached her, her heels clicking against the laminate flooring. "And you were very rude."

"No, I was just tired of you dictating my life to me, Janet. There is a difference."

"I don't think so." She curled her finger, motioning for Luciana to come closer. When she chose not to, Janet's eyebrow rose. "Have I taught you nothing in the years you've known me?"

"I'm not bowing down to you anymore." Luciana shook her head. "Please, just leave."

"I'm not going anywhere, sweetheart." Janet cocked her head, tugging the hem of Luciana's T-shirt and pulling her closer. "You should change. I have plans for us."

"I told you I'm busy." Luciana gritted her teeth as she stepped around Janet. As she reached the kitchen, her ex-client followed behind her, trapping Luciana against the kitchen worktop as she turned around. "Janet, please."

"What is your problem?" Janet's hand slid to Luciana's throat. "Why do you insist on pissing me off?"

"You were a client. You know we're not supposed to get attached." Luciana's eyes filled with tears. "I can put you in touch with one of the girls. Someone I know you'll love."

"I've had them all." Janet smirked. "And none compare to you, Alexis."

"I-It's not me," Luciana whispered. "What you expect of me... it's not me."

"You seemed to enjoy it enough when I introduced you to that world." Janet leaned in, taking Luciana's bottom lip and biting down. "Don't deny it. You wanted it."

"You've no idea what I want. You never thought about me long enough to care."

"Baby..." Janet's tongue trailed Luciana's bottom lip, sending a shudder down the younger woman's spine. "I had things to take care of. I'm back now and I'm here for you."

"Let go of me," Luciana cried as Janet's hand tightened around her neck. "Please?"

"Right, I forgot." Janet laughed. "You only like to be choked when I'm fucking you."

"I didn't like *any* of what you did to me." Luciana released a deep breath as Janet dropped her hand. "Why do you think I avoided you for so long after the first time it happened?"

"You told me you had work commitments."

"I'd have told you anything to stop you from leaving me bruised night after night."

"That's the world, Alexis."

"No, it's not." She shook her head. "I know people in your *supposed* world and they're *nothing* like you."

"Why do you insist on talking back to me?" Janet's nostril's flared. "Why do you think it's acceptable to speak to me that way?"

"You're not some powerful mistress." Luciana laughed. "You're just a whore who would fuck anything."

A sharp smack to the face brought Luciana out of her anger-filled state, her mouth falling open as her cheek burned. Her eyes closed as she attempted to stem the flow of fresh tears, her lip trembling.

"Get showered. Dressed. And do it quick."

Think!

"Okay." Luciana simply nodded her head, stepping out of the kitchen and towards the couch. "Give me twenty minutes. There's wine in the fridge." As she passed the couch, she took her phone from the cushion and disappeared into her bedroom. With a shaky hand, she dialled Sam's number, praying she would pick up.

"Hello?" Sam answered. "Luciana, I'm about to walk into my meeting. I can't talk right now."

"R-Right, yeah," she muttered. "Sorry I called."

"What's wrong?" Sam's voice held an element of concern. "Are you hurt?"

"Yes, I mean...uh, no. I'll be fine." Luciana sighed. "Maybe I'll see you tonight. I don't know what time I'll be home, or if you'll want to see me again."

"What's going on?"

"S-She's here. In my home," Luciana whispered, trying to compose herself. "She showed up, demanding I see her."

"Janet?"

"Yes, Janet."

"Tell her to leave," Sam said. "I can be there in an hour, but I really have to go into this meeting."

"It's okay." Luciana smiled, her heart sinking into her chest at the prospect of spending the night with the woman out in her living room. "I have to get ready."

"Get ready for what?" Sam lowered her voice. "Where are you going?"

"Wherever she takes me..."

"Tell her to leave!"

"She won't like that." Luciana laughed pathetically. "You should probably just go home when you finish at the office. I don't expect to be back before the end of the night."

"So, that's it?" Sam scoffed. "You're dropping me, for *her*?"

"You don't understand." Luciana shook her head, Sam's scent still on her body from the morning they'd shared together. "She isn't going to leave, Sam. I have to go with her."

"You said you're hurt?"

Luciana decided it would be easier to backtrack, telling Sam what she needed to hear so she could continue with her day. "No, I'm fine. I hope your meeting goes well. I'll see you soon, okay?"

"Luciana—"

She cut the call, leaving her alone with Janet once again. Luciana knew she was a coward. After all, she was supposed to be a strong firefighter. When Janet was in the picture, she felt anything but strong around her. She felt at her weakest. Vulnerable. Pathetic. The first few appointments she had with her had been perfect, ideal for what she was looking for, but as time wore on and she booked Luciana at any given opportunity, she saw a side to Janet that she wasn't so sure about. Though she promised to protect Luciana, or Alexis, as Janet still knew her, she had done anything but protect her. Her idea of protection led to abuse of her body, a body she had never felt the same about since. Sam, though...she made her feel completely different. Her touches were soft, safe and loving. Nothing like the callous hands Janet touched her with.

"Are you nearly ready?" Janet knocked on the bedroom door.

"Y-Yes." Luciana perked up. "Just be a few minutes."

"Good. I'd like to get this show on the road."

Sam paced back and forth in her living room, toying with her phone in her hands. All night she had continuously tried to contact Luciana, but so far, she had nothing. She was worried, of course, and now beginning to feel guilty for not cutting her meeting and going straight to her. The more Sam thought about it, the more the fear in Luciana's voice heightened. Was she in pain? Had Janet hurt her? Surely not. Janet Mason was a woman most didn't cross, but this? Sam found it hard to comprehend.

For the eleventh time in thirty minutes, Sam unlocked her phone and called Luciana's number.

Come on, please...

"Sam, hi." Luciana cleared her throat. "Sorry I've been unable to answer your calls. I left my phone at home."

"You're home?" Sam released a deep breath, placing her hand over her chest. "Oh, thank God."

"Yeah, I'm home." Something about Luciana's voice sounded off, but Sam wasn't sure if it was her own mind playing tricks with the worry she'd felt all night. "I was just planning to shower and get some sleep."

"You do remember that we were supposed to spend the evening together, don't you?"

"Of course, I remember."

"Yet you spent the evening with someone else," Sam said pointedly, unsure how to approach this conversation. "I mean, are we still a thing, or...?"

"I don't think it's a good idea." Luciana's voice broke. "Can I call you tomorrow? Explain myself? I just really need to sleep."

"Call me tomorrow?" Sam scoffed. "That's all I deserve? A call tomorrow..."

"No, you deserve so much more than that," Luciana cried. "But what you deserve... I cannot give to you."

"What are you talking about, Luciana?"

"I slept with Janet tonight."

Sam's heart fell into her stomach, pulling at her like a lead weight.

"I slept with her and I can never take that back, no matter how much I want to."

"I, uh..." Sam's forehead creased as tears slid down her face. "I thought you wanted this with me. I asked you repeatedly if you wanted me."

"I want you more than anything in this world."

"That's a lie." Sam closed her eyes, calming her breathing. "Just answer me one question. When you slept with me last night...was that your way of fulfilling your duty as my escort?"

"I'm sorry you feel that way," Luciana said with a sob, leading Sam to believe that not everything was as it seemed. "If I could see you now, I just..."

"Do you *want* to see me now?" Sam glanced at the clock; it was almost ten at night. She was angry that Luciana had gone out with Janet, but something felt off. How she spoke, the tremble in her voice, Sam believed there was more to the story. Rather than end the call, she chose to listen, hoping Luciana wouldn't shut down on her.

"All I wanted was to be with you tonight. I need you to know that."

"I have your address..." Sam allowed her words to filter down the line for a moment. "Should I use it or am I wasting my time?"

"I'm not the right person for you, Sam. I thought I was, that I could be, but after tonight...no."

"At least say that to me in person rather than over the phone?" Sam needed something more. In her heart, she didn't believe Luciana wanted to say these things to her. In her heart, she felt a desperate need to see her.

Sam heard movement, followed by a groan from Luciana. "I have to go."

"Wait!" Sam pleaded. Thankful when the line didn't go dead, she heard Luciana weeping on the other end of the phone. "I'm driving over now. Please, let me up."

"Okay."

Sam cut the engine on her Range Rover, resting her head back and preparing for the worst possible conversation with Luciana. She could deal with whatever she had to say, she knew that, but after last night, everything had changed for Sam. After falling asleep in another woman's arms, she wanted more of that. With Luciana, only. A single tear slid down her face as her eyes closed. Could she really lose Luciana from her life? Was that an actual possibility? Sam didn't want to believe that it could be true, but she had to be realistic. Sam, who had been around a lot longer than the younger woman she'd been spending time with, knew exactly how easy it was to lose those close to you. Important to you. Those who make your life brighter. While she had spent her time recently telling herself it would never last with Luciana, the realisation of that potential was terrifying.

Time to face this head on.

She climbed from her car and took the note from her pocket that held the code for the main door of Luciana's block. She appreciated the trust Luciana put in her by giving away the code, but she wished to be using it for different reasons. Not reasons that could come back to hit her in the face. As she approached the building, she keyed in the code and blew out a deep breath as the door bleeped, the catch releasing and allowing her entry. Sam had never considered herself to be a nervous person, but tonight she was. Tonight, she felt like her heart would leap out of her throat at any given moment. That, to Sam, meant she wasn't in control of the situation. She didn't like it.

She took the flight of stairs to Luciana's address and stopped at the end of the hallway, trying to remain as calm as possible. She'd thought about calling Lindsay before she left her apartment, but Sam had begun to realise that she couldn't rely on her sister whenever she had an issue. She'd done perfectly fine helping herself over the years, and now was the time to be that woman again. If Luciana no longer wanted to continue this, she would hold her head high and leave. It really was as simple as that.

She braced herself, approached the door she required, and knocked.

The lock clicked and the door opened slowly. Sam's forehead creased as Luciana refused to meet her eyes. "H-Hi," Sam croaked out. "Can I come in?"

"Yeah…" Luciana stepped aside and closed the door once Sam was safely inside her apartment. She didn't want to do this, not tonight, but Sam deserved answers. She deserved an explanation as to why this wouldn't work. "Can I get you something to drink?" Luciana wrapped her arms around herself, her focus remaining on the floor.

"No, thank you." Sam cleared her throat, taken aback by the change in Luciana's behaviour.

"Okay."

Sam noted how she remained distant, a void seemingly between them.

"Are you okay?"

"Fine, yeah," Luciana said barely above a whisper. "You didn't need to come all the way over here."

"It took me five minutes."

"Still…" Luciana shrugged. "I'm sure it's a waste of your time."

"Is it?" Sam stepped closer to her, but Luciana backed away. "Did something happen?"

"Something *always* happens."

"You look like you need to sit down." Sam held out her hand but Luciana refused to take it, a pained look on her face. *What the hell is going on?* "Look, I know I couldn't cancel my meeting earlier, and I know she's been here, but all I care about right now is that you're okay."

"I'm fine."

"No, you're not," Sam countered. "Did she say something? Threaten you again?"

"Sam..."

Sam closed the distance between them, wrapping her arm around Luciana's waist. When her body stiffened and her eyes closed, a tear fell down her cheek and a groan slipped from her mouth. Sam's heart shattered. Something was wrong. Very wrong.

"Luciana, I need you to tell me what the hell she's done to you."

"It was my own fault. If I hadn't spoken to her how I did when she came here, this probably wouldn't have happened." Luciana moved away from Sam, gingerly, and slowly took a seat on the couch. "Welcome to my home, by the way."

"It's beautiful." Sam's voice was hoarse with emotion. Watching Luciana, who appeared to be in pain, brought her a huge sense of sadness...and guilt. "Very homely."

I don't care about her home right now, Sam held back her emotion.

"Yeah." Luciana wrung her hands. "Are you sure I can't get you something to drink."

"No, I'm fine." Sam approached her. "Can I sit down?"

"Yeah."

Silently, Sam took in Luciana's appearance. A thick sweater hung from her body, and a pair of sweatpants covered her legs. For this time of year, it didn't make sense, but Sam hadn't shared this space with her before, so she couldn't be sure that this wasn't normal.

"I'm sorry," Luciana cried. "For letting you down tonight. For breaking your trust."

"Maybe you could explain what happened before there are any apologies."

"I-I don't think I can."

"I don't have anywhere to be." Sam swallowed hard as Luciana lifted the cuff of her sweater slightly, itching her skin. "What's that?"

"Oh." Luciana glanced down. "Nothing."

It doesn't look like nothing. It looks like rope burns. Sam's jaw instantly clenched.

"Can I see?" She settled her hand gently over Luciana's wrist, not wanting to pressure her to do anything at all she didn't want to do. "I won't hurt you."

"I know you won't." Her eyes finally found Sam's. Dull. Lifeless. Pained. "You've never hurt me."

"And I never would…" Sam slowly lifted the cuff, sliding it up Luciana's arm. Deep purple marks wrapped around her wrist, and as Sam glanced up at her, Luciana closed her eyes. "Look at me," Sam said, curling her fingertips under her chin. "Please?"

Luciana's eyes opened, glistening with unshed tears.

"Did she do this to you?"

Luciana simply nodded.

"What else did she do?" Sam's heart ached in her chest, but she also felt her anger rising from deep within. Her eyes landed on more bruising, this time around Luciana's neck. "Oh, God," Sam gasped. "S-She choked you?"

"That was before we'd even left here." Luciana offered a small smile. "I called you after she'd done it."

"Fuck," Sam muttered under her breath. "This is my fault. I didn't come to you, and this happened."

"No, don't blame yourself." Luciana squeezed Sam's hand. The thought of Sam condemning herself broke her heart; Luciana knew this was her own fault. "This is all on me. I never should have gotten involved with her. I should have stood up to her."

"Whether you choose to stand up to someone or not, it doesn't mean you deserve this. It doesn't mean she has any fucking right to lay a finger on you." Sam climbed to her feet, pacing the floor in front of the fireplace. "I'll fucking kill her."

"Sam, I'm okay."

"Get a bag ready." She stopped dead. "You're staying with me."

"You don't have to do that. I don't want to involve you in any of this."

"Is that why you told me you didn't want to do this anymore? With me?" Sam dropped to her knees in front of Luciana, cupping her face gently. "Is this why you said it wasn't a good idea?"

"You have to know that I don't want to let you go, Sam. But it *is* for the best."

"No." Sam's own tears fell. "No. I've only just found you... I'm not letting you go. Not like this."

"You can." Luciana turned her face, kissing the palm of Sam's hand. "You're amazing. Everything I could ever want...but my life is only going to bring you trouble and I wouldn't put you through that. You've been through enough."

"Let me help you, Luciana," Sam begged. "If at the end of this, you don't want to be with me, I'll walk away. But, please, let me help you."

"She still doesn't know about you."

"All the more reason for you to come home with me."

"I'm in pain," Luciana whispered, her eyes closing. "Everywhere."

"Come here." Sam climbed from her knees and took a seat beside Luciana. "At least let me hug you."

"God, I want that..." She winced. "But...my back."

Another wave of sadness coursed through Sam. Before this week was out, she would step over Janet's cold, dead body.

"Okay, let's get out of here." Sam stood up, straightening

herself out. "We will get you back to mine, get you cleaned up, and then call the police."

"No! No police." Luciana shook her head, her tone adamant. "Please, no police."

"I think you're making a mistake not calling them." Sam sighed. "They should really know."

"I was an escort, Sam." Luciana looked up at her, laughing. "Do you really think they will believe a word I say when I tell them my client tied me up and beat me?"

Sam's blood ran cold.

"Seriously? Do you think they will give a shit?"

"You have to try…" Sam ran her fingers through her hair. "Do you need to go to the hospital?"

"No. I just want to forget about it and pray I never see her again."

"And if you do see her again?" Sam's eyebrow rose. "If she comes here and does the same thing?"

"I'll look for somewhere else to live. I'll go back home to my parents. I used to commute to the station, I can do it again."

"You'd leave the city?"

"If it meant I didn't have to see her again, yes." Sam imagined the prospect of not seeing Luciana anymore, not partial to that possibility. However, this was Luciana's decision and she wouldn't force any of her own ideas on her. "What are you thinking?"

"Me?" Sam smiled faintly. "About how much I'm going to miss you…"

"I'm sure you won't." Luciana slowly got to her feet. "Like you said, you only wanted dinner and conversation. You'll forget I ever existed soon enough."

"No," Sam whispered as she shook her head. "I couldn't ever forget about you."

"That makes me feel a little better."

"Is there anything I can do while you're still here? I'd like to think I could make you stay…but only *you* know what you want."

Luciana's eyes brightened. She wasn't used to hearing those words from another woman, and after tonight, she hadn't expected them from Sam. How could she be so calm with her? After she'd openly admitted to sleeping with another woman, how could Sam even give her the opportunity to explain herself? *Because she's different than the rest,* Luciana thought. *She always was.*

"Can I stay with you tonight?"

"Of course." Sam smiled, wrapping her arms around her own body. "Whatever you need."

I need you, but this is a fucking mess, Luciana inwardly scolded herself, a slight relaxation settling in her shoulders.

"I'll just get some clothes together. Would you mind waiting?"

"I'm not going anywhere."

CHAPTER SIXTEEN

Sam sat in the window of her living room, her huge slouch chair enveloping her, comforting her. Last night played over in her mind, but she didn't know where to begin. What she wanted was to find Janet and make her disappear, but logically and realistically, it wasn't her business. Luciana chose not to tell Janet about their relationship, and she had to respect that. Her hope for this morning was that she could get Luciana to open up about what happened last night, but as with meeting at her flat, she wouldn't push her. If Luciana wanted to talk in her own time, Sam would be here waiting.

Her phone buzzed beside her, Lindsay's name on the screen.

"Hey," Sam breathed out. "You okay?"

"Haven't seen you for a few days…"

"I know, I've been busy." Sam's eyes focused on the river, the bright blue sky doing nothing for her mood. "I'm sorry."

"It's okay," Lindsay replied. "Did you want to meet for lunch today? Or I can come to the office…"

"I've cancelled my plans for the day," Sam said. "I have some other things to deal with that don't require being at the office."

"Oh, like what?"

"Nothing for you to worry about." Sam knew Lindsay was digging, but it was a waste of time. "Nothing for anyone to worry about."

"Mm, why don't I believe you?"

"I don't know. That's something you'll have to deal with yourself." Sam shrugged, hearing movement in the kitchen. "Can I call you later?"

"I suppose so." Lindsay sighed. "I miss you."

"I miss you, too." Sam smiled. "I'll have lunch with you tomorrow, I promise."

"I'll hold you to that."

"I promise. Bye, Linds."

"Bye, Sam."

She glanced back over her shoulder. Luciana appeared to be moving with a little more ease this morning. Sam didn't know the extent of her pain, or her injuries, but the thought of it made her stomach churn. How could anyone lay their hands on another woman? Someone they supposedly cared about? Sam was dumbfounded, she truly was.

"Can I get you some coffee?" Sam asked, not moving from her seat.

"I'm okay with water, thanks." Luciana rounded the counter with a glass of water and took a seat on the couch. "Did you sleep okay?"

"Could have been better..."

"Sorry about that," Luciana said, her eyes lowering. "What time are you leaving for the office?"

"I'm not." Sam faced her fully. "And I didn't sleep last night because I wanted you beside me."

It seemed the right thing to do last night when she offered Luciana her spare room, but once she climbed into bed alone, Sam regretted it. She knew Luciana needed space and that this wasn't about her own needs, but the last couple of days had been pleasant having her here, happy and enjoying one another's company.

"I am sorry that you got hurt, though."

"I didn't get hurt." Sam frowned. "You did, not me."

"I still slept with her, Sam."

"I'm not interested in that, I'm really not." Sam held up her hand. "But did you want to talk about what happened?"

"I don't know." She pushed her blonde hair from her face. "She's never been like that before. She was always dominating, more so in the last few months I spent time with her, but last night wasn't the same. It was violent."

Sam chose to remain silent, allowing Luciana as much time as she needed.

"She always told me that her interpretation of that life was the way it was supposed to be. I knew it wasn't. I mean, I have friends who are into BDSM, and it's fascinating. It's nothing like what Janet practices. Nothing."

"I don't know much about it, but I do know that it doesn't result in this," Sam said.

"It all changed about a year into our escort/client relationship. Before then, Janet had been perfect. In every sense of the word. Then she insisted we try something different. At first, it was just a little bondage. Sometimes a blindfold. It was quite enjoyable." Luciana side-glanced Sam, noting the shudder that travelled through her body. "We don't have to talk about this."

"No, please continue." Sam gripped her coffee cup, determined to be here for Luciana.

"That went on for a few months, and then she introduced other stuff. Things I didn't want to be involved in." Luciana chose not to go into too much detail. It wasn't needed and she wasn't sure she wanted to go over it again. "Then, once it got too full-on for me, I spoke to her about it. Explained that I wasn't willing to go any further with her if she continued to want what she was asking."

"That seems like a reasonable request."

"She didn't like that. She said we'd been meeting for long

enough and I should be able to trust her. One night, she booked me for dinner. She seemed different, closed off. I didn't complain; I was happy she didn't want me to go back to her place with her."

"I'll bet you were…"

"She said she would call the next time she wanted to book me. I didn't hear from her again."

"Until this week?" Sam asked.

"Until this week…" Luciana breathed out. "Last night though, I saw the evil in her eyes."

"What did she do?" Sam shifted closer, taking Luciana's hand. "You don't have to go into every detail, but I want you to talk about this with me." If Luciana wouldn't call the police, Sam needed her to open up in the confines of her home. She would always be safe here.

"She showed up at my door. Said she found me through one of the girls at the agency."

"Do you know which one?"

"No, and I don't care." Luciana sighed, the tension releasing slowly from her shoulders as Sam stroked her thumb over her knuckles. "She told me to get ready, that we had plans. I already had plans with you but she wasn't interested that I was already busy."

"Janet is a very demanding woman," Sam agreed.

"You don't have to convince me." Luciana snorted, a slight smile playing at the corners of her mouth. "She didn't like how I spoke to her and that's when she choked me. Then I received a smack for it, too."

"I'm sorry." Sam's voice broke. "I should have been there for you."

"I knew I shouldn't call you, that you were busy with meetings, but I just wanted to hear your voice. It calmed me, but once we'd been out to dinner, she took me back to her place and that's when this happened." Luciana stood up and lifted her T-shirt from her body. As she turned around, she prepared for the gasp from Sam but it never came. Instead, she heard sobs.

Sam couldn't comprehend what she was seeing. Deep bruising consistent with a whip plagued Luciana's back, her beautiful body hurting. This was far too much. Sam felt a heat rising through her, an anger she'd never felt before. She couldn't allow it to boil over, so she closed her eyes and released a deep breath.

"I have them on my legs too, but they're not as bad."

"Not as bad..." Sam whispered. "This couldn't be any worse."

"I just lay there and took it. Like I was supposed to." Luciana sat back down beside Sam, slipping her T-shirt back over her body. "I didn't want to do this with her, Sam. Please, you have to believe that. She didn't touch me, not like that. *I* had to pleasure *her*."

Sam took her hand and lifted it, pressing a kiss to her skin. "We're okay, I promise."

"How? How can we possibly be okay?"

"She won't hurt you ever again. I won't let her."

"I'm not sure even you can stop her."

"You underestimate me, beautiful." Sam pressed the palm of her hand against Luciana's cheek. "Trust me, okay?"

"I've always trusted you."

"I'm sorry I wasn't there to stop this." Sam held Luciana's face. "That won't happen again."

"I don't want to leave the city," Luciana admitted. "But I don't know what else to do."

"Stay here with me. I'll keep you safe."

"This isn't your problem." Luciana smiled softly. "As much as I appreciate it, you have a business to run. Not to be here looking after me."

"I won't be here looking after you. You're strong enough in yourself to do that, but I won't *ever* not be available for you again."

"You were doing your job," Luciana said. "You didn't intentionally leave me to get myself into this mess."

"Still, having you in my life... I have new priorities."

"I don't follow…"

"I want to make us exclusive." Sam smiled, running her thumb beneath Luciana's eye and catching a tear as it fell. "I want to call you mine."

"Yeah?"

"Mmhmm." Sam leaned in, pressing her lips to Luciana's. "If you want that, too?"

"I do." Luciana deepened the kiss, feeling something normal for the first time since she left Sam yesterday. "Can I shower before we spend some time together?"

"Do whatever you need to do." Sam released Luciana, her mind and heart settling knowing that this wasn't ending. "I just need to make a few calls to the office."

"I'll let you be then…"

"If you need anything," Sam said. "I'll be right out here."

"Thank you."

Sam released a deep breath as Luciana disappeared down the hallway. Hearing the bathroom door close, she took her phone from the coffee table and dialled Cheryl's personal number.

"Mrs Phillips?"

"Sam."

"Right, yeah. Is, uh…is everything okay?" Cheryl asked.

"Can you send me the contact details for Janet Mason, please? If she's working out of an office in the city, find it."

"Do you want me to call her and schedule an appointment? What project is this for?"

"Just…" Sam pinched the bridge of her nose. "Send over anything you can find." Cheryl worked harder than anyone Sam had employed, but sometimes she was too much.

"Yes, right away." Cheryl sighed. "To your personal number or business number?"

"Business."

"Okay. Bye." Cheryl ended the call as Sam sat back in her seat, a smirk forming on her mouth. If Janet Mason thought she could hurt someone Sam cared about, she was sadly mistaken. She couldn't help by seeking out the police, so Sam would use her business mind to lure Janet to her.

Sam stood outside a familiar restaurant deep inside the city centre. In a few short moments, she would come face to face with the woman who had hurt Luciana, her anger rising faster than she had anticipated. She didn't want to go inside all guns blazing, but she also wasn't sure how long she could make small talk, business talk, or any other kind of talk with this woman. Sam knew Janet when she had nothing, and in an instant, could take it all away again. She would make sure by the end of the night that Janet understood that exactly. Whatever it took, she wouldn't leave this restaurant without her knowing it.

Sam glanced down at her phone in her hands.

S: Meeting should only last an hour or so. Everything okay? X

Sam smiled when a little bubble instantly appeared beneath her read message.

L: Perfect. Just preparing the film so it's ready for when you get home. X

S: Sorry I had to go back on my promise of no business today. My client is leaving the city tomorrow and I wanted to finalise some things with them before they did. X

L: Go and be amazing. X

S: See you soon. X

L: Right here waiting...

Sam squared her shoulders and pushed the heavy glass door open. Finding Janet already waiting at their table, she smiled and waved at her as she weaved through the tables.

"Sam, I'm so happy you contacted me."

"Thought we could catch up." Sam chose to ignore the hand

that had been offered to her, instead sitting down and taking a menu. "Have you ordered drinks?"

"I ordered a bottle of red."

"Perfect." Sam smiled. "So, what brings you back to the city?"

"Personal things." Janet tapped her nails on the drinks menu in front of her. "My girlfriend is here, so I wanted to check in with her."

"Oh." Sam's eyebrows rose. "Have you been together long?"

"I kind of disappeared on her." Janet sighed. "I had to come back for her."

"You're lucky she hung around for you," Sam said. "Not many would in this city."

"I know. Thankfully, I got to spend the night with her last night. We had some making up to do."

Sam fell silent, the playful nature of the woman sitting in front of her too much to take. Janet didn't have any idea just what Sam knew, but she would soon. Sam was already done listening to her.

"Do you plan on disappearing again?" Sam smiled as the waiter filled their glasses.

"I have to." Janet took her wine and sipped. "I have a huge project in London."

"With who?"

"Wright-Peterson."

"Ahh, both good friends of mine." Sam nodded. "Say hi to them for me, won't you?"

"Of course." Janet relaxed back into her seat. "So, what's new with you?"

"Working. As always."

"And life at home? I hope it's beginning to get better." Sam noted the false tone in Janet's voice. In all honesty, this woman couldn't care less about Sam, but she knew that.

"Actually, it is." Sam beamed. "That's why this will only be a short meeting. I have to get back."

"Oh?" Janet smirked. "You have plans?"

"Big plans."

"I'm so happy for you, Sam." Janet reached across the table, squeezing Sam's hand. "It's about time you put yourself out there."

"Just had to wait for the right moment." Sam drained her glass and refilled it.

"Wow, you really are in a hurry." Janet watched Sam take a long sip of her fresh wine. "If you couldn't make it, you shouldn't have offered."

"No, she doesn't mind. I explained that I was catching up with an old friend I hadn't seen in *far* too long."

"It has been a while." Janet nodded. "So, do you have any projects on at the moment?"

"A lot, actually. You?"

"Just the one in London. Work has been...quiet."

"Really? Not here it hasn't."

"Perhaps I should come back full-time once I'm done with this one?"

"Oh, I don't know." Sam shook her head. "My current designer is more than doing his job."

"Do I recall you saying that you would always put the women before the men in your business ventures?"

"You would be correct." Sam checked her watch. "But Joseph is as gay as I am, so I class him as one of our own."

"That's very sweet of you."

"Just looking out for the people who matter in my company."

"I mattered at one time." Janet sighed. "Work really has been hard, Sam. You'll call me if you need an extra pair of hands?"

Not your hands, no. Sam held back a laugh she could feel bubbling away inside of her.

"Sure." She left money on the table and stood. "Walk with me? I do actually have something to discuss with you."

"Okay." Janet's eyes lit up. "Sounds interesting."

"Oh, it is. Very interesting."

Sam moved back through the tables and out onto the street, waiting for Janet to fall into step with her. What she had to say wouldn't take very long, so she decided to cut to the chase.

"Which way?" Janet asked.

"Oh, we'll take this alley. It'll get me home quicker."

"Fine by me." Janet laughed. "I don't like a frustrated Sam."

"And you shouldn't." Sam winked. "So, how much is this contract with Wright-Peterson worth to you?"

"A lot. It's my biggest project to date."

"Impressive."

"All the more reason to take me back on when it's finished." Janet nudged her shoulder, that playful nature returning and grating on Sam. "Don't you think?"

"Actually." Sam stopped dead, turning to face Janet. "How would you feel about it all ending in what..." Sam paused. "The next thirty seconds?"

"What?" Janet's forehead creased, her lack of Botox recently evident to Sam. "Are you offering me something better? I didn't even give you the figures."

"I couldn't give a fuck about the figures, Janet." Sam stepped closer, backing Janet up against the stone wall in the alleyway. "I'm not interested in anything you have to say."

"Sam, what the hell is wrong with you?"

"Shut it!" Sam's body pressed against Janet's, her hand forced against her chest. "My girlfriend was in pieces last night."

"Okay..."

"Because of you!"

"What? You've lost your fucking mind."

"You contact Alexis again...you so much as breathe the same air as her, and I'll know about it." Sam smirked. "She's not your girlfriend, she never was. You were her client and a pretty shit one at that."

"Alexis?" Janet's eyes widened. "What has she been telling you?"

"She didn't have to tell me anything. I saw the damage you did."

"She fucking loved it." Janet cackled, sending the hairs on the back of Sam's neck upright.

"It will take me one call, Janet." Sam's hand slid up to her throat. "One. Fucking. Call."

"Y-You wouldn't."

"And you're willing to test that?" Sam's grip tightened. "You're willing to play these games with the hope that I don't end your shitty career right now? I thought you knew me better than that."

"I don't know what you're talking about. Alexis has been fucking me since Lucia died."

"My wife's name comes out of your mouth again and I'll end it all for you right now."

"What would she think about this? Her perfect little wife shacking up with a whore?" Janet's eyes flickered, anger evident but also fear. "Sam Phillips cannot do any wrong." Janet rolled her eyes but it only encouraged Sam to grip tighter.

"You forget the people I know. The Mayor. The Chief of Police. Wright-Peterson."

"So?"

"So, they're fond of you, no?"

"They are," Janet agreed. "Very fond."

"One call is all it would take and I'd air your dirty laundry to every one of them."

"I don't think they'd care too much about me booking an escort."

"No, probably not. They would, however, find it hard to forgive you for abusing her. Beating her. Forcing yourself on her."

"My word against hers."

Sam was impressed by the resolve Janet seemed to possess. Anyone else would have crumbled by now, but not Janet. Sam knew this woman all too well, though.

"Maybe so, but in this industry...*my word* is gospel."

"W-What do you want?" Janet asked, the realisation of how powerful Sam was settling in. "Just tell me what you want!"

"Leave her alone. No contact. You leave the city first thing tomorrow morning and I don't see your fucking face again."

"And if I don't?"

"I have Peter Wright on speed-dial." Sam released her grip on Janet's throat. "I also have his wife on my side, who oversees a lot of projects in London."

"You really think you can destroy me?" Janet scoffed. "You truly believe you have the power?"

"No." Sam held up her hand. "I *know*."

"Fine."

"That's all you have to say? Fine!" Sam couldn't believe the disgust she held for this woman. "I want you out of here. Alexis may not be willing to go to the police, but I'm contacting my lawyer in the morning and having an order out against you. You touch my girlfriend again and you *will* be lying dead in this very alleyway."

"Threats?"

"Promises, Janet." Sam leaned in and brought her lips to Janet's ear. "Always promises from me."

CHAPTER SEVENTEEN

"Good morning." Sam leaned down behind Luciana, kissing the spot below her ear. "You made breakfast...again."

"Breakfast is the most important meal of the day." Luciana shrugged as she slathered her toast with butter. "I picked up some of those melon balls you love."

"You're too good to me." Sam sat beside Luciana, sipping her coffee as she made herself comfortable. "I never thought I'd get used to this again."

"Which?"

"Breakfast every morning with another woman." Sam popped a melon ball into her mouth, moaning as the juice slid down her throat. A week had passed since her encounter with Janet, her sole focus now to enjoy her time with Luciana. It did feel overwhelming at times, but she wanted her girlfriend here. Where she was safe.

"About that." Luciana cleared her throat, dropping her toast onto her plate. "How has it been for you?"

"What do you mean?" Sam faced her girlfriend fully.

"Has it been okay?" Luciana offered her a small smile, unsure of Sam's response. "I don't forget that you have a wife, Sam."

"Lucia would want me to be happy." Sam placed her hand on Luciana's. "It just took you coming into my life to realise that."

"That means a lot." Luciana upturned her hand. "Really."

"She would be happy." Sam lowered her eyes. "She'd like you..."

"You think?" Luciana beamed. "You really mean that?"

"My wife had a beautiful personality. She was friends with everyone. You actually remind me of her at times."

"I do?"

"Your mannerisms. The little things you do."

"Like what?"

"You sleep the way she did." Sam's lips curled upward. "On your stomach with your left leg bent and your right arm under the pillow."

Luciana smiled, enjoying this moment with Sam. Over the past week, spending so much time here, she'd wanted to ask about Lucia and how Sam felt, but she wasn't sure how upsetting it would be for her girlfriend.

"You twirl your hair 'round your right index finger when you're concentrating, and you watch me at night when we settle down together."

"Hard not to watch you." Luciana reached out, tucking Sam's dark silky hair behind her ear. "Don't ever think you can't do this with me."

"Do what?"

"Talk about Lucia. Remember her."

"You've been keeping me a little busy." Sam smirked. "It's been a welcome change."

"Thank you for being amazing this week." Luciana could never repay Sam for the kindness she'd shown since Janet arrived at her flat. Of course, it was in Sam's nature to be that woman, but Luciana hadn't expected it so soon into their relationship. While she fully expected Sam to run a mile, she hadn't. Sam had stayed and been everything she needed.

"You mean a lot to me." Sam plated up her breakfast. "And as your girlfriend, I'm allowed to be here for you."

"Yeah, I'm still trying to get my head around that." Luciana laughed. "Can't quite believe it."

"I know how you feel."

"Do you have much on today?" Luciana focused on the back of Sam as she stood and leaned over the table. "You look great, by the way."

"A few meetings. Some plans I need to take a look at." Sam returned to her seat. "And this is just my usual work attire. I know you hate it, but it's the professional look."

"H-Hate it?"

"You made a comment the first time I invited you to the office."

"Oh, that wasn't what I meant." Luciana pushed her chair back and approached Sam, straddling her legs. "I *love* a woman in a suit."

"Okay, that's hot." Sam blew out a deep breath, her hands falling to her girlfriend's thighs. "So, I should wear a suit more often?"

"Only if I'm the one who has the opportunity to remove it from your gorgeous body."

"Wouldn't have anyone else."

Luciana dipped her head, taking Sam's bottom lip between her teeth. As much as she wanted to continue this, it was her first day back at the station. She wouldn't be able to focus on the job if she didn't remove herself from Sam's lap. *That wouldn't be the worst thing in the world.*

"I should head off."

"Wait!" Sam gripped Luciana's jaw gently. "I'm not finished kissing you yet."

Luciana delighted in the feeling of Sam's tongue rolling against hers. The taste of this woman was enough to send her over the edge, regardless of the minimum contact they would likely have in the next thirty seconds.

"I'm hoping you'll never be finished kissing me."

"Tonight," Sam whispered against her lips. "I'll be here waiting for you. Suit included."

"Fuck." Luciana pressed her forehead against Sam's. "I'm counting down the hours."

Sam brushed her thumb against Luciana's cheek. "You're sure you're ready to go back to work?" She had tried to talk to her girlfriend about how she was feeling, but Luciana insisted she was fine. She hadn't gone into any more detail about Janet, claiming that she didn't want to think about her any more than she had to, but Sam was pleased with her progress. Unfortunately, she got the impression that Luciana was used to this type of behaviour. While Sam wanted the police and everyone else involved, her girlfriend had returned to normal life, not a care in the world. It didn't feel right and it didn't sit well with Sam, but she couldn't and *wouldn't* force Luciana to talk to the authorities, no matter how much she believed she should. Regardless of how much she hated the fact that Janet would walk away free, it was Luciana's decision and her decision alone.

"I'm sure. I'm fine. I haven't heard from her and you've looked after me so well that I'm feeling great."

"I haven't done much." Sam shrugged as Luciana climbed off her.

"Holding me was all I needed."

Sam smiled as her girlfriend approached the rucksack by the door and pulled it up onto her shoulder. Her usual work outfit hugged her in every right way; something about the black heavy boots she wore sent Sam into a spin. This feeling of waking each morning with Luciana in her home was quickly becoming normal for Sam, whether she once rejected the idea or not. The thought that she once wanted nothing more than a friendship with Luciana now seemed ludicrous, but moments like this...as she glanced back at her and blew her a kiss, these were the moments she was living for.

"Be safe."

Luciana threw her a wink. "Always."

S: Have you left the station yet? X

Luciana glanced down at her phone in her hand and smiled. She'd left the station on time but had since been sitting outside Sam's apartment building. For twenty minutes, she'd sat and thought about the woman upstairs, how good she was for her. For twenty minutes, her heart constricted in her chest when she thought about ever losing her. In those twenty minutes, Luciana had come to only one conclusion: She was falling in love with Sam. This wasn't how it was supposed to be, not so soon, but nobody had ever shown her so much respect or compassion, and Luciana knew that what she felt was genuine. It wasn't simply because Sam wanted her around—she wasn't that desperate to fall in love—but it was because everything felt so natural between them. It felt real and honest. For the last week or so, the thought of their age difference hadn't once entered Luciana's mind. It didn't matter to her. If people chose to talk, to judge, those people had little else to deal with in their tiny lives. The issue Luciana faced right now was that she was scared to go upstairs for fear of opening her mouth and those words falling from it.

L: Yes, I'm on my way. X
S: ETA? X
L: 10 minutes? X
S: Perfect. Dinner is almost ready. X

Luciana climbed to her feet and took her rucksack from the floor beside her. Checking her car was locked, the lights flashed and she turned, slowly walking towards the apartment block she'd spent the best part of a week residing in. Yes, she would one day have to go home, but for now…here was perfect. Until Sam kicked her out, sick of the sight of her, Luciana would continue to shower her with the same love and affection she'd been receiving.

She took the spare keys Sam had given her and used the fob to gain access to the building. The automatic lighting lit up the entrance immediately, shocking Luciana's eyes as they adjusted to the brightness of them. *Just another minute and I'll be safely inside with her.* Luciana sighed, smiling at the thought of being with Sam tonight. Her girlfriend may have promised to be waiting, completed by a suit, but just sharing dinner was good enough. It always would be.

Luciana took the stairs slowly, a mental image of her time spent with Janet flashing in her mind. Nothing had ever felt real with the interior designer, nothing worth holding onto, but Luciana recognised that long before today. It was the reason she'd never pushed to contact or find Janet once she fell off the radar. When her ex-client stopped calling, booking her, Luciana had felt a relief. With Sam, the opposite had happened. She knew she had to cut ties with her for her own sanity, but once she learned how Sam felt, that she wanted to continue seeing her, Luciana couldn't stay away. Their first meeting clouded her thoughts of Janet and a sense of happiness washed through Luciana's entire being. This, right now, was where she was supposed to be. Whether it lasted a year or a lifetime, Luciana was here and she planned to cherish every moment with Sam Phillips.

As she slid the key into the lock, the sight in front of her when the door opened caused her breath to catch in her throat. The lights were dimmed, and the strong aroma of Italian cooking sent Luciana's stomach into a frenzy. Sam stood with her back to her as she poured red wine into each glass on the table, dinner ready and waiting on the plates beside them. Sam's hair was pulled up into a ponytail, giving Luciana a hint of her neck. *Oh, wow.* But what caught her attention more than anything, was the same black suit from this morning. High-waisted navy pants sat around her midsection, an ivory silk shirt tucked into them. Her blazer had been shed, but it didn't matter. What mattered was that Luciana's heart was beating out of her chest, her brain having the inability to even croak out any sort of word.

Sam turned around, a ringlet of hair falling down the side of her face as she smiled. "That was quick."

"Y-Yeah." Luciana dropped her rucksack as she closed the door. "Didn't take me as long as I thought it would."

"Just in time for dinner." Sam crossed the room and stopped in front of her girlfriend. Her eyes were tired, her shoulders slightly slumped, but this was her favourite version of Luciana. Here, laid bare, was when she felt most connected to her. While Sam was fond of the first impression she had of Luciana, done up in her escort persona, nothing beat this. "Why don't you take a seat and I'll join you in a moment?"

"Okay." Luciana nodded slowly, unable to take her eyes off Sam. "Thank you for doing this."

"It's just dinner." Sam cocked her head. "Is everything okay with you?"

"Perfect. Great."

"Bad day?" Sam took her hand and guided her towards the dining table. "You look tired."

"I can push through." Luciana sat down, her grip tightening on Sam's hand. "Seriously, this food looks amazing."

"I figured I couldn't go wrong with Italian." Sam winked. "After all, I'm dating one..."

"Mm." Luciana smirked. "You are." She tugged Sam's hand, motioning for her to come a little closer. As Sam dipped her head, Luciana kissed her harder than she ever had. If Sam was surprised, she didn't show it. Instead, she moaned into her mouth, smiling against her lips. "I've wanted to do that all day."

"The suit, huh?" Sam pulled back.

"No. Just you. Everything about you." Luciana closed her eyes, savouring the taste of Sam on her lips. Moments like this mattered to her, more than she ever thought they would. Moments when the outside world didn't matter, just Sam and her devastating smile for company. "Hurry up. Dinner is getting cold."

"I'll just get the salad." Sam threw her thumb over her shoulder, refusing to break contact with Luciana's eyes as she slowly backed away from the table. "A-Anything else?"

"You," Luciana breathed out, every fibre of her being screaming to reach out and touch Sam once again.

Sam returned to the table and placed their salad down, sitting opposite Luciana. "Tell me about your day."

"Pretty standard." Luciana tore an edge from the focaccia bread sitting between them. "We had a Joey that we could have done without."

"A Joey?" Sam clasped her hands beneath her chin, listening intently.

"A hoax call."

"People actually do that?" Sam scoffed. "Do they have nothing better to do?"

"It's more common than you'd think." Luciana shook her head. "I fucking hate them."

"I can imagine," Sam said. "It must be infuriating."

"I used to get really wound up about it," Luciana agreed. "You know, I'd go home thinking about it and what could possibly possess someone to be so stupid..."

"Understandable."

"But tonight, I didn't." Luciana smiled, reaching her hand forward and taking Sam's. "Tonight, I left work at work, knowing I was coming back here to you."

"That's sweet."

"Now, I wanna hear about your day." She squeezed Sam's hand. "Anything interesting?"

"Actually..." Sam lowered her eyes. "I have to go away for a few days late next week."

"Okay." Luciana noted the shift in Sam's mood. She understood that being a businesswoman involved trips away and times when they couldn't be together. She'd always understood that. "You don't look too happy about going away."

"Can't say I'm looking forward to leaving you." Sam picked up her fork, bringing pasta to her mouth. "I'm hoping I'll only be gone for three days. Two if I can get everything out of the way quicker."

"Hey, don't worry about it." Luciana offered Sam a full smile. "I'll be waiting for you when you come back."

"You'll be okay?"

"I know you're worried about her, Sam. She hasn't been in touch, I promise."

"I'm not worried about her." Sam sighed. "I should have told you last week, but it wasn't my business and I didn't know if I'd done the right thing getting involved." Sam felt an anxiety settle within her. Luciana had asked her not to get involved, and while it seemed like a good idea at the time, she wasn't so sure now.

"You've lost me..."

"The night after it happened, I had that meeting." Sam glanced up, gauging Luciana's reaction. "Well, I'd arranged to meet Janet."

"You're going into business with her?"

"Oh, no." Sam laughed. "I arranged to meet her *after* I'd been to your flat."

"O-Oh." Luciana's face fell. She wasn't sure where Sam was going with this conversation, but panic coursed through her.

"I'm so sorry." Sam held her head in her hands. "I overstepped, but I believe I did the right thing. She's gone, and I don't regret doing it."

"Doing what, exactly?" Luciana dropped her fork to the plate and sat back in her seat.

"I threatened her with the contract she has in London." Sam cleared her throat. "That I knew what she'd done to you and I'd make the call to have her off the project."

"You did that for me?" Luciana's voice wavered. "You put yourself on the line...for me?"

"I explained that she could lose everything, that's all."

"Still, you didn't have to do that. I mean, why would you do that for me?" Luciana's pulse thrummed in her ears, the idea that she could fall for Sam only growing stronger as the minutes passed between them.

"Because I care about you, baby."

God, don't say things like that, Luciana thought as her entire being ignited with a sense of love she'd never felt before. *It's too soon to feel this way. Far too soon.* Luciana simply smiled, removing the image in her head of putting her foot in it and telling Sam something she couldn't possibly want to hear.

"And I know you're strong and someone who doesn't need my help, but I couldn't sit here night after night without telling that bitch what I thought of her."

"Thank you." Luciana pushed her seat back and approached Sam. "Thank you so much." She got down to her knees between Sam's legs and leaned up, kissing her softly. "You have such a beautiful heart, Sam. Don't ever forget that."

"As do you." Sam cupped Luciana's face, her bright smile widening. "I'm sorry I have to go away."

"Don't worry about it." Luciana dropped back on her knees, shrugging. "It's only a few days and maybe it will do you some good."

"Do *me* some good?" Sam arched an eyebrow. "Why would it?"

"I've been around a lot lately."

"I'm aware of that." Sam nodded.

"And I don't want this to burn out because you're sick of the sight of me. I have tomorrow to get through in work and then I'm all yours for the weekend."

"What are your shifts next week?" Sam asked as Luciana climbed to her feet and returned to her seat. The idea of asking her girlfriend to join her on her trip away had entered her mind, but she wasn't sure Luciana would go for it. With shifts to work, Sam wasn't completely up on the days and times she would be available.

"I have two earlies and two lates next week. Monday to Thursday. Once I finish on Thursday, I'll go home and sleep then head to Mum and Dad's on the Friday afternoon."

"That sounds nice," Sam said, returning to the food on her plate and attempting to seem as nonchalant as possible. "So long as you have plans."

"Well, I don't, but since you'll be gone, I should make use of that time to at least show my face to my parents."

"I just... I thought..." Sam paused. "Never mind."

"Is everything okay?" Luciana helped herself to a little more bread. "Babe?"

"I was wondering if you wanted to come with me on my trip?"

"Me?" Luciana asked, her eyes narrowed. "You want me on a business trip with you?"

"If you'd like to join me..."

"Wait! This isn't like an escort kinda thing, is it?" Luciana asked. "I mean, I'm going there as me. Not a friend or whatever?"

"You'd be joining me as my girlfriend," Sam said. "I'm not one of those women who require someone good-looking on her arm to make an impression. I made my impression in the business world a long time ago."

"That's hot." Luciana pointed her fork at Sam.

Sam blushed. "At least say you'll think about it?"

"I'd love to join you." Luciana's eyes lit up. "But I'm working until eight on Thursday night."

"I was originally going to leave Thursday but the next morning will be fine."

"You'd wait around for me?"

"Something tells me that you joining me on my trip will be beneficial." Sam hummed; just having Luciana's company would be a welcome relief.

"Oh, I'll make it worth your while. Don't worry about that."

"I don't doubt it."

CHAPTER EIGHTEEN

Sam focused on the black clouds rolling in, her mood currently better than it had been since Lucia died. Those two years since her death had been excruciatingly hard and lonely, but something good had come out of it. The nights when she lay awake, wondering if she would ever be happy again, had resulted in this. Luciana. A woman she had an immense amount of time for, and a woman who made Sam feel incredibly happy. Her nightmares had stopped, her anxiety had lessened, and her general mood had lifted. She no longer felt on edge, or short with people. Luciana had brought something out in her, something she thought had long gone. Over the last few days, Sam had tried to keep her feelings at bay, feelings she wasn't sure she deserved, but she couldn't. As she stood here this morning, she thought about her future. One that Sam wished would include Luciana.

The sound of humming in the kitchen made her smile. As she turned around, it widened when she caught sight of her girlfriend prancing around in nothing but a robe. A robe which left very little to the imagination. A robe which would, in moments, be on the floor.

"Good morning, beautiful," Luciana said huskily, her voice

body, the intoxication she felt whenever her mouth was on Luciana's skin. Sam slipped her tongue inside, gaining a guttural moan. In the short time she'd known Luciana, she'd come to find exactly what she wanted. How she liked to be touched. Everything felt so easy with her, but devastatingly overwhelming too. When she wanted to run in the opposite direction, Sam instead found herself running directly towards Luciana. The only woman to ever spark something within her other than her wife. The only woman to see Sam for herself and not her money. Her power. Her business. Luciana, God...she was everything Sam wanted and needed in her life.

Sam gripped Luciana's thighs, spreading her legs a little more, and plunged two fingers inside her. Luciana groaned, meeting every movement, every thrust. Her walls squeezed Sam's fingers as she curled them, hitting that spot she knew drove Luciana insane.

"Fuck, I'm close," Luciana whimpered as she dropped one hand from the window in front of her, taking her nipple between her finger and thumb. Tugging and pinching, she trembled as her impending release approached faster than it ever had. "Y-Yes," she cried.

As Sam pushed deeper, fresh arousal coated her hand, her thrusts not lessening. No, it only encouraged Sam to take her deeper and harder.

"B-Babe."

"Fuck." Sam sunk her teeth into Luciana's backside. "I can't get enough of you." She smoothed her hand over the bite mark, tugging her bottom lip between her teeth. As her fingers slipped out of Luciana, she turned and pulled Sam up to her feet.

"Bedroom, now!" Lifting Sam, her arms wrapped around Luciana's neck, her legs around her waist. "God, I'm going to fuck you until the sun goes down."

"Mm, sounds like my kind of day." Sam crushed her lips into Luciana's. "You're not going anywhere..."

"Never." Luciana knew there was a hidden message in Sam's

words, but that message was irrelevant. Luciana had no intention of leaving this woman. Not now. Not ever.

"Okay...this." Luciana spun around, holding up some very revealing white lingerie. "God, you'd look amazing in this."

"Oh, I don't know." Sam blushed as her eyes darted around the shop. "Can you *not* wave it in the air!"

"Why? My girlfriend is incredibly gorgeous and I want *everyone* to know she's mine." Luciana leaned in, kissing Sam softly. "Shoot me."

"Luciana, I uh... I'm not sure this is me." Sam lowered her voice, feeling a lack of confidence suddenly hit her. She didn't know why she was thinking about it, or why she was worried, but Luciana was beautiful and Sam was nearing forty. "It's beautiful, it really is, but I could have worn this ten years ago."

"You're not serious," Luciana deadpanned. "This. It's so you."

"Really?" Sam wrinkled her nose. "You don't think I'd look ridiculous in it?"

"Well, you won't be in it for long...but no, you'll look anything but ridiculous." Luciana placed her hand on the small of Sam's back. "My treat. If you don't like it, you don't have to wear it. But please, give it a chance?"

"Okay." Sam smiled. "If you think it will look okay."

"Come here." Luciana motioned for Sam to come closer, brushing her lips against her ear. "What's going on with you? Where has that woman gone who fucked me against the window this morning?"

"Baby, please..." Sam groaned.

"Too much?"

"You're always too much." Sam bit her bottom lip. "Always."

"We buy this and then I'm taking you for lunch."

"I'd like that," Sam breathed out, her body gaining a slight respite from Luciana and her flirting. "I could use some food."

"Me too." Luciana nodded as she headed for the till. "I worked up quite the appetite this morning." She threw a wink over her shoulder as she sauntered away, stopping at the cashier.

"Oh, this will look great on you." The cashier smiled, a flirtatious nature which likely came with the job evident. "Really great."

"Oh, it's not for me." Luciana smiled. "It's for my girlfriend." Sam stopped beside her girlfriend. "Tell her it'll look amazing on her."

"Hmm." The cashier narrowed her eyes before they landed on Luciana again. "No, this would look amazing on *you*."

Great, Sam groaned inwardly. *The twenty-year-old shop assistant thinks I'll look ridiculous.*

"Thank you." Sam smiled sarcastically. "I told you it wouldn't work." She lowered her voice. "Get it for yourse—"

"The black one," the cashier cut in. "This style, but the black."

"Oh." Sam's eyes widened. "You're sure?"

"Positive." Sam noticed the name tag she wore.

"Well, Gemma... I should go and get the black one. Wrap this one for her though." Sam cocked her head towards Luciana. "Everything looks great on her."

"You've got it."

Luciana watched Sam weave through the store, heading towards the display they'd spent twenty minutes at earlier. "Thanks for that." She turned her attention back to Gemma. "She was convinced it wouldn't look good on her."

"Nonsense." Gemma waved her hand between them. "She's gorgeous."

"She is." Luciana smiled softly. "Very gorgeous." Sighing, she turned back to find Sam moving towards her, her own smile gracing her features.

As Sam re-joined Luciana at the till, her phone started to ring in her hand. "I'll just take this outside." Luciana nodded as Sam hit the accept button. "Hi, Mum."

"Love, how are you?"

"Great. You?" Sam reached the fresh air and moved towards the edge of the walkway, peering over the ledge. "Just out, shopping."

"You're not at the office?"

"It's Saturday, Mum."

"That doesn't usually stop you from working incessantly."

"Well, things have changed. I'm taking the weekend off like I have been for the last few weeks."

"And why is that?" Sam's mum asked, her tone accusing. "Is everything okay?"

"Mum," Sam warned. "Everything is perfectly fine." She felt Luciana's presence behind her, a hand resting on the small of her back. "I just have plans. Did you call for something in particular?"

"Your dad was called away for the weekend. I thought I'd come into the city to visit you."

"Oh." Sam's eyes widened. "Well, I'm not home."

"I know that," Susan said. "So, I'll come and meet you."

"Mum, you can't just spring it on me. I don't know what my plans are for the rest of the afternoon."

"Lunch?"

"I'm going to lunch now." Sam sighed. "Look, can I call you later?"

"I guess that would be okay." Sam knew her mum was just trying to spend time with her, but Luciana was in her company today and she wished for it to remain that way. "Bye, love."

Sam glanced down at her screen as the call ended and sighed.

"Everything okay, babe?"

"Yes, it was just my mum."

"And is she okay?" Luciana asked. "It sounded like she wanted to meet up with you."

"She does." Sam nodded. "But I'm here with you."

"So?"

"So, I told her I'd rearrange." Sam locked her phone and shrugged. "She can't expect me to just be available."

Luciana lowered her eyes, realising what her girlfriend was saying. "You know, I can go home and just see you tonight or tomorrow."

"What? No." Sam laughed. "Why would I want you to do that?"

"I get it, okay?" Luciana gripped the bag of lingerie tight in her hand. "I don't expect everyone to be okay with this. Us. I just... I'm not bothered about people's opinions."

"Huh?"

"You don't want me around when it comes to friends and family." Luciana offered Sam a sad smile. "One day, I don't know..." She ran her fingers through her hair. "Maybe if you ever feel serious enough about us, I could meet them. For now though, I get it."

Sam's heart broke hearing Luciana say these things.

"I'm trying not to be completely in, I'm trying not to dive in head first..." Luciana leaned in and pressed a kiss to Sam's cheek. "Because I know it's not what you truly want, but I feel differently. I feel like I could spend my life doing this with you." Luciana backed away. "Call your mum back. Have lunch with her. I'll always be here whenever you want to lock us away."

"Don't go." Sam reached out and gripped her girlfriend's wrist. "I'm not ashamed of us. Of you."

"I know..."

A heat rushed through Sam's body, a desperate need to be honest making itself known. "I'm falling for you, Luciana. I'm falling for you and I know I shouldn't. I know I'm not lucky enough to have someone like you forever."

"Babe..."

"I didn't want to have lunch with my mum because she's infuriating." Sam sighed. "Don't ever think I don't want to introduce you to my friends and family because I do. I really do."

"I don't know where you get this idea of not having me forever from, because I see something completely different, but if it makes you feel better... I'm falling for you, too. I'm falling so hard and I don't care. I'm not pulling away from it anymore. I want you, Sam. I want you more than anything."

Sam blew out a deep breath, not expecting to hear those words from Luciana so soon, or at all. Just a few weeks ago, Sam was alone and committed to her company, but that one booking at the agency had changed her life. Whether this fizzled out or blossomed into something beautiful, she would always be thankful to herself for making the booking, and to Luciana for showing her that she still had the opportunity to be happy. To find love again.

"I didn't expect you to feel this way..."

"Do I look like I want anyone else, Sam?"

"Right now, no." *Why?* Sam thought. *Why do I insist on saying these things?* "I'm sorry."

"About what?" Luciana side-glanced at her girlfriend.

"Always doubting you..."

"I don't think that's what you're doing." Luciana pulled Sam away from the crowd to a quieter spot. "I think you're terrified about the future. The idea of giving yourself away completely scares you, but I understand."

"But in time, it will only push you away."

"I know you had another life before this. Before us. I know you had everything you could ever possibly need and you were happy."

Sam held back the tears forming in her eyes.

"I cannot change that. I cannot do anything other than make you happy *now*," Luciana said. "At least, in some way."

"You do make me happy." Sam guided them both to a bench. "I know I say things I shouldn't, and I know my words probably hurt you at times, but you have to know that you *do* make me happy. Happier than I've been in a long time."

"I spent time wondering if I could ever be enough for you." Luciana's intense blue eyes found Sam's. "I wondered if this was just a thing and whether you'd one day call it quits."

"Never." Sam shook her head, her voice barely audible.

"But then I thought about how you smile around me. How you relax against me at the end of the day. I know your smile is like nothing you had for Lucia, and I know it never will be, but seeing the difference in your mood since the first night I met you...it's good enough for me. Knowing I'm the one who has changed even just one tiny aspect of your life is more than good enough for me."

"You've changed more than one tiny aspect." Sam squeezed Luciana's hand. "Give yourself more credit."

"I don't need to rush into a life with you, Sam. It appears to be happening naturally."

"Yes, it does." Sam smiled as she stood up. "Come on."

"Where are we going?"

"I don't know, and I don't care." They walked hand in hand towards the dock. "This is my weekend with you, and I'm not spending it worrying about something that is out of our control."

"Out of our control?"

"Just...this is the last time I mention it." Sam held up her hand. "But promise me one thing..."

"Anything." Luciana beamed. "Anything at all for you."

"If you do one day meet someone else..."

"Sam—"

"Here me out," Sam interrupted. "If you do, promise you won't hurt me. I'm okay with you leaving me for someone younger or whatever else, but don't hurt me. Don't think you can't come to me and tell me you're unhappy. I don't want to come home one night to find out you've been seeing someone else. Please, just be honest with me from the start."

"I'd never do that to you." Luciana cupped Sam's face. "I'm very much a one-woman kinda girl."

"I know." Sam nodded as she leaned into her girlfriend's touch. "I'd love to still be doing this with you in years to come."

"Me too, babe."

"But I'm also a realist." Sam turned her head, pressing her lips to Luciana's palm. "And I know it isn't always that simple."

"I like simple." Luciana shrugged, taking Sam's hand once again. "Simple is beautiful."

CHAPTER NINETEEN

"You still haven't told me what I need to pack for this trip." Luciana stood at the foot of Sam's bed, her work clothes still covering her body. "I mean, are we going out of the country, or...?"

"No. I changed my plans," Sam said, her back to her girlfriend. "I hope you don't mind."

"Changed your plans? So, we're not going away now?" Luciana would be lying if she said she wasn't disappointed. She couldn't remember the last time she'd had the opportunity to go away and relax, even if it was a business trip in Sam's mind.

"Not quite." Sam turned around and faced Luciana fully. "I had something I wanted to talk to you about."

"Okay..." Luciana drawled out. Something about Sam's eyes told her not to worry about this conversation, but until thirty seconds ago, they were supposed to be leaving for a trip. "Then you should probably spit it out before I go insane."

"For a firefighter, you're not very patient."

"And that still doesn't make me feel any better." Luciana dropped down onto the edge of the bed. "Babe, what's going on?"

"I wanted to ask if you'd come somewhere with me?"

"Until a minute ago, I *was* going somewhere with you." Luciana's brows drew together. "I thought you had to meet with a contractor?"

"I did, but I sent someone else to deal with it." Sam shrugged. "I've had such a pleasant week with you, even if you have worked most of it, and I don't think I'm ready for it to end with a business trip."

"Right, okay." Luciana nodded. "So, where are we going?"

"Will you come home with me?" Sam's heart beat hard in her chest. The idea of going home, to her actual home, had been weighing on her mind since last weekend, but she wasn't sure she could do it alone. When she drove up the long path to her house out of the city, she wasn't sure what her reaction would be.

"Babe, are you feeling okay?" Luciana asked. "This *is* your home."

"It's not." Sam offered a small smile as she lowered her eyes to her lap. "I bought this place when Lucia died. My home...the real me, is out of the city."

"You didn't buy this to make work life easier?" Luciana asked, remembering their original conversation. "To make the commute easier?"

"No." Sam cleared her throat. "I bought this place when I couldn't face going home alone anymore."

"And now you want me to come with you?" Luciana couldn't believe what she was hearing. Sam, the woman she was falling head over heels in love with, wanted to show her a past life. A past home. "W-Why?"

"Because I feel like I'm ready to walk through the door again," Sam said. "But I can't do it alone."

"Okay."

"Okay?" Sam's head shot up. "You'll come?"

"You trust me enough to be the one you do this with, so yes. Of course."

"It's been two years since I walked out of there." Sam wrung her hands together. "Everything is still as it was when I left it."

"I don't think this is going to be very easy for you." Luciana wanted Sam to do what she thought was best, but she wasn't sure she could face seeing her girlfriend heartbroken. "Why do you want to do this now? Two years on, why are you planning to go back?"

"I don't want to be here anymore."

"Oh." Luciana's forehead creased. "Right, uh…"

"I don't mean it like that." Sam lifted her girlfriend's hand, pressing a kiss to her skin. "I hate the city. I hate this apartment, I always have."

"Really? I love it." Luciana glanced around. "It's gorgeous."

"So move your stuff into it." Sam shrugged. "But I won't be here."

"You're moving out of the city." Luciana nodded slowly. "And what will that involve? I mean, will I still see you often?"

"This doesn't change *anything* for us, Luciana. Nothing at all." Sam shifted closer. "What I'm saying is, having you in my life makes me want to go home. To show you the woman I am. This, the clinical walls and the chrome…it's not me. It never has been."

"When do you want to leave?"

"Tomorrow morning as planned." Sam smiled fully. "I want to spend my evenings with you in the house I built myself. Not here in some open-plan generic space."

"Yeah?" A tear slid down Luciana's face.

"I want to drink wine and talk about life out on the terrace…"

"Okay, you're going to have to stop that." Luciana wiped her face. "I'm really not a wine on the terrace person, Sam."

"Okay. A beer by the fire pit." Sam stood, gathering the clothes she'd folded on the bed. "Whatever works for you. I don't care."

"A beer by the fire pit." Luciana sighed. "Sounds perfect."

"Thank you for doing this with me." Sam stopped what she was doing and glanced up at her girlfriend. "I'm not taking you back home to show you the person I was. I mean, in a way... I am. But I'm taking you home to show you the real me and where I'll be. Where *we* will be one day."

"We?"

"I don't know what tomorrow will bring, or the next day." Sam reached behind her neck and flicked the clasp holding her sapphire necklace in place. The necklace she rarely removed in the ten years she'd owned it. "But I know that I want to build something with you." She took a long velvet box from her bedside table and secured the necklace to the hooks, holding it in place. "It may all go wrong, but it may not."

"It won't."

"Neither of us can be sure of that." Sam cocked her head and smiled.

"I can." Luciana folded her arms across her chest.

"While I love your enthusiasm, we can't say that." Sam closed the box in her hand. "One thing I've learned since I met you is that I have to take a chance. I have to open up to the potential life I could have if I stop closing myself off. I don't want to live alone. I don't want to wake up every morning and go through my usual boring work routine."

"What do you want?" Luciana swallowed hard.

"A future. A life. One that doesn't revolve around this apartment or every hour God sends at the office."

"And where do I stand in all of that?" Luciana's throat dried.

"At the front. Right at the front of all of it." Sam rounded the bed and set the velvet box down on top of her clothes. "You've shown me nothing but complete respect from the moment I met you." Taking Luciana's hands, she stepped closer. "I knew there was something about you the moment I met you. I knew I wanted you before you'd even opened your mouth to speak."

"You have a very good poker face."

"I didn't get to where I am without one, baby." Sam leaned in, smiling into a kiss. "Like you, I don't care about the opinions of others, their judgement. What I care about is our happiness. I want that with you, Luciana. Happiness."

Luciana opened her mouth to speak but fell short of any words.

"And I know I'll lie awake worrying about you at work, that's natural, but I also know you're perfectly safe. At least, it's what I tell myself whenever you leave for a shift."

"You know I'll come home to you." Luciana's thumb traced Sam's bottom lip. "You think I'd leave you?"

"I know you wouldn't." Sam chose to block out her wife's death. She'd spent two years playing it over in her mind, and now it was time to put those thoughts to bed. Lucia was gone, but Luciana...she was very much here. Sam couldn't change her past, but she could guide her future. "I worry that this is moving too quickly, but I'm not sure I care anymore."

"Everything happens for a reason..."

"I'm a firm believer in that." Sam nodded in agreement. "It's been what? A month..."

"The most beautiful month of my life," Luciana whispered. "Stop fighting it, Sam. If this is what you want, if it feels good, let it."

"I am."

"Fuck the timescales and what society believes." Luciana took a fistful of Sam's hair and gently tilted her head back. "Because I know exactly how I feel about you. Nobody can take that away from me or tell me it's wrong."

"No." Sam's eyes closed. "No, they can't."

"And if I want to spend my time, my days, falling harder for you...then I will do that." Their lips met fervently. Luciana needed this woman to know exactly how she felt, what she dreamt of. A moan fell from Sam's mouth as their lips parted, and when her eyes opened, Luciana noted the tears welling. "Don't cry, beautiful."

"For once, they're happy tears."

Luciana held Sam close, their bodies slowly swaying. "I wasn't looking to settle down with anyone when you came along," she said. "I was content with fighting fire and meeting beautiful women."

"What changed?"

"Everything." Luciana pressed a kiss to Sam's hair. "When I walked into that tapas bar and saw you, God... I can't explain it."

"Try..." Sam said. "For me, try."

"You know when you get those intense butterflies in the pit of your stomach? I felt them all over my body." Sam tilted her head and watched the smile form on Luciana's mouth. "I watched your every move all night. Just the little things. How you held your wine glass. How you people watched. How sad you were..."

"Keep talking." Sam guided them to the bed and lay down, pulling Luciana down beside her. She curled her body around her girlfriend, nuzzling her face in the crook of her neck. "Please, keep talking."

"When you'd finished that night...when it was time to leave, I'd never felt so disappointed," Luciana said. "I wanted more time with you. To know you. To listen to your voice. God, I just didn't want the night to end."

"But I booked you again. The next night."

"You also ran out on me not even an hour into it..."

"The night I'd fought with Lindsay." Sam nodded. "Remind me to call her in the morning before we leave."

"Is she okay?"

"She's fine. I want her to arrange coming to visit."

"That'll be nice."

"With my parents."

"O-Oh." Luciana's stomach somersaulted. "W-When I'm working?"

"No, baby. Not when you're working." Sam's hand slid beneath Luciana's tank top. "I want you to meet them all."

"Phew."

"Nervous?" Sam sat up on her elbow smirking. "I don't think I've ever seen you nervous."

"I'm about to meet the woman of my dreams parents."

"*I'm* the woman of your dreams?" Sam laughed. "Seriously?"

"Damn right you are." Sam suddenly found herself on her back, with Luciana straddling her hips. "We met when we were supposed to. And everything that came after it...it was meant to happen."

"I beg to differ," Sam said. "Janet. She didn't need to happen."

"Janet was around long before you." Luciana waved off Sam's comment. "She is the least of my concerns."

"Good." Fisting her hand in Luciana's tank top, Sam pulled her girlfriend down against her. "How about we go back to you telling me all about how amazing I am?"

"Gladly," Luciana growled, dipping her head and kissing her way up Sam's stomach. "But first, there is something I need to do."

"What's that?" Sam squealed as her girlfriend nipped at the skin below her breast.

"Touch you." Sam arched up into Luciana's touch. "Taste you." She whimpered as lips enveloped her nipple. "Make you come."

"Oh, God." Sam buried her head into the pillow.

"Sound good to you?" Luciana husked, lost in everything that Sam was.

"Do it!"

The rain outside the window did nothing to ruin Luciana's mood. If anything, it only encouraged her to snuggle up with Sam and wish the hours away. After spending the best part of last night tangled up in one another, they'd somehow managed to pack what they needed for their weekend break at Sam's *other* place. Now, as her girlfriend finished showering, Luciana had the opportunity to think about the things Sam said to her last night. She was shocked when the suggestion of going to Sam's original home came into the conversation, but she felt thankful too. Thankful that her girlfriend would want to take her to a home that meant so much to her, and thankful that Sam thought so much of their relationship. Luciana would admit to feeling, at times, unsure about their future, but Sam had put her mind to rest last night during their pre-sex conversation. It felt good, having Sam lay in her arms and discussing life. It was a positive step hearing Sam talk about what she wanted in the future. Wants that included Luciana. She fully understood though. If the tables were turned, Luciana would feel sceptical about a younger woman wanting a relationship with her. It wasn't necessarily odd these days, but it still didn't happen as often as it should.

Luciana, in this moment, had never felt more certain about the outcome of her relationship. Of course it would be hard at times. Of course people would have comments to make and opinions they felt mattered, but above all that... Luciana just wanted a happy life with Sam. What that life included exactly, neither of them knew, but as each day began, she felt a little more of Sam's insecurity slip away. With every touch, she felt Sam relax into this exactly how she knew she should. Today would be interesting for them both, but Luciana was fully prepared. Whether she had to take a step back and allow Sam to process being in her old home, or whether Sam chose to take her mind off it in other ways, Luciana was ready and willing to be whatever her girlfriend needed. A shoulder. A lover. A friend. So long as Sam continued to talk about it, they couldn't go wrong.

"Okay, I think I have everything we need."

"Great." Luciana turned in the slouch chair to find Sam dressed comfortably. Jeans and pumps were a change to her usual attire, but Luciana was definitely feeling it. "Looking beautiful, as ever."

"Stop." Sam blushed, shaking her head. "Another coffee before we head off?"

"Perfect."

Luciana watched Sam move around the kitchen, her skinny jeans moulding to her slender body. While Sam may be significantly older than her, Luciana was in awe of how in shape she was. It didn't matter to her either way, but damn...her girlfriend looked like a masterpiece this morning.

"For you." Sam handed a coffee over. "Can I join you there or is that now *your* seat?"

"Depends." Luciana narrowed her eyes. "In order to sit in this seat, a kiss from a beautiful woman is required."

"Well then, I guess I should take the couch." Sam shrugged, smirking. "Enjoy."

"Hey!" Luciana suddenly gripped her wrist, careful of the coffee in her other hand. "In my lap, NOW!"

"Yes, sweetheart." Sam smiled sarcastically as she carefully climbed into her girlfriend's lap. "Are you looking forward to today?"

"Honestly, yes."

"Me too."

"You know, if at any point it becomes too much for you...just say."

"Planning to take my mind off it?" Sam's eyebrow rose, her flirtatious nature beginning to come through more as the days passed. "Anything in particular you can think of?"

"I need to see what I have to work with first." Luciana held up a hand, sipping her coffee. "You know, the layout and furniture."

"Mm." Sam's eyes crinkled at the corners as her smile beamed. "I'll leave that to you."

Though it would be a sad day for her girlfriend, Luciana didn't want to dwell on that fact too much. If she could keep Sam's mind occupied before they arrived, she was less likely to back out of their visit as they approached the house. "You really have a fire pit?"

"I do."

"Amazing."

"Really?" Sam scoffed. "It's just a pit."

"Which makes fire." Luciana wiggled her eyebrows. "You know I love me some fire."

"I wish you wouldn't joke like that." Sam swatted her girlfriend's shoulder. "It's not funny."

"Sorry, babe."

"Don't be. I'm joking." A light knock on the door pulled Sam from her conversation, her brow furrowed when she looked at the clock. "Who the hell is that?"

"Um…" Luciana pressed her index finger to her temple and closed her eyes. "Give me a moment."

Sam stared.

"Nope. Can't see through the door."

"You're a real joker this morning, aren't you?" Sam rolled her eyes playfully. "Maybe if we're quiet, they'll go away."

"Maybe if you kiss me, I won't care who it is." Luciana gripped Sam's jaw gently and brought her into a kiss. "Mm, perfect."

Before they had time to pull apart completely, the sound of a key in the lock sent Sam's heart rate through the roof. "Um…" The door opened, and in walked her mother. "Mum?"

"Sam, good morning." Susan's eyes landed on Sam before switching to Luciana. "And you are?"

"Oh, uh…" Luciana set her coffee cup down and lifted Sam out of her lap. "Mrs…"

"Priestly," Susan said, her eyes landing on her daughter. "What's going on, Sam?"

"Pretty self-explanatory, Mum." Sam laughed. "This is Luciana. My girlfriend. Coffee?"

"Why am I only just hearing about this?" Susan's eyes darted between them both. "How long has this been going on?"

"Babe, did you want me to go and busy myself?" Luciana lowered her voice as Sam approached her. "I don't mind."

"Oh, no. You're staying here." Sam gripped her hand. "Mum, Luciana. Luciana, my mum, Susan."

"Lovely to meet you." Luciana stepped forward and held out her hand. "Wonderful daughter." She threw her thumb over her shoulder, her nerves settling in too quickly for her liking. "Can we get you some coffee?"

"We?" Susan's eyebrows rose as she dismissed the hand being offered to her. "We, Sam?"

"Yes, we." Sam furrowed her brow. "What the hell is wrong with you, Mum?"

"Can I speak to you for a moment?" Susan disappeared into Sam's bedroom. "Sam? Now!"

"Mum, that was really rude." Sam closed her bedroom door. "Why are you behaving like this?"

"This is why you've been avoiding me?" Susan scoffed. "Because you have a child in your home?"

"Excuse me?"

"She must be what? Eighteen?"

"Twenty-five, actually." Sam crossed her arms, her anger rising. "And how dare you! I'm not sure what the hell is going on, but how dare you come here and accuse me of such a thing!"

"She's virtually a child compared to you!"

"Get out!" Sam swung the door open. "I'm not listening to this. You wonder why I don't call. Why I don't visit. This is the reason."

"Sam, love." Susan sighed. "Just give me a moment."

"No, I'm not standing here listening to you bash my relationship." Sam threw her hands up. "I can't win with you. One minute you tell me I'm lonely, the next you accuse me of being a predator."

"Don't you think she's a little young for you, love?" Susan smiled softly. "I'm sure she's a lovely girl, but we both know why she's here, don't we?"

"I know why she's here, yes. I'm not sure *you* even know what day it is."

"Close the door, Samantha."

"This is ridiculous." Sam slammed the door shut, startling her mum. "There is nothing you can say to me which will forgive what you've just said."

"Lindsay is worried about you."

"Lindsay?" Sam deadpanned.

"She came to me last night. Worried she hadn't seen you in over two weeks. You don't answer her calls. You arrange to meet her and don't show. What does this woman have on you, Samantha?"

"What woman?" Sam asked, confused. It was one thing for her mum to react how she did, but to know this was Lindsay's doing... it hurt.

"The woman in your living room!"

"You've got to be kidding me." Sam burst into a fit of laughter. "She doesn't have *anything* on me."

"Then you will ask her to leave and come home with me."

"And you really have lost your mind. I'm thirty-seven, Mum. You don't really have the option of telling me what to do. Back off!"

"If my daughter is being hurt, emotionally or physically, I have every right!"

Sam froze. Did her mum and sister honestly believe Luciana was here, hurting her? Surely not. Lindsay knew Luciana. Lindsay encouraged this to happen. Sam didn't understand how it had come to this, but she wanted answers from her sister, and she wanted them now.

"Where is she? At home?"

"She's downstairs," Susan said. "The poor girl is terrified to come up here."

She's doing drugs again. She has to be.

"Go and get her," Sam demanded. "I want her here now!"

"No, love. Ask your friend to leave and we will all discuss this like a family. Calmly."

"Because you came in here calmly before, didn't you?"

"I'm sorry, Samantha." Her mum approached her. "But I won't watch someone hurt you. I can't. Lucia would never forgive me."

"Nobody is hurting me and in case you forgot, Lucia is dead." Sam dropped down onto the edge of her bed, her head falling to her hands. "I don't believe this. I really don't."

"I know, love. Some people only want one thing, though." Sam's eyes found her mum's. As she studied them, she realised her mum really did believe that something was wrong here. In her home. With the woman she was falling in love with. "Should I ask her to leave myself?"

"No, Mum." Sam smiled weakly. "No, I don't want you to do anything."

Sam stood up and calmed herself. There was no use being angry with anyone. Lindsay had some explaining to do, but she knew they were only worried about her. Completely unnecessary, and she would make sure they knew that, but she loved her family for who they were. Most of the time. Rather than arguing with her mother, Sam chose to remain silent. As she left her bedroom, her heart settled knowing Luciana would be waiting for her. Also probably worried, but still waiting for her.

When Sam reached the open space, she sighed. Luciana was nowhere to be seen, or her bag which had sat by the door since last night. *Great. She's gone.* Sam turned around to find her mum behind her, a stone look on her face.

"I think you should leave, Mum." As she ran her fingers through her hair, Sam bit back a sob. "I have things to do."

"Where is your friend?"

"She wasn't my friend." Sam lowered her eyes. "She was my girlfriend."

"Well, whatever she was...she's not here."

"And I have you to thank for that." Sam moved into the

kitchen and made a fresh coffee for herself. "Tell Lindsay I'm fine. It was nice seeing you. Bye, Mum."

"Samantha…"

"Not now, yeah?"

"Where are you going?" Susan asked when her eyes landed on the packed hold-all. "Anywhere nice?"

"I'm not going anywhere."

"But your bags…"

"I was going home." Sam's eyes fluttered closed but a tear managed to escape. "With Luciana. She was helping me through today."

"H-Home?"

"That's what I said." Sam smiled. "Seems those plans are out the window."

"Then I'll come with you."

"You don't get it, do you? I don't *want* you to go with me. Or Lindsay. Or Dad. I don't want anyone to go with me. I was perfectly happy doing this with Luciana, but you just couldn't help yourself, could you? You had to come here saying those things you did!"

"Sam, she's too young."

"No, I'll tell you what she is." Sam dropped the spoon in her hand and approached her mum. "She's the woman I'm falling in love with, Mum. She's the only one I've so much as looked at since Lucia. *She's* the one I was prepared to plan a future with."

"I'm sorry…"

"Me too." Sam brushed a tear from her jawline. "Because now you've just fucked that chance for me."

"Watch your language," Susan admonished.

"Get out of my home!"

"Babe?" Sam's front door opened. "You almost ready?"

"I, uh…" Sam's forehead creased. "I thought you'd left."

"I put my bag in your car and ran to the shop for today's crossword. Thought we could do it together on the way."

"You did?" Sam's lips curled. "Come here." She held out her hand. "Thank you." She cupped Luciana's face, their lips colliding. "I thought you'd left. I just...thank you."

"I told you I wasn't going anywhere." Their foreheads pressed together. "I found someone downstairs..."

"Don't say my sister." Sam clenched her jaw.

"Sam..." Lindsay cleared her throat. "Can we talk?"

"No, we can't." Sam spun around. "What the hell did you think was going on here? How could you send Mum here?"

"I thought something was wrong. Every time I called, you dismissed me. When you were supposed to meet me, you'd cancel. Why? You never cancel our plans."

"I've just been busy, Linds." Sam sighed. "It wasn't my intention to cut you off, but I've been busy."

"You're always busy, but you've never not made time for me."

"It was time to make time for myself." Sam stood hand in hand with Luciana. "You know I'm always here for you, but what about me? You kept telling me to be happy. To find someone. And I have."

"I know." Lindsay smiled weakly, dropping her gaze. "Luciana said you're going home..."

"I am." Sam nodded, studying her sister's face. "And I *was* going to call you before I left so we could arrange for you all to visit. That's when I was going to introduce everyone to this one here." Sam cocked her head at Luciana. "I guess that won't be happening now. Not since some people can't accept it—"

"Give me time, love," Susan cut in. "That's all I need."

"You do what you need to do. All of you." Sam took her keys from the kitchen counter. "But me? I have plans and I'd like to get them going." She dragged Luciana away from the kitchen and towards the door. "Do we have everything?"

"I think so." Luciana nodded, unsure as to what had just transpired here. She glanced around before taking the remaining bags from the floor and lowered her voice. "Is everything okay?"

"Everything is perfect." Sam leaned in. "I really need to get out of here."

They both stepped out into the hallway and Luciana gripped Sam's hand. She needed reassurance that everything would be okay, but she wasn't sure she would like the answer. "Your mum doesn't like me, does she?"

"What?" Sam laughed. "Of course she does."

"You don't have to lie to me, babe. I'd rather you were just honest with me."

"She can't *not* like you. She doesn't know you…"

"She's not happy, I know that much." Luciana's shoulders slumped. "What does she think was going on here?"

"Honestly, I don't know," Sam said. "But we have plans and I don't want to hang around here a minute longer…"

"Don't you think we should go back inside and maybe clear the air?"

"If that's what you want to do…" Sam's arms slid around Luciana's waist as she brought her lips up to her ear. "But I can think of a million and one things that are so much more fun."

"Yeah, me too." Luciana grinned. "Let's go."

CHAPTER TWENTY

Luciana's breathing slowed as Sam drove up a graveled path surrounded by trees and thick bushes. She couldn't see any buildings yet, but the calmness and serenity out here were impressive. It left her with one question: why did Sam ever leave her original home? Luciana knew it had been due to the death of her wife, but this location appealed to her and how she imagined she would cope with such heartbreak. They were two very different people, that was clear from the outset, so she relaxed her mind and sat back, desperately praying she would soon see the masterpiece Sam had once created.

"So, a little about this house..."

"I'm listening." Luciana sat up in her seat.

"We built it with the environment in mind. It sits on a private lake, the entire building is made from sustainable, natural materials."

"Impressive."

"When I thought about building something of my own, it was always what came to mind. It's a bungalow style, but very deceiving. It doesn't look as big as it is from the outside, but it was my sanctuary. God, I loved being here."

"You left..."

"I had to." Sam gripped the wheel of her Range Rover. "I felt like I had no other choice."

"That's fair enough." Luciana nodded. "Thank you for bringing me here. I can't wait to see it."

"I want you to feel comfortable here. Relaxed. It's the reason this place exists, and you'll see why when we get there."

"When *will* we get there?" Luciana shifted in her seat. "I know this is an emotional day for you, but I'm too excited to wait much longer."

"I don't think it'll be as emotional as I once thought it would be."

"Why?"

"Because I have you here with me." Sam reached her hand over, taking Luciana's. "Knowing that you'll be here with me... when you can be, it doesn't seem so daunting."

"Oh God." Luciana squeezed Sam's hand. "Is that it through the trees?"

"That's the place." Sam blew out a deep breath, focusing her eyes on the pathway. "Just another minute and you'll be inside."

"Shit." Luciana's breath caught in her throat. "Holy..."

Luciana had no words. Nothing. Sitting on a lagoon-style body of water, Sam's home was surrounded by timber slat panelling and floor-to-ceiling panoramic windows. Elevated on a docking platform, the decked area led down to the edge of the water, as calm and still as it could possibly be. Luciana had been impressed with Sam's city apartment, but it was a hovel compared to the beauty towering over them as the car came to a stop.

"Welcome to my home," Sam said, her voice barely above a whisper. "Enjoy it. Go and take a look. Make yourself at home."

Luciana climbed from the car, her mouth still hanging open from moments ago when they pulled off the gravel path. Sam sat quietly, a small smile on her face. Luciana motioned through the window for Sam to join her, but she declined, simply waving

Luciana away. She knew Sam was processing being here, so she wouldn't push. She wouldn't beg her to let her inside her home until she was ready for that moment herself. This was a private space and one that Sam shared with her wife; every memory she had here would likely be from before that devastating day when Lucia's death was confirmed.

She took the few steps onto the decking, peering through the panoramic windows at the interior design of the place. Beauty, absolute beauty. While she wanted to lounge around here for the rest of her life with Sam, Luciana wasn't sure she was worthy of it. This home had to be worth an absolute fortune, and the thought of touching anything terrified her.

"So, what do you think?" Sam appeared behind her girlfriend, her hands shaky. "Did you want me to let you inside?"

"Not until you're ready to go inside too." Luciana turned to face Sam. "This is your home. Not a toy for me to play with."

"I appreciate that, but I'm not sure when I'll be able to go inside." Sam slid her key into the lock and pushed the door open. "You go ahead. I'll sit out here a while."

"Okay." Luciana nodded as she watched Sam turn around and walk away. *I can't do this without her.* She shook her head and gave Sam a moment to herself, silently watching on. She took a seat at a step on the decking and brought her knees up to her chest. Luciana's heart broke for her girlfriend, but she wasn't sure Sam wanted her right now. This was a moment when she was truly lost. She watched Sam place her forehead against her knees, her shoulders shaking. *I should go to her,* Luciana warred with herself. *No, I should let her be.* She slowly moved closer to Sam, listening to the sobs carried through the light breeze around them. As she quietly took a seat beside Sam, she settled a hand on her shoulder and remained silent.

Sam leaned into her girlfriend, thankful that she wasn't alone. She hadn't known what to expect when she arrived here, but the emotion was too overwhelming. The memories hit her like a tonne of bricks. Here, she could see Lucia. She could feel her. She knew when she walked inside her home, she would likely still smell her, too. As much as Sam missed those moments, she'd spent a long time forgetting them. Lucia's perfume, her shampoo. She had to block them from her mind a while back or she'd have gone insane.

"You know, we can always go back," Luciana whispered, pressing a kiss to Sam's temple. "We don't have to do this right now."

"No." Sam smiled as she lifted her head and wiped the tears away. "No, I want to do this with you now."

"Okay." Luciana nodded. "Well, there's no rush. We have all day."

Sam squared her shoulders and released a calming breath.

"Come on." She stood up and pulled Luciana to her feet. "It's now or never."

"Babe..."

Sam was pulled back. "Yeah?"

"Are you sure you can do this?" Luciana asked. "You're one of the strongest people I know, but you don't have to prove anything by coming back here. Especially not to me."

"I know." Sam kissed her girlfriend softly. "I'm not trying to prove anything. I'm just trying to come home."

"Then lead the way."

With their hands laced tightly together, Sam took a few determined steps and reached her front door. The smell of vanilla wafted through the open space as she stepped inside the entrance hall, her spiral staircase standing directly in front of her.

"Wow, that's impressive." Luciana looked up at it, open-mouthed. "You really have one hell of a talent."

"I wouldn't usually take all the credit for something, but yeah..." Sam nodded. "This was all me."

"This is the complete opposite of your apartment."

"*The* apartment." Sam held up a finger. "I may own it, but it doesn't feel like mine."

"What will you do with it?"

"I'd thought about giving it to Lindsay, but after this morning... I'm not sure she deserves anything from me ever again. I bailed her out once and this is how she behaves."

"Bailed her out?"

"That's a conversation for another day." Sam moved through the lower level of her home, inspecting every inch of it. Her finger trailed along the marble worktops in the huge kitchen, satisfied that minimal dust was evident. "It's good to see my cleaner has kept on top of this place."

"You have a cleaner?"

"Well, no." Sam turned around to find Luciana standing in the middle of the entrance and looking as though she was unable to move. "I hired someone to take care of this place for me." Sam frowned. "Is there a particular reason why you're still standing over there?"

"Scared to touch anything." Luciana shoved her hands in the pockets of her jeans. "I'm good here."

"Don't be ridiculous." Sam laughed from deep within her belly. "Come here and stop being so weird."

"I'm not." Luciana stalked towards her. "This is just a completely different side to you I didn't expect to see."

"You can have any side you want." Sam winked. "You just let me know which you prefer."

Luciana cleared her throat. "Oh, I think we both know which side I prefer..."

"Okay, picture this." Sam waved her hand in front of her dramatically. "You lounging around here when you have a day off. Me coming home from the office."

"I'm listening." Luciana grinned.

"You in nothing but a T-shirt and boxers...me in a suit."

"And I think I just died." Luciana swallowed hard. "Shit. How do you do that?"

"Do what?" Sam stepped closer to her girlfriend, knowing full well that she was teasing.

"Be all professional and explaining this magnificent home... and then BAM! You're this gorgeous, extremely hot woman that I want to take here and now?"

"Guess my mind just works in funny ways."

"Well, I love your mind... amongst other things." Luciana took Sam's bottom lip between her teeth. "And as much as I love where this is probably going, I want to see more of this place."

"Follow me..."

Luciana relaxed back in an oversized porch chair, her legs dangling over the edge. There wasn't a sound around her, just the light humming from Sam coming from the kitchen, the bi-folding doors wide open and creating a feel of the house being at one with nature. She may love the buzz and the business of the city, but here? In the middle of nowhere...she could definitely get used to it. Hell, she *was* used to it. Sam had cooked an amazing dinner for them, but Luciana was struggling with the right words to thank her. Not only for dinner, but for opening her eyes to such a beautiful tranquil place.

"Can I get you another glass of wine?" Sam asked, her voice low and relaxed.

"I'd love another." Luciana reached forward and took her empty glass from the table. "Are you going to join me out here?"

"Oh, yes." Sam smiled. "Give me two minutes and I'm all yours."

"Perfect." Luciana's eyes followed Sam back into the kitchen, her girlfriend visibly relaxed as the night wore on. She had worried that this would be an overly emotional visit for Sam, but other than her moment when they first arrived, Sam looked as though she was thrilled to be back in her home.

"So, what did you think of dinner?"

"Beautiful." Luciana shifted, allowing Sam some space to join her on the chair. "We didn't bring all this stuff with us, though."

"The woman I have keeping a check on this place went out and got some things in for us."

"You had this planned?"

"Only from the moment you agreed to come here with me." Sam looked out over the lake in front of them. "I didn't think you would agree, to be honest."

"Hey!" Luciana's hand found Sam's. "I'd go anywhere with you."

"I'm beginning to realise that." Sam side-glanced at Luciana. "You like it here, don't you?"

"Love it."

"Maybe one day, it could become permanent." Sam chewed her bottom lip, studying Luciana's features. She wanted nothing more than to call this place home for both of them, but she knew it wasn't that simple. Luciana had a life back in the city, and a family who didn't know Sam even existed. While it didn't seem to be a huge obstacle, Sam couldn't be sure how Luciana's parents would react to their dating. She never thought her mum would be so against it, so it was perfectly possible that the rest of their friends and family would be hostile, too.

"I'm not sure I ever want to leave..."

"This place does that to you." Sam sighed. "I've enjoyed it here so much this evening that I'm wondering how I ever left."

"It was a different time for you." Luciana squeezed her hand. "Different circumstances."

"Yes, it was."

"Besides, had you not moved to the city...we may never have met."

"You don't think?"

"Well, I don't think there would have been much call for an escort up here with you." Luciana laughed. "I mean, I'm sure you'd have been content with your life as it was. You wouldn't have dreamt of booking an escort."

"Do you miss it?" Sam asked. "Escorting?"

"Not even slightly." There wasn't a hint of hesitation in Luciana's voice. "I haven't thought about it once."

"Really? You just let it go like that?"

"I guess I found what I'd been looking for."

Sam rested her head on Luciana's shoulder and sighed. "I didn't see myself back here."

"I'm glad you chose to come back. This home is beautiful, Sam."

"I did miss it," Sam admitted, a light breeze whipping around them. "But once I'd got over the initial leaving, I tried not to think about it. You know, what I'd left behind."

Luciana pulled a blanket from the back of the slouch chair and draped it over them both. "I think you're more relaxed here," Luciana said. "You've smiled more since being here than the entire time I've known you."

"It's where I'm supposed to be." Sam curled up beside her girlfriend, the clear star-filled sky above them catching her attention. "Even if only for a view like this."

"There's definitely something about this place." Luciana followed Sam's line of sight. "And being here with you only makes it all the more special."

"I was going to sell it."

"What?" Luciana's head shot around. "This place?"

"At one time, yes." Sam offered a small smile. "Foolish I know, but I saw sense before it was too late."

"Things were really bad for you, weren't they?"

"I'm not sure I've ever felt so broken." Sam propped her head in her hand. "I didn't know what to do each morning when I woke up. I'd sit there at the island with breakfast in front of me, and I'd just stare at it."

"I can't imagine what you went through."

"Then I got angry." Sam scoffed. "At Lucia. At myself. Basically, at anyone who dared to even look at me."

"Anger is natural, babe."

"How natural?" Sam arched an eyebrow. "We once had an old wooden canoe in that lake. It was more just for decoration but worked perfectly fine." Sam pointed her wine glass towards the still water. "I set fire to it and now it's at the bottom."

"Y-You set fire to it?" Luciana's eyes widened. "You're not serious."

"Doused it in petrol and lit the fucker." Sam drained her wine glass. "I was sick to death of looking at it."

"You could've just got rid of it."

"I did." Sam smiled. "With fire."

"Okay, remind me never to get on the wrong side of you." Luciana smirked.

"You're the one who has kept me sane," Sam said. She may not have been going through a bad time like she once was, but Luciana had really shown her what she was missing. Without knowing it, either of them, Sam's mindset had dramatically improved.

"I wish I could have been there for you." Luciana finished her wine and climbed from the seat, tucking the blanket around Sam. "Just as a friend."

"I was a monster."

"Still, the thought of you being here alone and hurting, I don't like it."

"I survived, baby." Sam curled her finger, beckoning Luciana to come closer. "I made it and I'm so glad that I did."

"Me too." Their lips met softly, a slow, building passion between them. "This is just the beginning and the thought of not having you in my life terrifies me."

"I'm not going anywhere if you're not," Sam whispered against soft lips. "I'm enjoying this too much to even think about walking away."

"Don't ever walk away." Luciana's thumb brushed Sam's

cheek. "I'm getting more wine and then we're sitting out here until the birds are singing."

"I thought you weren't a wine on the terrace kinda person?" Sam quirked an eyebrow.

"Seems you just bring it out of me." Luciana leaned down behind Sam, kissing her head. "Don't move."

Sam sighed, content with her evening so far. "Don't plan to."

Sam's eyes bored into the flames dancing in the fire pit, warming her as the air around them cooled. Time had passed by quicker than she would have liked, but their evening showed no signs of ending just yet. Luciana lay beside her on the plush outdoor swing bed, her eyes focused on the stars above them. This silence was just what they both needed given the busy schedule they'd faced in the last month. Sam's only regret tonight was that she hadn't brought her girlfriend here sooner. When Janet was around, this could have been the ideal place to recuperate. To forget the world around them existed. To focus fully on one another.

As the night wore on, Sam found herself thinking less about her past here, only good memories forming as Luciana lay in a pair of shorts and a baggy hoodie. Comfort. Contentment. An element of love. That's exactly what Sam felt in her old home. Her idea of returning here and falling apart had all but faded, the woman beside her the reason for that. Sam didn't need to dwell on what was. Instead, she chose to focus on what she could control. Her life *now*. The sense of love she felt whenever Luciana's arms enveloped her, holding her securely. Nothing and nobody could take that feeling away from her, and she sure as hell wouldn't be the one to ruin what was blossoming. She'd thought about their relationship running away with itself too quickly, but like Luciana, she truly didn't care. Whatever happened, *however* it happened, Sam was ready to take the full force of it head-on. Why hold back when everything in her life felt ideal? Beautiful. Something special.

Her hand trailed Luciana's stomach beneath her hoodie. "I could lie with you like this forever."

"Me too, babe." Luciana turned her head, capturing Sam's lips. "We should just quit our jobs and stay here."

"Mm, that sounds ideal." Sam held Luciana closer. "But we still have the small matter of introductions."

"Introductions?"

"Well, you've already met my mother." Sam rolled her eyes. "But what about yours?"

"Oh, they're easy."

"Have you told them about me?"

"Maybe." Luciana turned on her side, taking in Sam's features as the fire flickered and illuminated her deep, dark eyes. "Would you be bothered if I had?"

"Not at all."

"I may have mentioned it to my mum when I went home a couple of weeks ago."

"And what exactly did you mention?" Sam asked, her eyes narrowed. "Fill me in."

"I just told her I was dating." Luciana tucked Sam's hair behind her ear. "A gorgeous woman."

"Who is a lot older than you?"

"Well, I didn't mention that part." Luciana laughed. "You know, since it's irrelevant."

"Mm, tell that to my mother." Sam scoffed. "Sorry she was so off with you this morning. I didn't expect her to react like that at all."

"She's your mum. She's bound to be worried about you."

"That doesn't matter. She was rude to you." Sam lowered her eyes. "She'll come around, I know she will."

"She should." Luciana nodded, not overly concerned about Sam's parents. "Because she's pretty much stuck with me."

"Is that so?" Sam's eyes darkened, her fingertips trailing Luciana's skin.

"Mmhmm."

"Was she always supportive of you? Your mum?"

"Yeah, they knew before I'd even come out." Luciana delighted in the sensation Sam was creating through her body. Every touch lit up her skin. "Claimed they knew before I did and all the usual stuff."

"I don't think I actually ever came out. I just introduced a girlfriend to Mum once and that was that." Sam laughed. "I don't think she cared either way, to be honest."

"We're lucky really..."

"We are," Sam agreed, her eyes closing momentarily. "*I'm* lucky."

"How so?"

"I'm here with you. Just us. It's perfect."

"I've had relationships in the past. One or two," Luciana said. "I've had the time of my life with some of them, but you..." She studied Sam's face, taking in her every feature. "I've never felt how I feel when I'm with you."

"No?" A smile played at the corners of Sam's mouth.

"Not like this. Not even close." Luciana's voice wavered. "Do you believe that everybody has someone out there waiting for them?"

"I do."

"I think I've found my someone." Luciana's eyes welled with tears. "And I know you've had your someone, but maybe there is more than one person out there for us."

"Forget about my past, Luciana." Sam shifted closer, her voice low. "I don't want you to *ever* feel second best."

"No, I don't."

"Still, I want you to do this the way I am."

"And how's that?" Luciana's brows drew together.

"New. Fresh. No past included," Sam said. "The life I had with my wife was what I wanted, it was beautiful. But you and her, you're different people. Different times."

"Yeah..."

"I went about this all completely the wrong way, I'm aware of that, but when I tell you that I want you in my life... I mean it. I'm sure about you, okay?"

"I know you are." Luciana's eyes shifted from Sam's to her lips. "I guess I just hope that one day I can be your everything."

"And what makes you think that *one day* that will happen?"

"I mean, it's okay if you never feel that way about me—"

"If I already feel that way now..."

"Don't say something you don't mean, Sam." Luciana looked pointedly at her girlfriend. "I'm a big girl; I can take your honesty."

"That *was* my honesty." Sam propped herself up on her elbow. "You've brought so much to my life, so much more than I thought anyone could give me."

"Okay." Luciana rolled her eyes playfully. "You're going to make me cry if you carry on."

"So cry." Sam shrugged. "Because you better believe that the worry and the apprehension stop now. From me. From you. Tonight has been fucking beautiful with you."

"God, you're killing me."

"Now, move your arse..." Sam dragged her girlfriend up to her feet. "Because this place needs christening and I'm done waiting."

"Did I ever tell you how much I love this demanding side?"

"Tell me when your legs are wrapped around my head!" Sam pulled Luciana's body against her, swaying as they collided. "Upstairs, now!"

CHAPTER TWENTY-ONE

Silence. Peace. A sense of belonging. Luciana, in this moment, felt exactly that. The sun beat down on her face, aviator sunglasses covering her eyes. Sam milled about somewhere inside, preparing lunch, but she found herself unable to move. Luciana couldn't bring herself to head inside, not when the view she was offered was so ideal for a Saturday morning. Sam hadn't said much since they woke up, but Luciana assumed she was processing being here. It was one thing to come back to your old home, but to wake the following morning in a bed you once shared with your wife? It had to sting. It had to bring back a mountain of memories, and some not necessarily good ones.

She glanced back. Sam was preparing a salad, her white tank top covering her body. Luciana struggled to remain composed around her girlfriend regardless of her choice of dress, but something about a relaxed and comfortable Sam made her smile harder. Longer. Wider. Returning to the view of the lake in front of her, Luciana's heart fluttered. Not for a reason in particular, but it fluttered, and she felt it intensely. This view and the silence that came with it allowed her to think. To breathe. To just be. Her life was always so fast-paced that she hadn't ever truly stopped and thought about where she was headed. Now that she had the opportunity to do that, it was overwhelming. It gave her a reason to sit and evaluate everything she'd been through...and everything she could potentially have. Luciana didn't make a habit of fucking up in life, and she knew she had to continue that if she had any hopes of truly keeping hold of Sam. It's all she wanted. As she sat here, her feet tucked away underneath her on the swing bed, it was all she saw in her future. Take away the worries, the past, their age...and life was as close to perfect as it could ever be.

Nothing about this suggested pressure or uncertainty. The only thing Luciana felt this morning was happiness. Complete, earth-shattering happiness. Did Sam feel the same? She didn't know. Life had been incredibly hard for her girlfriend in recent years, but Luciana hoped that Sam felt just an ounce of what she did. It didn't matter how long it took for this to all fall into place; she wasn't going anywhere.

The sound of tyres on gravel caused her to look away from the lake, her forehead creasing. "Um, babe?"

"Yeah?" Sam called back, tossing the salad in a homemade vinaigrette. "Everything okay?"

"Someone's here to see you."

"Unlikely. Nobody knows I'm here."

"Well, somebody does." Luciana stood up and moved to the edge of the decking. "Red Volvo? Ring any bells?"

"Yeah." Sam sighed, wiping her hands on a towel. "It's the family."

"Your parents?" Luciana's eyes widened. "Shit! I'm not dressed for meeting parents."

"I wouldn't worry." Sam appeared behind her girlfriend, placing her hand on the small of her back. "They show up unannounced. They'll get what they're given."

"Still..." Luciana backed up. "I should change."

"You look beautiful." Sam tugged her wrist, pulling their

bodies closer together. "And you've caught the sun." Their lips met, softly. "Mm, I could do this all day."

"Well, you'd better remove that thought." Luciana cleared her throat. "Your mum looks like she's about to strangle me."

"Are you ready for this?" Sam asked. "For whatever may happen?"

"Will I still have you at the end of it?"

Sam nodded, her lips upturned. "You know you will."

"Then I'm ready." Luciana pushed out her chest, laughing. "Hit me with 'em."

"Sam, love!" Susan waved as she took the steps to the decking. "We thought we'd find you here."

"Yeah. Since I told you I'd be here," Sam mumbled, rolling her eyes. "Hi, Mum."

"Sam, it's about time you came home." Sam's dad, Bill, cradled a bouquet of flowers. "It's good to see you, love."

"You too, Dad." Sam pulled her father into an embrace. "And you, Linds."

"Hi." Lindsay held back, her hands shoved in the pockets of her jeans. "Happy birthday."

What? Luciana's heart sunk. *How could Sam keep this from me?* "Um, come again?" She faced her girlfriend fully, her eyebrow raised. "It's your birthday?"

"It is." Sam nodded. "And it's not a big deal. I don't celebrate."

"Sure you do." Bill approached his daughter, pushing the flowers towards her. "Happy birthday, love."

"Thanks, Dad." Sam smiled sheepishly at Luciana. "Dad, this is my girlfriend, Luciana. Luciana, this is my dad, Bill."

"Lovely to meet you." Bill held out his hand. "Susan tells me you're the one who encouraged our Sam to come home..."

"Oh, I don't know about that." Luciana lowered her eyes as she took Sam's father's hand. "But I'm happy she chose to come back."

"You're doing something right." He winked. "She's not been here in years."

"I believe so." Luciana wore a crooked smile, still reeling that Sam had chosen to hide the fact it was her birthday. She didn't have a thing here. Not a card or a gift. Nothing. Now, she felt like a shitty girlfriend. "Hi, Susan." Luciana smiled. "Lindsay."

"Hi," they both said in unison, Susan a little less enthusiastic.

"Can you excuse me a minute?" she asked Sam. "I need to use the bathroom."

"Of course." Sam leaned in, kissing Luciana's cheek. She suspected her girlfriend was unimpressed by the news she had just received, but Sam had no intentions of celebrating her birthday. It wasn't important. "Are you okay?"

"Fucking great," Luciana muttered under her breath. "Won't be long."

Sam watched as her girlfriend's shoulders slumped, feeling marginally cruel for not disclosing this day to her. It hadn't been intentional, but all the days rolled into one as far as Sam was concerned. Her only hope was that Luciana wouldn't worry about it all day. She had a heart of gold but being here was good enough. In Sam's eyes, being in her life was the greatest gift she could ever receive.

"How is it being back?" Susan asked, catching her daughter's attention.

"Great, yeah." Sam's fingers trailed her hair as she turned around and went inside. "Can I make anyone coffee?"

"I'd love one," Bill said, propping himself up against the kitchen counter. "It's great seeing you here, Sam. Isn't it, Sue?"

"Yes, it is." Susan's smile widened as she approached Sam. "About yesterday... I'm sorry."

"I don't want to discuss it right now, Mum. Maybe later, yeah?"

"If that's what you want, okay."

"I just want everyone to be okay with this." Sam placed the

bouquet down at the side of the sink and braced herself against the unit. "I don't want her to feel out of place here, so if that's what you've come here to do, I'd rather not hear it."

"That's not why we're here." Susan shook her head.

"What's going on?" Bill asked. "What have you said, Sue?"

"Nothing, Dad." Sam turned around, smiling. "Wires just got crossed, is all." Sam's eyes found her mother's. "Isn't that right?"

"Perfectly right," Susan agreed. "Why don't I make that coffee while you check on your girlfriend? I think she's a little angry with you."

"Yeah, I have a feeling you could be right." Sam excused herself from the room and took the staircase. She found Luciana perched on the end of the bed, her phone in her hands. "Baby?"

"I don't know what's available around here." Her shoulders sagged. "No florists. Nothing like that."

"For what?"

"A shitty gift which will be seen as an afterthought." Luciana scoffed. "Why didn't you tell me?"

"Because it's not important."

"It is to me." Luciana's brows drew together. "These things matter to *me*."

"I'm sorry." Sam crouched down, taking her girlfriend's hand. "I am, I'm sorry."

"It's a bit late now."

"Having you here...this time we've spent alone...is more than I could have asked for this weekend." Sam cupped her face, stroking her thumb across Luciana's bottom lip. "I don't need gifts to know that you care. I just need you."

"This really isn't okay." Luciana closed her eyes, a tear slipping from them. "Not by any stretch."

"But?"

"Your parents and Lindsay are downstairs so we should go back down."

Luciana stood out on the decking at the edge of the water. Sam's parent's had been at the house for the last few hours, her girlfriend relaxing as time wore on. Susan hadn't made any remarks about their relationship, but Luciana had kept her distance nonetheless. Bill seemed like a great man, and Sam was evidently closer and more at ease with him. She'd caught their private jokes, his eyes mirroring those of his daughters. Those dark, deep brown depths that Luciana often found herself lost in.

"Mind if I join you?" a quiet voice asked.

"Of course not." Luciana glanced over her shoulder to find Lindsay shifting uncomfortably.

"You seem quiet."

"Hard to be anything else here."

"Beautiful, isn't it?" Lindsay sighed. "I just wish Sam wasn't mad at me."

"She's okay," Luciana said, reassuring Sam's sister.

"No, she's not." Lindsay shook her head. "When she came home, I was supposed to be the one here for her. I was supposed to be proud of her."

"And you're not?" Confusion flickered in Luciana's eyes.

"I am. It just doesn't feel the same. She won't even look at me."

"You really thought I was keeping her from you? Hurting her?" Luciana struggled with those words, but she knew it was how Lindsay felt. If they were ever to move forward, they would have to face the accusation head-on. Sam hadn't wanted to divulge the things her mother had said, but Luciana appreciated her honesty once she'd finally brought herself to say the words. "Really?"

"I just got used to her always being around," Lindsay admitted. "I did some stupid stuff last year. Sam was there for me...day and night."

Luciana remained silent.

"Sam bailed me out when I hit rock bottom and we grew closer. We'd always been close, but after Lucia died, I felt like I'd lost a piece of my sister. I *did* lose a piece of her. The state she was in terrified me, Luciana. I couldn't sleep at night. I constantly worried that she would disappear. That we'd get a call to say her body had been pulled out the river."

Luciana felt for Lindsay. She hadn't ever been in a situation like this. "And how did you cope with that?"

"I didn't." Lindsay scoffed. "I did drugs. Got myself into debt. We both realised what life was doing to us and promised to come out of the other side. That we'd always have each other."

"And you do." Luciana nudged Lindsay's shoulder, smiling. "She loves you so much."

"I panicked. I couldn't understand why she kept cancelling our plans. I just feared the worst. I'm sorry."

Luciana understood Lindsay's worries, to a degree. Nobody knew her, nobody knew she existed until yesterday when Sam's mum showed up at the apartment. While she hated being thought of as someone who could potentially hurt Sam, Luciana knew the truth. Deep down, Lindsay did too.

"That's my fault." Luciana sighed, wrapping her arms around her body. "I'll take a step back. Give you both that time together. I know it's important to you."

"No, don't do that."

"Honestly, it's okay," Luciana said. "I'm not going anywhere. If being around every minute of the day is putting a strain on you two, I can cool down. I'll always be around, waiting."

"Please, no," Lindsay begged. "Since you came into her life, she's happy. She smiles and she laughs like she used to."

"I appreciate that, but—"

"But nothing," Lindsay interrupted. "She needs you. God, I've been waiting for this moment."

"What moment?"

"This. You." Lindsay beamed. "I have to let her go so she can find love again. With you." She paused. "I know you wouldn't hurt her. I see how you look at her."

"I love her." Those words fell effortlessly from Luciana's mouth. "And I don't care how long it takes for her to feel the same way."

"She does." Lindsay squeezed Luciana's shoulder. "She loves you, too."

"She told you that?" Luciana's pulse thrummed in her ears.

"Sam doesn't need to tell me anything. I *always* know how my sister feels. Trust me."

"Well, I uh..." Luciana's throat dried, a lump rising. "Thanks."

"Thank you for finding her." Lindsay wrapped her arms around Luciana. "Thank you for making her happy."

"She found me," Luciana said, her voice close to breaking. "She found me when I didn't know I was looking."

"It all seems to be a match made in heaven." Lindsay linked arms with Luciana, guiding her back towards the house. "*Or* sent from heaven."

"You've lost me."

"Oh, come on!" Lindsay laughed. "You must see it, too?"

"See what?"

"Luciana, the firefighter." They made their way up the decking, Luciana's heart fluttering when she caught Sam laughing, her head thrown back. "My sister lost her wife, *Lucia*, in a *fire*."

"I try not to think about it."

"I'm telling you. You two were *always* supposed to meet."

"Maybe." Luciana suppressed a grin, knowing Lindsay was right. "Maybe."

Sam approached the door, receiving a hug from her mum as she opened it. They'd had the opportunity to talk earlier, but Sam decided against it. She didn't need to rehash their previous conversation, not if it wouldn't change anything, but her mum's apology when they arrived had settled her. Whether that apology would stick remained to be seen, but Sam felt as though it was genuine. She felt like her family were okay with the time they'd spent at her home. With Luciana.

"Thanks for a wonderful day, love."

"Any time, Dad." Sam kissed Bill's cheek. "Don't leave it so long next time."

"I believe we were playing to *your* schedule." He gave his daughter a knowing look.

"I know. I'm sorry," Sam said. "Things are going to change."

"She's a bloody angel." Bill threw his thumb over his shoulder in the direction of Luciana. "A bloody angel."

"She is." Sam smiled. "Love you, Dad."

"Love you, too." He stepped out onto the porch. "Luciana, you're welcome in our home any time, okay?"

"Thanks, Bill." She approached Sam, her hand settling on the small of her back. "Safe trip home, okay?"

"You've got it." He nodded. "Come on, Sue."

"Luciana..." Susan cleared her throat. "I know we got off on the wrong foot, but I want us to start again."

"I'd like that."

"Those things I said, it was in the heat of the moment," Susan continued. "You've brought my daughter back to life and I will always be thankful to you for that."

"I look forward to more days here with you all." Luciana leaned in and hugged Susan. "We should do it more often."

"We will." Lindsay stepped forward. "If Sam can forgive me?"

"Come here." Sam ushered her sister closer, wrapping her arms around her. "I'm sorry I haven't made any time for you."

"It's okay." Lindsay held her sister close. "I understand."

"Monday night," Sam said. "Come over to the apartment. I'll cook."

"I'm sure you have plans already." Lindsay glanced at Luciana.

"I won't be there." Luciana shrugged. "And even if I was, it wouldn't make any difference."

"Call me, okay?" Lindsay focused her attention on Sam. "Call me on Monday if you're available."

"Expect a call." Sam nodded. "Plan to be with me at the apartment."

"Okay." Lindsay disappeared onto the decking, glancing back and smiling. "See you both soon, okay?"

"You will." A worry settled inside Sam and she quickly pulled Lindsay back inside. "Hey, is everything okay with you?"

"Of course, yeah."

"Linds." Sam looked pointedly at her sister. "Is something going on?"

"You mean…am I taking drugs again?" Lindsay's shoulders slumped. "No, Sam. I'm not."

"Promise me everything is okay…"

"Everything is perfectly fine." Lindsay kissed Sam's cheek and rushed off, the sound of the car engine startling her. "Bye." Lindsay threw a wave over her shoulder as Sam stepped back, releasing a deep breath.

"I think she's fine, you know…" Luciana started. "She seemed fine when she cornered me on the deck earlier."

"Cornered you?"

"Joking." Luciana smiled. "She came out to talk to me. I can understand why you worry about her, but I think she's doing good."

"She told you about last year?" Sam's eyebrows rose. "About her addiction?"

"She did." Luciana closed the door and guided Sam further inside. "She didn't go into great detail, but she told me enough for me to understand the bond you two have."

"I worry about her every minute of the day." Sam sighed. "I know it's not healthy to feel like that, but she's my little sister and I saw the mess she got herself into last year."

"Did she ever tell you why she did what she did?"

"Sort of. A bit. I don't know." Sam ran her hand over her face. "Whatever the reason, I still had to pay five thousand off a debt she had with the city's biggest drug dealer."

"She thought she was going to lose you."

"Me?" Sam frowned. "Why would she lose me?"

"Because you were in a bad place." Luciana stepped closer, taking Sam's hand. "You made a promise to one another."

"We did." Sam smiled. "She spent six months living with me and it was the most beneficial six months of my life. Hers too, I think."

Luciana noted the look in Sam's eyes. The love she had for her sister. The only thing missing from her own life was a sibling, but she appreciated the connection Sam and Lindsay had.

"I don't want Lindsay to ever think that I'm keeping you away from her, Sam."

"S-She doesn't. She was just worried."

"Still, that thought was there. That I could be hurting you."

"You? Hurting me?" Sam laughed. "Not in a million years."

"We know that, of course we do, but Lindsay still thought for a split second that something could have been wrong. I don't like that."

"So, what are you saying?" Sam swallowed hard. "You're not leaving, are you?"

"No, babe." Luciana's hand settled on the side of Sam's face. "But you two should spend more time together. I can disappear for a few days when we get back to the city. It's not the end of the world."

"I don't want you to do that."

"Do you think we've been spending too much time together?" Luciana asked, her tone soft. "Honestly?"

"I don't think we've spent *enough* time together." Sam fisted her hand in her girlfriend's tank top, pulling her painfully close. "This, what we have, I don't want it to disappear."

"It won't."

"But it might." Sam's voice broke. "The little things like this... Lindsay's worry, it could push you away."

"Nothing and nobody is pushing me anywhere." Luciana's lips pressed gently against Sam's. "God, I have so many things I want to say to you, but I'm scared."

"Say them..."

"Not yet." Luciana shook her head. "This feels too perfect for me to go and say something stupid, so please, not yet."

"I don't think you could say *anything* that would ruin this." Sam shrugged, aware that her girlfriend didn't want to rock the boat. "Today went well."

"It did." Luciana rounded the kitchen island. "Fresh coffee?"

"Please." Sam smiled. "We have to leave tomorrow..."

"I know. Back to work for us both."

"I won't know what to do with myself when you go back on shifts."

"I'm sure you'll survive." Luciana cocked her head.

"Doesn't mean I have to like it."

"Can I do something nice for you tomorrow when we get back or do you have plans?"

"Why would I have plans?" Sam narrowed her eyes.

"Birthday plans with friends. I don't know."

And there it is. Sam smiled faintly.

"Can *I* celebrate with you or do you have other arrangements?"

"Of course I don't." Sam took Luciana in her arms. "Please don't be offended. I've been so busy with you that I forgot today was even a thing."

"Sure." Luciana sighed. "I just would have liked the opportunity to buy you a terrible card, anything."

"I've really hurt you, haven't I?" Sam pulled back, her eyes finding intense blue.

"Just wish I'd known."

"Come with me." Sam pulled her girlfriend away from the kitchen and out onto the decking. The early evening sun bounced off the still water, not a soul around for miles. "Sit down." She nudged Luciana down onto the swing bed. "Birthdays mean nothing to me. They never have." Sam climbed beside Luciana. "I don't enjoy celebrating the fact I'm getting older. Especially now that I have a gorgeous younger woman in my life."

"Sam—"

"I've had the perfect weekend with you. That's what matters."

"It matters to me, too." Luciana ran her fingers through her hair. "Sorry, I just felt really shitty about it."

"Don't feel anything about it." Sam kissed Luciana softly. "Please?"

"Okay." Their foreheads pressed together.

Luciana lay back, lacing her fingers behind her head. Rather than beating herself up about something she couldn't change, she relaxed her body and her mind. "Have you decided when you'll officially move back in here?"

"A month or so, I think."

"Why that long?"

"I have quite a few projects on at the minute. It just makes sense to be in the city until things settle down."

"Okay. Whatever works for you."

"*You* work for me." Sam laid her head on Luciana's chest, the sound of her heart beating in perfect rhythm making her smile. "God, you *really* work for me."

Luciana simply smiled as she ran her fingers through Sam's soft hair. This weekend had been more than she could have hoped for, it truly had. Yes, she'd been angry about Sam's choice to dismiss her birthday, but did it really matter? In this moment, no...it didn't. She would remember this day, this date, forever, so she knew she would have plenty of opportunities to spoil Sam in the future.

"Tell me about the plans you had for this place."

"Plans?" Sam lifted her head, her brow knitted.

"What did you imagine your future here would look like? You must have had plans."

"Well, I was hoping to retire at forty-five," Sam said. "I work too much."

"Sounds perfect."

"The layout inside…" Sam paused. "It's a broken open plan. You know with the timber sliding doors? I designed it that way so it would work better when the time came to have kids. Give them free reign of the house."

Luciana continued to listen. Sam didn't often open up about her past, but the more she heard, the more she wanted to know.

"I wanted to try once I'd turned thirty-five, but we took on a big contract and time just disappeared."

"I'm sorry."

"It is what it is." Sam's fingertips trailed Luciana's bare arm. "That was my chance and I blew it by putting the business first."

"I'm sure that's not true."

"No, it is." She smiled weakly. "We fought about it. I came across as the cold, heartless, work-driven bitch. It wasn't about that, though. I just wanted to secure our future so we could stop it all one day and never have to leave this place if we didn't want to."

"You can have whatever you want, Sam. The world is yours for the taking."

"Oh, no." Sam shook her head. "I made peace with the fact I'd never have a family of my own some time ago."

"Because?"

"Time is ticking away."

"So?" Luciana snorted. "You're thirty-eight, not eighty-eight."

"Okay, so I'll just turn up at a clinic? Go through a pregnancy alone because I couldn't lessen my load a few years ago?"

"No, of course not." Luciana's voice wavered, the idea that Sam thought she would do it alone breaking her heart.

"I'm fine with my decision. I had the chance and I messed it up."

"Right. Yeah."

"And by the time I prepare everything...the business, this place, clinics and appointments, I'll be too old."

"That's ridiculous." Luciana scoffed. She wanted to scream from the rooftops that she would be by Sam's side, but it was too soon for that. Luciana had always imagined herself with a family, but she wasn't one-hundred percent sure that it was still in Sam's future. She wanted to believe it could be, one day, but Sam's eyes told a different story.

"No, it's the truth." Sam looked pointedly. "I know my age doesn't faze you and I love that, but it's still there. My age *does* still matter."

Luciana felt emotionally drained. She wanted to continue this conversation, but Sam still had that look in her eye. A look that told her she was wasting her time.

"Okay." Was all she could muster up.

"How about we spend the evening in front of the TV?"

"Yeah." Luciana sighed. "TV sounds like a good choice."

CHAPTER TWENTY-TWO

Music blared around Luciana's flat, the bass sending her body into a frenzy as she bopped away to the beat. Three weeks had passed since her weekend away with Sam and life was good. Great, even. They'd fallen into a pattern of never being apart, but for three days, she'd missed her girlfriend. Work commitments at the station meant that Sam had to leave for a trip to London alone, and now Luciana waited for her to return, her body begging for the only woman to ever make her feel like she was on top of the world. They'd spoken at any given opportunity, but twelve-hour shifts didn't make it easy. When Sam was awake, Luciana was sleeping. When Sam was beginning her day, Luciana was ending hers at nine am. Today, she'd finished her early shift and headed straight home, sleep being the last thought on her mind. All she wanted was to hold Sam. To tell her how much she'd missed her. How she never wanted to be without her again.

Luciana had at first been wary about returning to her flat, but she'd made a promise to herself to spend the weekend here when she wasn't working so she could get back into a routine. Sam would soon be leaving the city for her home on the outskirts of Liverpool, and it wouldn't always be possible for Luciana to be there. When she worked a night shift, it made more sense to come back to her flat and sleep while Sam worked at the office. One day, she hoped that would all change, but for now...this was perfect. Ideal. Heavenly.

The sound of her buzzer broke her from her energetic movements in the kitchen, her heart stopping. Nobody knew she was here, only Sam. The problem was, it couldn't be Sam. They'd spoken half an hour ago and her girlfriend explained that she wouldn't be back for at least another hour or so, motorway roadworks preventing her from getting into the city any earlier. She cleared her throat, lowered the volume on the radio and lifted the receiver.

"H-Hello?"

"SURPRISE!"

A familiar voice filtered through the handset, but it wasn't the voice she hoped she would hear.

"Mum?"

"Let me up, love," Jackie said. "I only have a few hours before my train leaves to go home again."

Luciana granted her mum access to the block, thankful that it was a familiar face rather than the abusive one of Janet. Until this moment, Luciana hadn't realised that the other woman still unnerved her, but she did. She always would. Opening the door, she returned to the kitchen and flicked the switch on the kettle.

"Hello?"

"Come in, Mum." Luciana stood in the kitchen, her smile beaming as her mum poked her head around the door. "How are you?" She crossed the flat and hugged her mum tight. "I didn't know you were coming."

"Decided to hop on the train an hour ago and here I am."

"Dad not with you?"

"No, he had to work again." Jackie offered her daughter a small smile. "But one of us is better than none of us, wouldn't you say?"

"Definitely." Luciana released her grip and stepped back. "I, uh... I kind of have plans this evening."

"Out with the station?"

"No." Luciana blushed. "My uh, my girlfriend is due here in about an hour."

"Girlfriend?" Jackie's eyebrow rose with surprise. "I knew you were dating, but a girlfriend?"

"I didn't want to jinx anything, Mum. You know what I'm like."

"Don't worry about it." Jackie dropped her handbag onto the couch. "So, her name?"

"Sam."

"Have you been together long?"

"About six weeks or so." Luciana eyed her mother, expecting a reaction.

"So long as she makes you happy..."

"She's thirty-eight." The words left Luciana's mouth before she could process them. In all honesty, she didn't know why she *had* said them.

"Are you telling me that because you want my opinion or are you just giving me some information to work with?"

"Honestly, I've no idea." Luciana laughed. "I don't care for people's opinions, as you know."

"And you know I would never say anything to hurt you." Jackie approached her daughter. "If she makes you happy, that makes me happy."

"I knew you wouldn't mind."

"It's your relationship, my love." Luciana's mum pulled herself up on a stool at the breakfast bar. "And you know I'm always here if you need to talk...though I don't expect you will."

"Things are really good here, Mum."

"You look happy." Jackie reached her hand out, taking her daughter's. "You look happier than you have in years."

"Because I am." Luciana squeezed her mum's hand. "I didn't

think I needed a relationship to make me feel that way, and I know it isn't the be all and end all of everything, but I couldn't imagine not having her in my life now."

"Can I meet her?"

"Do you want to meet her?" Luciana countered. "I mean, you won't do or say anything to put her off, will you?"

"Would I do anything to jeopardise a relationship of yours?"

"No, you wouldn't." Luciana knew in her heart that her mum would always have her back. It's why they'd always been so close. "Let me text her so she knows you're here. She's been away for three days."

"Sounds interesting."

Luciana grabbed her phone from the worktop and tapped away at the screen.

"She's a property developer."

L: Mum has just arrived. Is that okay? X

"Lovely." Jackie chose to take over the coffee duties while her daughter arranged with her girlfriend. "Usual two sugars?"

"Please." Luciana glanced up momentarily before returning to her phone.

S: Looking forward to meeting her. If you want that? X

L: More than anything. ETA? X

S: At a service station grabbing coffee. I'm dead on my feet. Should be with you in the next half hour. Should I bring anything? X

L: Yourself. X

S: I've missed you. X

L: I've missed you more. X

S: Should I let myself up? X

L: Yes, you definitely should. I'll keep Mum company until you arrive. X

Luciana placed her phone down and looked up to find her mum staring at her, smiling. "What?"

"You only sent her a text but your face looks like she's just promised you the world."

"Don't be ridiculous." Luciana felt the tips of her ears heat.

"You're in love with this woman," Jackie observed. "Head over heels in love."

"Mum, please don't say that in front of her." Luciana felt a sudden panic set in. "I've been trying to figure out when the right time to tell her is... I still haven't found the courage to say it."

"That's not like you." Jackie carried two cups into the living room. "What's wrong? You can't be having second thoughts."

"No, I'm not." Luciana dropped down onto the couch. "No way."

"Then what is it?"

"Sam, she's married." Luciana tucked her legs under her. "Her wife died two years ago."

"Oh, love." Jackie sighed. "That's awful."

"I'm just trying to take it slow and not say or do anything to ruin the moment. You know?"

"But if you love her, she should know that."

"I know, and I will tell her one day." Luciana nodded. "I just have this worry that she won't feel the same way. I try not to think about it too much and I try to imagine us together in the future, but saying I love her seems to be impossible for me to do."

"Of course you're scared. That's perfectly natural," Jackie said. "Not only is she older than you, but she's had a life experience nobody should go through so young. She has you now though and all you can do is show her who you are, because I know she will love you back. You have a wonderful heart, Luce. Sam would want to know how you feel."

"At times, I feel like the universe brought us together in some way."

"Explain..."

"Her wife was called Lucia. She died in a fire." To this day, it sounded incredibly strange to say that out loud. Luciana struggled to comprehend how something so devastating could be so similar to who she was. "I wasn't looking and neither was she."

"Then yes, I do believe the universe brought you together." Jackie smiled. "Fate. If you believe in that stuff."

"I suppose I do, in some way." Luciana nodded. "She just... God, she's perfect, Mum. Everything about her. I'm yet to find a single fault. And I know, I know everyone has faults, flaws...but Sam is everything I believe I want and need in my life. We just fit together so perfectly. Nothing feels forced."

"That's when you know you've found true love."

"You think?"

"I do." Jackie nodded slowly. "But only you know what you want, love. Nobody else can tell you what to do."

"What *would* you do?"

"If that was how I felt?" Jackie paused. "I'd grab it with both hands and never let it go, Luce."

"Thanks, Mum."

"Our time on this earth can be short; Sam knows that better than anyone. Your job...you run towards danger every day."

"Mum—"

"Hear me out." She held up her hand. "How would you feel if something happened, to either one of you, and you never had the chance to tell Sam that you loved her?"

"Devastated."

Luciana knew what her mum was trying to say. In her line of work, everything could disappear. One wrong move. One incredible fire. It could all be over. All it took was a locked door, a roof collapse. Running towards fire may be exhilarating to Luciana, but the consequences of nights when it could potentially go wrong could be earth-shattering. She knew that, and she knew her mum was right.

"I'll build myself up to it soon, I promise."

"Or you could just let your relationship bring it out of you when you least expect it." Jackie's eyebrow rose. "Don't think about saying it. When it feels right, when it's on the tip of your tongue, say those words."

"God, I didn't realise how much I needed to talk to you about this."

"You know I'm only down the road."

"I know. Life just got in the way...and now here we are."

"I'm so happy you're thriving here, Luce." Jackie pulled her daughter into a hug. "So happy."

Sam blew out a deep breath as she reached the top of the stairs. Her eyes landed on her girlfriend's front door, but something prevented her from moving closer. Sam was ready for this. Of course she was. So why did she feel as though all oxygen had been stolen from her lungs? Why did her legs falter as she attempted to move? Because this mattered, that's why. Luciana meant the world to her and this meeting was important. Sam knew all too well how much a first impression mattered. They'd discussed meeting Luciana's parents on more than one occasion, but Sam never imagined she would feel this anxious about it when the time finally arrived. She was a successful businesswoman, for the love of God. A meeting with someone's parents shouldn't spook her like this. It was ridiculous. Luciana wasn't just someone, though. She was Sam's everything.

Okay, just go inside. Sam glanced down at the keys in her hands. *There is nothing to worry about.* She ran her fingertips over the silver key, a heart keyring attached to it. Smiling, she pushed her hair from her face and took a step closer. *It's just her mum.* She reminded herself. *If she's anything like her daughter, this will be great.*

Sam steeled herself and slid the key in the lock. The sound of laughter caught her attention, and in turn, unexpectedly settled her worry. When she opened the door, the sight in front of her caused her breath to catch. Luciana lay sprawled out on the couch, her baggy sweatpants accompanied by her white racer-back. That gorgeous blonde hair sat atop her head in the form of a messy bun, and her eyes... God, her eyes absolutely shone. Sam had fallen in love with her girlfriend's eyes the moment she met her, but after three days away, they begged her to move closer.

"Babe?" Luciana brought Sam from her stare. "You doing okay over there?"

"Oh." Sam's eyes widened. "Yes, sorry." She cleared her throat, closing the door.

Luciana climbed from her position on the couch and took Sam in her arms. "I've missed you." She leaned in, her lips ghosting over Sam's. "So much."

"Baby," Sam whispered, her eyes closing momentarily. "We have company."

"Right, yeah." Luciana spun around. "Mum, this is Sam."

Jackie beamed. "The woman my daughter hasn't stopped talking about."

"Oh." Sam blushed.

"Jackie." Luciana's mum held out her hand, still smiling from ear to ear. "An absolute pleasure to meet you."

"You too." Sam took her hand, internally chastising herself for ever worrying about this moment.

"I won't stay too long," Jackie said. "I'm sure you two want to relax. Luce said you've been away."

"Three days." Sam blew out a breath as she dropped her handbag to the floor and removed her jacket. "I don't plan to do it again unless completely necessary."

"Yeah, I wish," Luciana cut in, handing Sam a glass of her favourite red wine.

"No, I mean that." Sam smiled. "Mm, I needed this." She licked the wine residue from her lips.

"How was your trip?" Jackie asked, enamoured by the interaction playing out in front of her.

"Miserable." Sam moved into the living room. "I had zero interest in being there."

"Everything okay?" Luciana's brows drew together as she sat beside Sam. "You go on multiple trips."

"I wanted to be here with you." Sam took her girlfriend's hand, sitting back and crossing her legs.

Luciana salivated as her eyes followed Sam's luscious, long legs. It wasn't often Sam wore a skirt, but damn, she wore them well. The black heels Sam chose had to be at least six inches in height. Luciana struggled to maintain clean thoughts, only images of a naked Sam in heels now firmly in her mind. Spread out on her bed. Writhing. Moaning.

"Wouldn't you agree?" Sam squeezed Luciana's hand.

"Um..."

"That the bungalow is perfect. So much more than being out here in the city."

"Oh, yes." Luciana managed a smile, but Sam narrowed her eyes, smirking. "It's gorgeous, Mum."

"It sounds it." Jackie relaxed in her seat. "Maybe I could visit one day?"

"If I'm there, yeah."

"Why wouldn't you be there?" Sam asked.

"Well, I just... I don't know." Luciana found herself unable to concentrate. "Work. Stuff. I don't know."

"Oh, about that." Sam's eyes brightened. "I noticed your car was making a horrific noise when you started it last week."

"It's been making that noise for the last six months." Luciana laughed. "But it's still going."

"Mm, but I don't want you getting caught at work one night because it won't start. You'd have no way of getting back."

"I can just come here, it's fine."

"Of course." Sam chose to shelve that conversation until later. That was the second time Luciana had refrained from the potential excitement of the bungalow on the lake. "How long will you be staying, Jackie? You'll be staying here with us..."

"Oh, I have a train to catch in an hour." Luciana's mum smiled. "Just a flying visit this time around."

"That's a shame." Sam sat forward, setting her wine glass down. "But I can take you home. No need for trains."

"That's very kind, Sam." Jackie held up her hand. "But you've been driving all afternoon."

"It's no problem."

"I know, but the train will be fine tonight." Jackie offered a thankful smile. "Luciana has missed you. Enjoy what's left of your night together."

"Be right back." Luciana stood up, disappearing into the bathroom.

Sam watched the door close and shifted in her seat, clearing her throat. "You are okay with this, right?" While Sam loved Jackie's enthusiasm, she couldn't be sure it was completely genuine. She'd expected this reaction from her own mother and got the opposite, so she had to ask. "I'd understand if you were wary of me."

"Would it matter if I had an issue?" Jackie's eyebrow rose.

"Well, I'd like to say that it wouldn't, but you're Luciana's family and I only want her to be happy. If this would put a strain on your relationship..."

"I have no issue at all, Sam," Jackie said with a sincere voice. "Luciana is happier than I've ever seen her."

"She is?" Sam's pulse thrummed in her ears.

"My daughter doesn't need much in life, but this? Love? She deserves it," Jackie continued. "She spends her life helping people; the least she should receive in return is her own happiness."

"You really do have an amazing daughter." Sam glanced at the closed bathroom door. "I don't think she understands how much she means to me."

"Maybe you should tell her." Jackie winked. "She's a big girl. She can handle whatever truth you have to offer her."

"I may have it all." Sam sighed. "But the thought of losing this, her, it would finish me off."

"What makes you think that you're going to lose her?" Jackie's forehead creased.

"If I tell her how I feel, she's going to run." Sam wrung her hands together in her lap. "She says she's not going anywhere, but what we have... I'm not sure I can risk it."

"Luciana doesn't run." Jackie shook her head. "She told me about your wife."

"Mm, understandable." Sam sipped her wine.

"She also told me how you worry about her job."

"Hard not to." Sam smiled weakly. "When she's working, I fully expect a call, you know?"

"I did at one time," Jackie admitted. "So much so that she left home and moved here."

"Oh." Sam lowered her eyes. "I'm managing it, how I feel. I know she's safe and I know she's trained."

"She also wouldn't do anything to put herself in danger. Luciana plays by the book." The sound of the bathroom door opening caught their attention and Sam smiled.

"Thank you." Sam said, lowering her voice.

"Any time." Jackie stood up, squeezing Sam's shoulder. "Love, I should head off to the station."

"You're sure you can't stay?" Luciana cocked her head. "It's been nice having you here."

"I think you both have some much-needed time to spend together."

"Call me when you get home, okay?"

Jackie nodded, taking her handbag and moving towards the door. "Sam."

"Visit the bungalow any time you like." Sam pulled Jackie into a hug. "Luciana *will* be there. I can promise you that."

"I know," Jackie said, her eyes switching to her daughter. "And she does, too."

"You two are being weird." Luciana rolled her eyes. "Promise you'll let me know when you're home?"

"I'll send a text." Jackie kissed Luciana's cheek. "Bye, love."

"See you soon, Mum."

"Bye, Sam."

Sam smiled as she watched Jackie step out into the corridor. "Lovely to meet you, Jackie."

Luciana closed the door, turning to face Sam as she flicked the lock. Their eyes met, both hungry for the moments they'd missed with one another. Luciana's mind wandered back to her explicit thoughts when Sam arrived, her bottom lip firmly between her teeth.

Sam remained speechless. Over the three days during her trip away, she'd struggled to focus, to work, to be the businesswoman she knew she was. Her mind played Luciana's voice on a loop, the evenings the worst when Sam thought about packing up and heading home. It didn't matter that she had a job to do. It didn't matter that she was in London to work. Luciana wasn't with her and it hurt. Those moments when she had the opportunity to talk to her, she grabbed them. It didn't matter that a client had invited her to dinner—she needed to hear Luciana's voice.

"H-How was your trip?" Luciana stuttered, her eyes travelling the length of Sam's body. "Good?"

"I don't care about my trip." Sam stepped closer. "I don't care about your car or the fact that I've bought you a new one." Her fingertips reached the hem of Luciana's racer-back. "I don't care that we should probably discuss the fact that your mum was here or how either of us feel about it."

"Babe—"

"All I care about is that I'm home and I'm here with you." Sam's heels clicked against the laminate, sending Luciana's heart rate through the roof. "That you're mine. Always."

"I am." Luciana's breath caught as Sam pushed her against the door.

"I've spent three days needing you. Missing you. With so much I want to say."

Luciana's heart slammed against her ribcage.

"And I know..." She paused. "I know this could all fall apart around us, but I don't care. I don't care about *anything* other than you and how much you mean to me."

"Sam." Luciana bit back a sob.

"Do you know?" Sam's breath washed over Luciana's lips. "Do you know how much you mean to me?"

"I-I..."

"I love you, Luciana." Sam pressed her forehead against her girlfriend's. "God, I really love you."

"I love you, too." Luciana wasn't sure if she'd actually uttered those words, but her mouth certainly moved.

"And I know I'm the luckiest woman in the entire world to have found you. Knowing that you even see me is beyond my wildest dreams...but you don't have to say it back." Sam offered the smallest of smiles, her eyes holding unshed tears. "I just had to tell you. That I love you."

Sam's thumb trailed Luciana's bottom lip.

"You really don't have to say it back. If it's not how you feel..."

"But I did." A smile played at the corners of Luciana's lips. "I did say it back."

"What? When?"

"Somewhere between your rambling."

"You said it back." Sam's knees weakened. Everything within her told her to fall to the floor, but as Luciana wrapped her arms around her waist, she felt safe. Safe in her arms and safe with the knowledge that she was loved.

"You love me?" Sam blinked as tears fell freely down her face.

"I think I've loved you since the moment I met you," Luciana whispered. "I do, Sam. I love you."

Luciana had never been so sure about anything as she was in this moment. Their time together may have been brief, but what they had to come outweighed every worry in her mind. Initially, this was an arrangement, dinner and conversation, but as time passed and Luciana saw behind those deep brown eyes, she fell harder than she thought possible.

"I want so much for us." Luciana gripped Sam's body. "You deserve *so much*." Her eyes flickered closed as her voice trembled. "I've known since the first encounter that I needed more with you." She brushed a tear from Sam's cheek. "You're the only woman in this world who has ever shown me what love feels like. And I know, I know, I wasn't looking when you appeared in my life…but I'm so happy it was you who was sitting in that tapas bar. I'm so happy you gave me the chance to know you. To see the real you. To love you."

"You've shown me I can have this. That it's okay to move on." Sam's lip trembled. "I don't ever want anyone else. You…you're my second chance. My only chance."

"I want it *all* with you." Luciana searched her girlfriend's face. "I need you to know that."

"All?"

Luciana brought her hand up to Sam's face, caressing her soft skin with her thumb. Nothing had ever felt so relaxed. So certain. "Everything."

TO BE CONTINUED

SIGN UP TO WIN

Sign up to my mailing list to be the first to hear about new releases, and to be in with a chance of winning books!

WWW.MELISSATEREZEAUTHOR.COM

DID YOU ENJOY IT?

THANK YOU FOR PURCHASING THE ARRANGEMENT.

I HOPE YOU ENJOYED IT. PLEASE CONSIDER LEAVING A REVIEW ON YOUR PREFERRED SITE. AS AN INDEPENDENT AUTHOR, REVIEWS HELP TO PROMOTE OUR WORK. ONE LINE OR TWO REALLY DOES MAKE THE DIFFERENCE.

THANK YOU, TRULY.

LOVE,
MELISSA X

ABOUT THE AUTHOR

Oh, hi! It's nice to see you!

I'm Melissa Tereze, author of The Arrangement, and other bestsellers. Born, raised, and living in Liverpool, UK, I spend my time writing angsty romance about complex, real-life, women who love women. My heart lies within the age-gap trope, but you'll also find a wide range of different characters and stories to sink your teeth into.

SOCIAL MEDIA

You can contact me through my social media or my website. I'm mostly active on Twitter.

Twitter: @MelissaTereze
Facebook: www.facebook.com/Author.MelissaTereze
Instagram: @melissatereze_author
Find out more at: www.melissaterezeauthor.com
Contact: info@melissaterezeauthor.com

ALSO BY MELISSA TEREZE

ANOTHER LOVE SERIES
THE CALL (BOOK TWO)

THE ASHFORTH SERIES
PLAYING FOR HER HEART (BOOK ONE)
HOLDING HER HEART (BOOK TWO)

OTHER NOVELS
ALWAYS ALLIE
MRS MIDDLETON
IN HER ARMS
BEFORE YOU GO
FOREVER YOURS
THE HEAT OF SUMMER
FORGET ME NOT
MORE THAN A FEELING
WHERE WE BELONG: LOVE RETURNS
NAKED

CO-WRITES
TEACH ME

TITLES UNDER L.M CROFT (EROTICA)
PIECES OF ME

Printed in Great Britain
by Amazon